THE REVEREND'S SECOND CHANCE

SECOND CHANCES IN HARMONY SPRINGS ~ BOOK TWO

LAURALYN KELLER

WILD HEART
BOOKS

ISBN-13: 978-1-963212-34-1

To Mom and Dad: thank you for being supportive and encouraging of my dream to write.
I'm so thankful for you both.

CHAPTER 1

November 1888
Montana Territory

*G*rief always hit at the most inopportune moment.

A lump formed in Lydia Jefferson's throat as she watched a group of her students work on their science project. The classroom boasted plenty of windows, letting natural light into the small one-room schoolhouse that provided education for the children of Harmony Springs. She faced one of those windows and drew in a long breath. Wind blew through the straw-colored grass, long dried up for autumn. The sky had turned gray, matching her mood. With a sigh, Lydia turned her attention back to her students. Their happy faces, so bright and innocent, tugged on a piece of her heart she tried to keep hidden. Most days, it worked. Today, though...

"Mrs. Jefferson?"

Lydia fumbled with a piece of clay before dropping it to the table. She found a smile for the child in front of her. "Yes, sweetie?"

Ruby Calhoun blinked up at her with wide hazel eyes, so like Lydia's own. Many people had marveled at the way the two of them resembled each other. Both with black curls, hazel eyes, and porcelain skin. Ruby had been mistaken for her daughter many times.

And she looks so much like...

Lydia clamped down on the thought. It would do no good to remember now. Not when she was in class.

Ruby held up a tangle of dried grass and sticks. "I made a nest."

"It's perfect, Ruby. Where are the clay birds to go with it?"

"Isaiah and Alice have them." Ruby smiled shyly, then made her way to the other youngsters in class.

Isaiah Brooks grinned as his classmate approached. Alice giggled and waved. The two girls were six and Isaiah seven, the three youngest in her group of twenty-five students, and they'd bonded over their similar age.

Lydia followed Ruby. She knelt beside the small children. "Isaiah, Alice, Ruby tells me you made the bird."

Alice nodded, her blond curls bouncing with each shake of her head.

"Uh-huh." Isaiah pointed to a lump of clay on the table. "It's a robin."

Look, Mama! The first robin of spring.

Stabs of pain radiated from Lydia's chest. She rubbed a hand over her heart, hoping to dull the ache. Not now. She couldn't fall apart now.

Isaiah stared at her, his little brow furrowed. "Mrs. Jefferson, what's wrong? Are you sad?"

She gave him a smile. Maybe it appeared less weak than it felt. "Nothing's wrong, Isaiah. You made a wonderful robin. Shall we put it in Ruby's nest?"

Isaiah's brown eyes remained on Lydia as if he knew she hid something. She'd learned quickly last year that her student possessed a keen understanding of people. Unease settled over her, as much from the child's gaze as from the fact that she was indeed hiding something. She abhorred lying— yet here she was, lying to a student.

With a small sigh, Lydia looked Isaiah in the eyes. "Actually, something is bothering me, but I'll be all right. Especially with sweet students like you who care."

He darted forward and threw his arms around her neck. She pressed her toes against the floor to remain upright, then hugged him back. This sweet innocence, the pure affection of a child, was the best part of her job.

"Can we put the birdie in now?" Ruby's voice piped up.

Lydia smiled, surreptitiously wiping a tear from her eye. "Yes, we can."

Ruby put the nest on the table and arranged a few sticks that had come loose. Then she peered up at Isaiah. "Can I help put him in?"

"Sure."

Isaiah took Ruby's palm in his before placing the bird in hers. They lowered it into the nest and spent the next minute arranging it just so. He then did the same with Alice. Pride swept over Lydia as she watched their careful movements. These children were more meticulous than she'd have thought possible in ones so young.

"Mrs. Jefferson, can you help me?"

Another student called for her attention. Lydia rose, but not before smiling at her young charges. "Wonderful work, you three. I'm impressed."

Isaiah and Alice beamed while Ruby blushed and ducked her head. Lydia pressed a hand to Ruby's shoulder in a silent show of support before heading to her other student.

By the end of the school day, Lydia almost forgot her lingering sadness. Almost.

One by one, her students filed out of the small schoolhouse.

Each of them said a polite goodbye. Isaiah waved with a smile before bounding outside. Lydia followed at a more sedate pace, hoping to say hello to his mother.

Her friend grinned when Lydia came out the door. Ella Brooks's red waves were pinned up under a pretty bonnet. She held her eleven-month-old daughter in her arms. Isaiah had found his other two siblings, and the three were engaged in a game of chase around the yard.

Ella shook her head. "How those children have so much energy is beyond me." She turned her gaze to Lydia. "Did Isaiah behave himself today?"

"Always."

A flash of amusement crossed Ella's face. "I'm glad he's so well-behaved for you. At home, he has a stubborn streak the size of Montana."

Lydia laughed. "I have yet to see that."

Isaiah raced up to them, breathing hard. "Mama, ask Mrs. Jefferson if she's okay. She was sad today." With that declaration, he darted off again.

Ella tilted her head, a frown creasing her brow. "Lydia?"

All the grief crashed into her again. So much for trying to keep it at bay. Traitorous tears burned her eyes. She swallowed hard. Twice.

A comforting arm slid around her shoulders. Ella hugged her close, not saying anything. Twin trails of moisture worked their way down Lydia's cheeks before she swiped them away. She drew in a ragged breath before attempting to speak. "It's just...today is a hard day."

"Today as in the present, or because of something that happened in the past?"

Ella's tone held warmth and compassion. Lydia drew strength from that. She fidgeted with the sleeve of her dress, keeping her gaze down. "Something that happened in the past."

"Do you want to talk about it?"

"I..." Lydia shook her head. "Thank you for asking, Ella, but I'm not sure I want to dredge it up."

Her friend opened her mouth, then snapped it shut. She touched Lydia's shoulder. "You know I'm always here if you need to talk."

Yes, she knew. Ella had been a steadfast friend ever since Lydia moved to Harmony Springs eighteen months ago with her mother-in-law. So why did she still find it hard to confide her deepest pain to Ella?

"I know."

Maybe someday.

Little Rosie began fussing in her mother's arms. Ella bounced the baby. "We should get going." She put a hand on Lydia's arm. "Will you and Dorothy like to join us for supper on Saturday?"

Her mother-in-law would love a visit with the Brooks family. Lydia nodded. "That would be great."

After saying farewell to Ella and the children, Lydia walked back into the schoolhouse. She stopped short at the sight of Ruby still at a table. "Ruby! What are you doing here, sweetie?"

The little girl had a thumb in her mouth, but she pulled it out to reply. "Granny didn't come yet."

Odd. Pearl was never late. Though the woman had to be in her seventies, she always came down the mountain to pick up her great-granddaughter.

Oh, Lord, please let nothing be wrong.

Even as the prayer welled up inside, Lydia's chest constricted. Her instincts buzzed with trepidation. Fighting it down, she found a smile and held out her hand to Ruby. "Would you like me to take you home?"

Ruby bounced up from her chair. "Yes, please." She slipped her hand into Lydia's, looking up at her with total trust.

Lydia tried to ignore the anxiety rising inside. Pearl had to be all right. She'd taken on custody of her great-granddaughter after Ruby's parents and baby brother died of cholera.

Ruby couldn't lose anyone else.

~

"Next stop, Harmony Springs."

The conductor's loud proclamation jerked Samuel Allen out of a restless sleep. He yawned and stretched as best he could in the cramped seat. A few minutes later, the train slowed its pace. Another few minutes and it came to a stop with a creaky groan.

He waited for the family seated beside him to disembark. The mother gathered up her four children while the father gave Samuel a tired smile, hoisting several bags. "Pleasure meeting you, Pastor Allen."

"The pleasure was mine. Enjoy the visit with your in-laws."

The man grimaced, but his lips tugged up in a smile. "Pray for me."

"Of course."

Once most of the car had emptied of passengers, Samuel stood and reached for his luggage. One bag held all his worldly possessions. He considered it a blessing, seeing as his vocation as pastor provided him with a home and a flock. This town was his first assignment on his own. He'd spent the past few years assisting his mentor, John Rivers, at a parish in Chicago. Now, he was to shepherd the people of Harmony Springs, the first permanent pastor the town had seen.

He didn't feel ready. But, as John often said, God would lead the way.

A rush of nerves tightened his belly. Samuel pushed them away. It wouldn't do to be swept away by emotion. He was all too familiar with that sensation.

Memories tried to rise in his mind. Samuel deliberately

ignored them, turning his attention to getting off the train. John said he'd be met by the town's sheriff. Apparently, that office was the highest position of governance in many small towns of the American territories.

As he stepped off the train, his gaze landed on a tall, broad man in a cowboy hat with a star pinned to his vest. Dark hair peeked out from under his hat. Samuel walked forward confidently. "Sheriff Doyle?"

The man nodded with a friendly smile. "Pastor Allen?" His voice carried a familiar brogue.

Samuel's brows rose. "You're Irish."

"That I am. Parents came over from the old country before I was born, but I grew up among Irish immigrants." He pointed at Samuel's bag. "You got any more of those?"

"No, sir. This is everything."

The sheriff chuckled. "My name's Travis, young man. Unless we're in formal situations, feel free to call me by that name."

Young man? Samuel tilted his head, studying Travis. He couldn't be more than five or so years over Samuel's own twenty-six. Maybe they could become friends.

The thought lightened Samuel's heart. He loved making friends. His parents always said he'd need an occupation that involved getting to know people. Becoming a pastor had been perfect for that.

"And you can call me Samuel."

"All right, then. Let's get you to the parsonage."

Travis headed toward the street. Samuel fell into step with him. Wooden buildings lined the dusty main street, fitting his image of a small western town. Horses stood tied to hitching posts outside many of them. People milled the streets, the men in cowboy hats, the women in bonnets. Several noticed Samuel and offered polite smiles or tips of the hat.

He had a feeling he was going to like it here.

~

*R*uby's great-grandmother wasn't well.

That became clear within moments of entering the small cabin where the only remaining members of the Calhoun family lived. The old woman lay in her bed, a cough wracking her frail body.

Lydia knelt by the bed and took the woman's hand. "Pearl?"

Pearl opened her rheumy eyes. "Mrs. Jefferson." She inhaled sharply, leading to another coughing fit before she wheezed out, "Am I late pickin' up Ruby?"

"I'm here, Granny." Ruby climbed onto the bed. "Mrs. Jefferson brought me home."

Confusion swirled over Pearl's face before she relaxed. "Thanks, ma'am. I'm sorry I missed pickup today."

Lydia eyed the throbbing vein in Pearl's throat. "Do you know what ails you?"

The woman shook her head, leaning back against her pillow with a tired sigh. "It's been comin' on slowly but surely. I probably need a doc, but we ain't got one no more."

Fear slithered through Lydia's heart. With Doc Grady having retired and gone farther west to be with his eldest daughter, Harmony Springs was left without a physician. A traveling nurse came through on occasion, but without a doctor in residence, emergencies had become a true problem. And this could become an emergency.

"Is there anything I can do for you?" Lydia asked.

Pearl smiled and gave Lydia's hand a pat. "No, thanks. I just needed a little rest." The elderly woman pushed back the covers and struggled to sit up. Lydia reached out to help, but Pearl waved her away. "Now, young lady, I've done this thousands of times before. I'll be fine soon enough." Her eyes flickered to Ruby. "Sweetie, can you fetch Granny a cup of water?"

Ruby squeezed Pearl's hand and dashed off. Pearl fixed her eyes on Lydia. "There is one thing you can do for me."

"What's that?"

Pearl nodded toward Ruby. "If something should happen to me, take care of my girl. It's only a matter of time before the Lord calls me home. I don't want her goin' to an orphanage."

Only a matter of time? Lydia stared at Pearl.

The other woman held her gaze, her mouth set in a firm line. "Please, Mrs. Jefferson. Ruby adores you. I know she'd be in good hands."

The woman talked as though her death was imminent. Chills made gooseflesh rise on Lydia's skin. "Pearl, is there something you're not telling me?"

Pearl dropped her gaze with a short exhale. "I'm seventy-eight, Mrs. Jefferson. I've already lived longer than most folks in these parts." She lifted one shoulder in a half shrug. "This sickness could do me in."

How could she say those words so factually? No despair marred her tone, no regret evidence in her words. She looked at Lydia with a calm steadiness that said Pearl had thought this through.

"I..." Lydia swallowed a lump in her throat. Her gaze found Ruby. How could she say no? She didn't *want* to say no. But could she raise a child on her own?

Pearl gripped her hand. "Please."

The single word broke through Lydia's reservation. If it came to that, she'd figure something out. She gently pressed Pearl's hand and took a breath.

"I will."

CHAPTER 2

*L*ater the evening of his arrival, Samuel sat in Travis's parlor, the scents coming from the kitchen making his mouth water. The sheriff's wife, Cassie, owned the only café in town. According to Travis, she was the best cook this side of the Rocky Mountains. Samuel was inclined to agree by smell alone.

Travis lounged in a chair across from him. A little boy, about one year old, bounced up and down on his father's lap. Connor had Travis's hazel eyes and his mother's blond hair. With chubby cheeks and a ready smile, the child was adorable.

"You like kids?" Travis asked.

Samuel grinned. "Sure do. I'd love to have a passel of them someday." *If I can ever get over...*

He cleared his throat, pushing the memory away.

Travis nodded, seemingly unaware of the sudden turmoil boiling in Samuel's heart. "There are a few single women in this town, but the men outnumber them handily. Quite a few folks here resort to taking mail-order brides."

"What's this I hear about mail-order brides?" Cassie bustled into the room, hands on her hips. "Trav, are you already trying to get the preacher married off?"

Samuel hid a smile. He raised a hand. "Don't you worry, ma'am. I have no intention of marrying any time soon. My focus is on my new flock."

She turned her blue eyes on him and tilted her head. "Well, now, nothing wrong with that. But if love should come your way sooner, make sure you answer the call."

"I'll keep that in mind."

Cassie plucked Connor from her husband. "Supper's ready. I hope you're hungry."

"Very." Samuel stood along with Travis. "It smells delicious."

"Thanks." Cassie beamed. "We're having roasted rosemary chicken with root vegetables, and there's dried apple pie for dessert."

That sounded like a little slice of heaven. Samuel followed the Doyles into the kitchen, where a sturdy table sat laden with food. They sat, and Travis asked Samuel to say the blessing.

Bowing his head, Samuel prayed, "Lord, thanks for the bounty before us. Thanks for Travis and Cassie's generosity in opening their home to a stranger. Please bless the food and the hands that made it. Amen."

After the food had been served and he'd had a chance to savor a few bites—which were every bit as succulent as they looked—Cassie turned to him. "So...what do you think of the parsonage and the church?"

"Both are much more spacious than I expected. The church seems well maintained, and the parsonage is particularly comfortable. I'm surprised there were two bedrooms instead of one."

"Oh, that's because those who built it thought a family might stay. Some feared it would be too small for a preacher's family." Cassie smiled at him. "You'll have space for guests if anyone were to visit."

Samuel laughed. "Thank God for that. My mentor is coming out next month to see how I'm getting along. He'll be happy to know he can stay with me."

"Who's your mentor?" Travis asked.

"Pastor John Rivers. He's wanted to see the Montana Territory for some time. My coming here provides him with the perfect excuse."

Cassie fed Connor a bite of potato. "We'll be sure to welcome him when he arrives. Will he stay long?"

"I'm not sure." Samuel enjoyed some chicken before continuing. "He's talked about visiting friends in the Dakota Territory, so he might travel there after coming here."

After supper, Cassie served generous portions of pie. Samuel bit into his and groaned. "Cassie, I've never had pie this good before. Your cooking is even better than Travis said."

She gave Travis a tender smile. "He says the sweetest things." Her attention turned back to Samuel. "Thanks for the compliment. I'm happy you like it."

Once he'd finished, Samuel tapped his fingers against the table. "I'd like to introduce myself to folks around town, get to know the people before I officially start pastoring. Where should I start?"

Travis leaned back in his chair. He rubbed a hand over his neatly trimmed beard, a reflective look in his eyes. "Well, any business owners would be a good bet. Maybe you could start by visiting each one tomorrow. It shouldn't take too long to say howdy. Oh, and knowing the schoolteacher would probably be good too. I'd be happy to take you around."

"That's a generous offer. I'd appreciate your company."

Travis nodded, then hiked a brow at Cassie. "Am I missing anyone?"

She shook her head. "That's a good start. Once you've met

the townspeople, you could ride out to the ranches. My brother owns one of them, and I know he and his wife expressed interest in meeting you before the first Sunday service."

"Of course. I'd love to meet them." Excitement grew in Samuel's chest. "I look forward to getting to know the residents of Harmony Springs. I enjoy making new friends."

Travis chuckled. "Good quality in a pastor." He clapped Samuel's shoulder. "You shouldn't have a problem with that. People here are pretty friendly."

"Good. My mother always said I could charm a tree from its roots."

His comment made the Doyles laugh. Cassie grinned, mischief written on her face. "Then perhaps you'll catch some woman's eye before you know it."

Samuel rolled his eyes with a grin. "Something tells me you're a matchmaker, Mrs. Doyle."

Her answering smile told him he was right.

Travis shook his head, giving his wife a fond expression. "Cass is a romantic."

"So am I."

The admission came out before Samuel thought the better of it. Two sets of eyes regarded him with curiosity.

Cassie spoke first. "Is that so?"

He nodded, sheepish. "When I fall in love, I intend to make my beloved feel like a princess."

"Aww." Cassie put a hand over her heart. "How beautiful. The future Mrs. Allen is a lucky lady."

Samuel's cheeks heated. He ducked his head. "Thanks, ma'am. But as I said, it'll probably be some time before I meet her."

His hostess's lips turned up. "We'll see about that."

*B*y three o'clock the next day, Samuel's head swam with information on all the shopkeepers he'd met. Travis had taken him to fifteen local businesses. Everyone was eager to meet the new preacher. He'd handled more questions about his history and credentials than he expected. It seemed the people of Harmony Springs wanted to make sure their pastor had a good education. Thankfully, he had.

As they left the bank, Travis slipped his hat back on his head. "All that's left on Main Street is Mrs. Holt's shop. She's the milliner. After we visit her, we can make our last stop to see Mrs. Jefferson at the school."

"Sounds good," Samuel said. "Everyone here is as kind as you said."

Travis chuckled. "Glad you think so." His eyes twinkled. "I should probably warn you about Mrs. Holt, though."

"Warn me?" With its window boxes and freshly painted blue trim, the hat shop exuded as much welcome as any of the other businesses.

Travis's chuckle became a full laugh. "Oh, she's a lovely lady. A lovely lady with a sharp tongue and two single daughters of marriageable age."

Samuel suppressed a wince. "Ah. I don't suppose this will be a quick meeting, then?"

"I wouldn't count on it."

They entered the shop, a bell clanging overhead as one had in every store in town. A woman with graying hair and large brown eyes emerged from the back. "Welcome, Sheriff! Good to see you." Her gaze landed on Samuel. "Hello, sir. Are you visiting the Doyles?"

Travis swept his hat from his head. "Mrs. Holt, allow me to introduce Pastor Allen. He arrived yesterday."

"Oh!" Mrs. Holt's lips curved into a smile. "What a blessing! I'd heard we were getting a preacher, but we've heard that

before and nothing came of it. I'm so happy you're here, Pastor."
She glanced over her shoulder before her smile turned...calcu-
lating? "Please wait right there. I'd love for you to meet my
girls."

"Here we go," Travis muttered under his breath as Mrs.
Holt disappeared in a flurry of swishing skirts. "Prepare
yourself."

"What do I do?" Samuel asked, a brief bout of panic seizing
him.

"Declare your intention to fall in love with one of them?"

Samuel opened his mouth to give a sharp retort, only to
calm when he realized the sheriff was teasing him. "Very
funny." He doubted he'd be able to fall in love anytime soon.
Not when his heart still belonged to—

"Here they are!" Mrs. Holt flounced into the room as
dramatically as she'd left it, but now she had two young women
in tow. "These are my daughters, Francine and Abigail. Girls,
this is Pastor Allen."

The young women murmured their greetings. Both had
brown hair and brown eyes, their dresses tailored to them
perfectly. They smiled at him in unison. Francine and Abigail
were quite pretty, but nothing stirred in his heart, just as he
predicted. He gave them the same smile he'd given every other
person in town. "Ladies."

Francine stepped forward, her lashes fluttering faster than
should be possible. "I'm looking forward to hearing your first
sermon, Pastor. Do you enjoy giving them?"

Why did that question sound like more than it was? Samuel
cleared his throat. He resisted the urge to tug at his collar. "Yes,
I like it just fine."

"Will there be a social to welcome you?" This question from
Abigail, who glared at her sister as if indignant that she'd
managed to speak first.

"Uh..."

Travis cut in. "Of course. We'll give him a potluck lunch to celebrate his first Sunday as our preacher, right after services."

The ladies tittered their agreement in a chorus of giggles. Even their mother joined in. "Well, that should make for a wonderful community event," Mrs. Holt said, her smile bright. "Both my girls are excellent cooks. We'll be sure to bring a couple of tasty dishes."

"Great." Samuel pasted what he hoped was a convincing smile on his lips. "It's been a pleasure, ladies, but we have one more stop to make."

Francine took another step closer. "Oh? Heading to the mercantile?"

"No, ma'am. The schoolhouse."

The three women exchanged glances. "To visit...Mrs. Jefferson?"

Why were they suddenly acting strange? And what did those looks mean? Before he could ask, Travis nodded and opened the door. "See you at church on Sunday."

Samuel echoed the sentiment before hurrying outside. When the door shut behind him, he released a breath of relief. "Well. That was something."

"Get used to it. You're a single man in a frontier town. But don't worry too much. Every woman has five men courting her."

"Really?"

Travis shrugged. "That might be a bit of an exaggeration, but not much."

"Hmm. Then it's a good thing I don't plan on marrying soon, isn't it?" Samuel grinned. It soon faded when he remembered the Holts' reactions to his upcoming visit. "Travis, why did the ladies act funny when I mentioned Mrs. Jefferson? She's married, isn't she?"

"Nope. As far as I can tell, she's a widow."

"Ah." Something turned in his gut. "She's young?"

"Yep."

Great. "Am I going to have to deflect flirting again?"

Travis laughed. "From Mrs. Jefferson? No. She's not so much as looked at a man since moving here in May of '87. I don't think you have anything to fear there. She is a wonderful lady, though. I think you'll like her."

Samuel relaxed. "Then I can't wait to meet her."

❧

"Thanks for your help, Ella," Lydia said, swiping a cloth over the blackboard to erase the white chalk marks. "I wasn't sure how I would sort through all these books on my own."

"I'm happy to help. Cody will be working for several more hours, and the kids love playing in the schoolyard." Ella tugged the box of books closer. She peered inside, her eyes widening. "All this was a donation?"

"An anonymous one. Johnny at the mercantile brought it over before school this morning. Said a wealthy patron wanted to do some good."

"A wealthy patron? In Harmony Springs?" Ella's forehead crinkled. "Are there any rich people here?"

"You mean other than you?" Lydia shot her friend a grin.

Ella chuckled. "My *parents* are rich, not me." She fell quiet, her eyes closing briefly.

Lydia let her process. Over a year ago, Ella's family attempted to force her into marriage with an abusive man. When she fled to Montana and married Cody instead, her father and ex-fiancé tried to get her back by threatening her and her new family. Lydia first met Ella when the woman's ex-fiancé kidnapped her and left her tied up in a hotel room in

Helena. The man had been killed in a scuffle that followed after Ella was rescued. Her father, though, never faced charges, as it was impossible to determine his involvement in the attacks on Ella's family. There were rumors that he'd face charges in Boston for swindling clients, but according to Ella's sister, nothing had come of that either.

People with lots of money rarely received justice. A hard fact of life.

Lydia bit back a sigh. She dropped the cloth and skirted her desk to give Ella a hug. "I'm glad you're here."

Ella sniffed, swiping at a tear before hugging Lydia back. "Thanks. I'm glad we're friends." They pulled away and started unpacking the box. The box was emptied and the sorting halfway done when Ella turned to Lydia. "You seem a little recovered from yesterday."

That sharp pain that was all too common in November pierced her anew. Now, though, she longed for release. Maybe it was time to reveal a bit of her past to Ella. Dorothy often told Lydia speaking about the pain could diminish it. Hopefully, her mother-in-law was right.

With a long exhale, Lydia looked Ella in the eyes. "You know I was married."

Ella blinked a couple times, then nodded. "Yes." She studied Lydia a moment. "You told me once you knew what it was like to lose someone. Your husband?"

"Yes. His name was Frank. We'd been married for several years when he got influenza. The doctor couldn't do anything for him. I nursed him as best I could, but a week later, he was gone."

"Oh, Lydia." Ella slipped an arm around her shoulders. "I'm so sorry."

Lydia bit her lip, her throat tightening. "It was hard enough losing Frank. We'd been friends since childhood. But that wasn't the worst of it." A sob choked her next words. Tears flooded her cheeks, and to her horror, she wept uncontrollably. If it weren't for Ella's arms holding her up, she'd be a bawling heap on the floor.

Her cries startled Rosie from her nap on a blanket near the table. The baby's wails soon joined hers. Ella bit her lip, helplessness written on her face.

Lydia inhaled as much air as she could, hiccoughing between words. "You...should...see...to...her."

Ella picked up her daughter. "But..."

"Mama!" Isaiah burst into the classroom, followed closely by his five-year-old brother, Jonah. "Addie fell down and is crying." He froze, staring at Lydia. "Mrs. Jefferson, what's wrong?"

She pulled out a handkerchief, giving her eyes and cheeks a good drying. "I was just telling your mama about Mr. Jefferson." And had been about to tell her about someone else, but for now, it seemed her moment of sharing secrets had ended. She put a hand on Ella's arm. "I'll see to Addie."

"Are you sure?"

"Yes." She punctuated her reply with a smile. "Thanks for being there, Ella. Maybe we can talk more another time?"

Ella nodded, rocking Rosie in her arms. "Perhaps you can come over after school tomorrow?"

"All right."

Feeling a little better, Lydia made her way into the schoolyard. Addie sat on the ground, sniffling with tear marks down her cheeks. Lydia crouched beside her. "Are you okay, Addie?"

The two-year-old pushed out her lower lip. "Ouchy."

"Where does it hurt?"

Addie pointed to her arm.

Lydia picked her up, wiping dirt from the child's dress. "Would a kiss make it better?"

A small giggle came from the little girl, along with a shy nod. Lydia lifted Addie's arm and placed a gentle kiss there. "There. All better. Shall we go in and see your mama?"

At Addie's nod, Lydia turned for the school steps. She entered the building to see Jonah and Isaiah running around the classroom. Ella gave her a sheepish chuckle, cradling Rosie in one arm. "I think they've hit their limit. We should probably head home."

"Of course. I understand." Lydia smiled at Addie, then Ella. "This little one is fine. She wants to see her mama, though."

"Come here, precious," Ella cooed. She held out her free arm, and Addie practically jumped into her mother's embrace.

"Here, let me take Rosie." Lydia reached for the baby.

"Thanks, Lydia." Ella kissed Addie's cheek. "You ready to go home, sweetie?"

"Home," Addie repeated with a nod.

Ella called to the boys. "Time to get in the wagon."

"Okay, Mama!" Isaiah bolted for the door, Jonah close behind him. As Lydia and Ella headed in the same direction, Jonah's voice floated in from the yard. "It's Uncle Travis!"

"Travis?" Lydia came to a stop at the top of the school steps. "I wonder what brings him here."

Ella shook her head. "Good question. Hopefully, everything's all right. Oh...he has someone with him."

Travis raised a hand in greeting, the newcomer a few steps behind him. "Howdy, ladies. We've got ourselves a new preacher, and I wanted to bring him by for introductions."

The pastor stepped up beside him. Lydia's gaze turned to the tall man. Their eyes locked, and she forgot how to breathe.

Curly light-brown hair. Sparkling blue-green eyes. A confident stance. The years fell away as she stared at the one man she'd never thought to see again.

"Sam."

His name escaped her lips in a breathy whisper. Dark spots

danced in her vision, blurring the shock covering his face. Old feelings poured over her in a rush of confusion. They vied for dominance until one burned hot above the others.

Anger.

Without a word, she spun and marched back into the school.

CHAPTER 3

*H*e'd seen a ghost. Samuel was sure of it.

That was the only possible explanation for imagining Lydia Davis standing at the top of the school steps. Must be all that talk about love over the last two days. He blinked hard and shook his head before focusing on the woman holding a toddler. "Mrs. Jefferson, I presume?"

The redhead frowned, her gaze darting at the school, then back to him. "No. I'm Ella Brooks." She held out a hand. "Nice to meet you, Pastor."

"You as well." They shook hands.

Travis crossed his arms over his chest. "Ella is my sister-in-law. Cassie's brother married her almost two years ago."

Samuel tilted his head, taking in the three children obviously over the age of two. Ella must have seen his confusion because she smiled. "Cody and I adopted our children."

"Adoption is an admirable calling, ma'am."

The oldest boy stepped forward. "Yeah. My first mama and papa died in a riding accident. My new papa used to be Uncle Cody, and she was Aunt Ella." He pointed at his mother. "But now we're all Brooks, and we even got a new sister, once she finally came out of Mama's tummy." He glanced around. "Hey, where'd Mrs. Jefferson go with Rosie?"

The woman he'd seen on the steps. Samuel swallowed. Would a second look reveal her to resemble his Lydia less? And why in the world had she spun back into the building after the introduction?

Ella bit her lip. "I'm not sure." She gave Samuel an apologetic smile. "Lydia is usually very collected. I wonder if she isn't feeling well. She whispered something before going inside. I'll check on her. Travis, would you mind holding Addie?"

Lydia.

Samuel's heart lurched. Could it be...? But no. That was impossible.

Travis introduced him to the children while Ella disappeared into the school. Samuel found a smile for the boys despite his roiling feelings. They chatted for a few minutes. When footsteps sounded from the school, Samuel looked up, wondering if Ella had brought the teacher with her.

She hadn't. Instead, Ella held a baby on her hip and a deep frown on her face. She came to a stop beside Samuel and Travis. "Lydia said she isn't up for company right now."

"She's not?" Travis squinted. "Is she all right?"

"I...don't know." Ella tilted her head, her green eyes turning on Samuel. "I'm sorry you came all this way for nothing."

Something glittered in her eyes, something he couldn't read. Before he had a chance to analyze it, Ella said a polite goodbye and gathered her children into a nearby wagon. Travis helped her get them settled. As the family drove away, the sheriff turned to him. "I need to get back to the office. Do you want some company walking home?"

"No, thanks." He needed to think through this strange encounter. "The parsonage isn't far. Thanks for all your help today, Travis. I appreciate it."

"No problem."

The men shook hands. Travis headed back toward town. Samuel began walking in the direction of his new home, but movement at one of the school windows made him pause. A woman stared back at him for one long second. His heart skipped a beat before thudding painfully hard. She ducked back, but there was no doubt.

Lydia was here. *His* Lydia.

Waves of emotion pulsed through him. Joy. Hesitation. Surprise. What was she doing here? Why had she left their hometown all those years ago without a word?

And why didn't she want to see him?

A whisper coursed through his heart, the memory of the last time they'd seen each other flashing through his mind. Shame filled him. Maybe he did know why she didn't want to see him.

Still...it had been a long time. Surely, she'd forgiven him by now. Even if he couldn't quite forgive himself.

Indecision warred inside. Did he leave her to her classroom, or should he get the answers to questions that had haunted him for seven years?

His feet made the decision for him. Before he knew it, he was striding toward the school, his legs eating up the steps two at a time.

~

*L*ydia's hand trembled. She shouldn't have peered out the window. Samuel saw her, and he wasn't going to let it be. Moments later, his footsteps shook the small schoolroom. She turned to the wall, unprepared to face him.

"Lydia."

That voice. The one she'd heard time and again since she was five years old. It was deeper now, more masculine, but still familiar—and it held an intimate warmth she'd forced herself to forget.

A shiver danced down her spine. She held herself rigid. The polite thing to do would be to turn and greet him. But how could she? He'd abandoned her when she needed him most. The anger bubbled up again.

Samuel's footsteps drew closer. "Lydia? It is you, isn't it?"

She inhaled a sharp breath and spun around. "What do you want, Mr. Allen?"

He froze. "Mr. Allen?" A frown turned his lips down. "Since when is there such formality between us?"

"If you can't figure it out, I have nothing to say to you." Her throat burned.

His blue-green eyes sparked with fire. "I'm not the one who disappeared without a word. If either of us has reason to be upset, it's me."

"You?" she hissed. "How dare you!"

He crossed his arms over a broad chest. "Where'd you go, Lydia?"

"It's Mrs. Jefferson to you. You lost the right to call me by my first name when you abandoned me."

His brow furrowed. "Abandoned? I went to seminary. How is that..."

"Don't act innocent," she snapped. "You left and let someone else pick up the pieces of my life."

The confusion in his eyes only made her angrier. "Oh!" Lydia threw up her hands. "Never mind. You may leave."

He didn't move. His eyes moved back and forth slightly in a manner that said he was putting together a puzzle. She spun again, packing her things into a small bag to take home.

"Mrs...Jefferson."

Lydia slung the bag over her arm. She took a deep breath before facing him again and raising her brow.

Samuel stared, his mouth falling open. "You married *Frank*?" Hurt flashed over his features. "Why? When?"

So he didn't know she'd married his childhood best friend. Not that she'd had much choice, thanks to him. And he dared ask why?

Lydia gritted her teeth. "Figure it out, Mr. Allen. Good day." She stomped down the aisle and out the door.

When she'd made it halfway across the yard, Samuel caught up. He clasped her wrist, pulling her to an abrupt stop. The momentum of his grip propelled her into his chest. For a moment, time faded away and she was eighteen again, snug in the embrace of the man she loved. The man she was going to marry.

Reality crashed in with all its awful implications. Lydia shoved away from him. "Don't touch me!"

"Lydia, please. We need to talk."

"No, we don't. There's nothing left to say." She walked away at a brisk clip.

He jogged after her. "There's plenty to say. You're not making any sense, and I'm more confused than ever. I need answers."

She stopped. Her chest felt as though it might burst as she glared at Samuel. How did he not understand? He tore out her heart and trampled it, and now had the audacity to pretend she owed him answers? "You left. I married Frank. There's nothing more to tell." Her tone turned icy. "Now leave me alone."

Angry tears blurred her vision as she stomped away. Thankfully, Samuel didn't follow. It seemed he'd finally taken the hint.

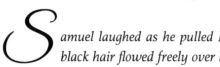

amuel laughed as he pulled Lydia toward the barn. Her black hair flowed freely over her shoulders in long waves, her hazel eyes flashing with joy. "What's this surprise you promised me, Sam?"

"You'll see." He squeezed her hand. "I think you're gonna like it."

"If you came up with it, of course I will."

Words like that melted him. Samuel shut the barn door behind them and immediately took her in his arms. His lips found hers, pouring his heart into the kiss. She returned it with an innocent passion that drove him crazy.

When he finally pulled back, Lydia laughed softly. She traced his lips with her finger. "I'm going to miss you so much while you're away at seminary."

His grip on her tightened. "We'll write each other. Often. I don't think I can last more than a week without hearing from my Lydi."

She wrinkled her nose. "Aren't nicknames supposed to be shorter? Just dropping the 'a' doesn't seem to make much difference."

"It makes enough for me." He tapped her nose. "I like calling you Lydi from time to time."

She tipped her head forward, joining their lips once more. Samuel could quite happily kiss her until he left tomorrow, but that didn't seem prudent. With one more brush of their lips, he took her hand again. "C'mon. The surprise is in the loft."

They climbed the ladder. Lydia's soft gasp when she reached the top made him grin. "You like it?"

"Sam!" She turned in a slow circle, hands clasped against her chest. "It's beautiful."

The loft was aglow with lanterns. Late-summer flowers adorned vases placed strategically around the room. In the middle of it all was a large blanket, and on top, a picnic basket full of food.

Another surprise awaited Lydia at the bottom of the basket. Samuel could hardly wait to present it. But first, dinner.

He seated her on the blanket before plopping down beside her. "I got your favorites from the café. Roast chicken sandwiches, watermelon, lemonade." He pulled each item from the basket as he spoke. "And cinnamon jumbles for dessert."

They ate and talked and laughed, much as they'd done since they were children. But somewhere along the way, Samuel had fallen in love with Lydia. To his astonishment—and joy—she returned his feelings. All that was left now was to ask her to be his permanently.

Samuel reached into the basket, his hand closing over the small black box inside. He withdrew it as Lydia took her final bite of cookie.

"Mmm." She smacked her lips before taking a sip of lemonade. "Everything was so good, Sam."

"One more thing." He took a deep breath before getting on one knee. Lydia's eyes widened, her gaze darting between his and the box in his hand. Samuel held it up. "I know we're young, Lydi, and I'm about to leave for a few years. But I know you're the only woman for me. I love you and want to spend my life with you. It might be a lot to ask you to wait, but I hope you feel the same." He opened the box. A diamond ring sparkled in the light of the lanterns. "This ring is my promise to you. Will you marry me?"

Tears shone in her eyes. She laughed and tackled him in a hug. "Of course I will!"

Samuel managed to keep his balance as he chuckled. "I thought you'd say yes, but I didn't expect that much enthusiasm." He grinned, pulling the ring from its box and slipping it onto her finger.

Lydia's gaze rested on the ring only a moment before she framed his face in her hands. "I love you, Sam. I'm glad we're going to spend forever together."

"Me too."

He kissed her for a few sweet moments before forcing himself to pull away. "All right. Should we clean up? I can walk you home."

She shook her head. "My parents are still away, and this is the last time we'll see each other for over a year." She gazed out the loft window. A gentle breeze blew in, lifting the waves framing her face. "Can we sit here and watch the moon rise? And count the stars like we did as kids?"

"No argument here." Samuel settled against a hay bale. Lydia curled up beside him, resting her head on his shoulder.

No words passed between them for a half hour while they watched the moon rise. Then they talked quietly, dreaming about their future when Samuel returned to Aspen Grove as a pastor.

When the moon climbed high in the sky, Lydia sighed. "I suppose it's time to go."

Sudden desperation swept over Samuel. He wouldn't see her again for such a long time. Tugging her close, he pressed his lips to her. Lydia responded as always, with her sweet innocence. Samuel took the kiss deeper. He'd never allowed his passions to get out of hand, but with him leaving on the morrow, he couldn't seem to get enough of his new fiancée.

After a minute, Lydia drew back with a gasp. She gaped at him with wide eyes. "Sam, I need to go."

"Not yet. Just another minute, Lydi, please."

Indecision flittered over her face. Slowly, she settled against him again. "I guess one more minute wouldn't hurt."

Samuel jerked awake. He groaned. The reality of his dream cut through his heart. It was one he'd had more than once, an exact memory of the last time he saw Lydia. She'd trusted him, trusted that he meant it when he said one more minute. But one minute turned into two, and two into more, and by the time the sun rose over the horizon, irreparable damage had been done. He could never forget the feeling of shame that weighed on him that morning. Far worse had been the stricken look in Lydia's eyes when she first saw him in the light of day.

He'd hugged her close and tried to comfort her.

"It'll be all right, Lydi. We're getting married. No one has to know what happened."

She swallowed hard. "But Sam...what if there's a baby?"

A brief moment of panic threatened. Could there be from one encounter? He rested his forehead against hers, inhaling deeply. "If there is, I'll come back and marry you right away."

"But you'd get kicked out of seminary."

"We'll figure it out if it comes to that, okay? I promise."

He walked her home. They shared a final embrace. He waited until she got to her front door. Just before she went inside, she looked back. The grief on her face felt like a punch in the gut. Samuel wanted to run to her and reassure her once more, but she disappeared inside and shut the door.

He'd never seen her again. They wrote back and forth for four months before her letters stopped. He kept writing, but with each unanswered letter, panic built stronger. His parents visited at six months. Samuel asked for news of Lydia. Dread took hold when they'd exchanged a telling glance. His mother placed a hand on his arm.

"Her family left town, Samuel. No one knows where they went. I'm sorry."

The pain that slashed through him in that moment was worse than he'd ever imagined possible. He nearly left seminary to search her out, but his parents convinced him to continue his studies.

"She's gone, son. They could have traveled anywhere. You'd be on a wild goose chase in this massive country."

His father's words were wise. That didn't mean they'd been any easier to take. Alone and heartbroken, Samuel threw himself into his studies. Over the years, his classmates tried to set him up with various women, but Samuel never lost his love for Lydia. He even searched for her, looking desperately for any clues as to her whereabouts.

His search was fruitless.

Before receiving his first assignment, his mentor suggested he try to find a wife. But he couldn't. He doubted he'd ever feel for another woman what he felt for Lydia.

Now she was here. In the same town. And she wanted nothing to do with him. Clearly, he'd hurt her worse than he thought with his youthful indiscretion. She trusted him to keep her purity safe, and he'd broken it instead.

Guilt slithered through him. He owed her an apology. The only question was, would she listen?

CHAPTER 4

*A*fter school the next day, Lydia sat in Ella's parlor.
Anxiety rippled through her to the point she could no
longer sit. While Ella made tea in the kitchen, Lydia paced the
room, Rosie nestled in her arms. Samuel's arrival in Harmony
Springs couldn't have come at a worse time. Not that any time
would have been good, but this week of all weeks?

"Here we are." Ella's cheerful voice reached the parlor
before she did. "I've got some cookies to go with the tea. I made
shortbread." She placed the treats on a table beside the sofa.
"Why don't you lay Rosie down on her blanket? She's fast
asleep."

Indeed. Rosie's lips puckered in a small O, her eyes closed.
Lowering herself to her knees, Lydia did as Ella suggested
before getting up again and joining her friend on the sofa. Ella
poured a cup of tea and handed it to her. Lydia inhaled the
comforting aroma of lemon and citrus. The scent calmed her
nerves a bit. She took a sip and closed her eyes. For a moment,
she could pretend there was nothing wrong.

"Thank you for inviting me over, Ella. I needed this." She

bit into one of the cookies. Butter and sugar melted in her mouth. Another comfort.

"I'm glad you came," Ella said. "It's too bad we were interrupted yesterday. It sounded as though you needed to talk."

Guilt nudged Lydia. "It's something I should have talked about a long time ago. I'm sorry I've kept this to myself."

Ella shook her head and reached for Lydia's hand. "No need to apologize. I didn't speak of my abuse to anyone for years, so I understand. Sometimes the words just won't come." She gave Lydia's hand a gentle squeeze before letting go. "Does the new pastor have anything to do with your story?"

Samuel's face flashed through Lydia's mind. Time had been kind to him. He'd always been handsome, but he had lost the soft edges of youth and turned fully into a man. Her stomach flipped. Lydia pressed a hand there, stunned at the unexpected reaction. Yes, she'd loved him once, but no more. Not since he'd broken her heart.

"Lydia?"

She blinked hard. "Sorry. I was just thinking." Blowing a strand of hair away from her eyes, she sighed. "Yes, Samuel is a part of my story."

Ella raised her brows but remained quiet.

Lydia took another sip of tea, then placed the cup and saucer on the table and turned to face her friend. "I told you I lost my husband but that losing him wasn't the worst thing that happened." She drew in a fortifying breath. "Two days after he passed, my daughter died too."

"Your daughter?" Ella sucked in a breath. "Oh, Lydia. I am so sorry." Her gaze fell on Rosie while her throat worked. "I can't even imagine the pain that caused." She swallowed hard. "How old was she?"

"Four." Lydia closed her eyes. "There was an outbreak of influenza. So many people were sick. I'm not sure how Frank caught it. He was ill for three days before Charlotte got it too." Her voice broke. "I tried everything to save them. I prayed while nursing them, desperately begging God to spare my family. But...for whatever reason, He chose to take them home." A tear slipped down her cheek. She brushed it away. "Mother also got sick, but she recovered."

"And you?" Ella asked quietly.

Lydia shook her head. "Nothing. I was one of the few who escaped the illness." Her throat tightened. "But I would have given anything to trade places with my little girl. It killed me watching her fade away. She was the light of my life." She lifted her teacup but didn't raise it to her lips. "Ruby looks just like her."

"Does she?" Ella studied Lydia for a moment. "That makes sense. You and Ruby could pass for mother and daughter. Charlotte must have taken after you, then? Not your husband?"

Lydia's hand clenched around her cup. "She couldn't have taken after Frank." She braced herself for Ella's reaction. "Charlotte wasn't his daughter."

A minute of silence followed her statement. Ella watched her, head tilted to one side. No judgment appeared on her face. Instead, she appeared contemplative. When she spoke, her voice was soft. "Is that how Pastor Allen comes into the story?"

Familiar shame crept into Lydia's heart. "Yes." She put the cup down again and stood, pacing the floor. "Samuel and I were childhood sweethearts. I can't remember a time I didn't love him. Everyone thought we'd get married someday, just like they knew he'd be a pastor. We had our lives figured out. The night before he left for seminary, he asked me to marry him. I said yes."

Ella gasped softly.

Lydia stopped pacing, pressing a hand to her stomach. "We let ourselves get carried away after his proposal. Three months later, I realized I was pregnant."

"Did you write to Pastor Allen?"

"I did." Anger sparked again. "At first, I didn't know what to do. I was scared. Samuel's parents were going to visit him, and I made a decision to trust them with the truth. They were surprisingly understanding and agreed to take a letter to him explaining my condition." Her fingers gripped the material of her skirt. "But when they came home, there was no return letter. Mrs. Allen told me Samuel denied the child could be his at all. He wanted nothing to do with the baby...or with me. When I needed him most, he abandoned me. He abandoned our little girl." A tear rolled down her cheek. "The worst part is that he'd promised me if I became pregnant, he'd leave seminary and come home to marry me immediately. But when it came to that, he refused to do the right thing. He condemned me to a shattered reputation and life as a single mother, not taking any responsibility for what he'd done."

Ella's mouth hung open. Indignation flashed in her eyes. "That's awful."

With a deep sigh, Lydia pressed on. "You can see why his arrival here upset me. I thought never to lay eyes on him again." She pinched the bridge of her nose in an effort to alleviate the headache that had started to throb. "Frank was a friend of ours. He'd made plans to move west into the Dakota Territory with Dorothy. When he found out about my pregnancy and what Samuel did, he offered to marry me to protect my reputation and give my child a father. I married him, and my parents joined us in our journey west. Neither of us expected love. It was a convenient marriage. Frank never so much as kissed me in our five years together. We had great affection for each other as friends...but nothing more. He was a wonderful father to Charlotte. She was well loved by us both." Tears threatened again. "And now they're both gone." She sniffed. "Yesterday was two years since Charlotte's death."

Ella scooted closer and enveloped Lydia in a hug. "I'm so

sorry, my friend. What pain you've been carrying." When Ella pulled back, her eyes shone with concern. "How are you going to handle Samuel being in Harmony Springs?"

"I thought about asking Mother if we could pick up and move again. We only came to this town because it's where her husband was from. We could have gone to the Dakotas where her daughter and grandchildren are. But I can't leave my students. They're like family to me." She summoned a smile. "And I wouldn't want to leave my favorite friend either."

Ella smiled back. "I'm glad you're staying, but Lydia, you're going to run into the pastor a lot. Will you be able to handle it?"

"I'll have to." Lydia raised her chin. "It was seven years ago. Perhaps Samuel has changed. But he broke my trust along with my heart. We'll never be what we once were."

The front door opened. Little feet scampered into the room. Jonah hurtled toward them. Excitement danced over his happy face. "Papa's home early!" He pointed toward the entryway. "See?"

Cody rounded the corner, a smile on his face. "Howdy, Lydia." He tipped his hat before removing it to hang on a peg. His gaze turned to Ella, his smile turning soft. "Hi, darlin'." He came close and planted a kiss on his wife's upturned lips.

Ella's hand went to his cheek, and for a moment, they were lost in each other's eyes.

They made love seem so easy. Lydia's chest ached with longing. If only she could find that again.

Cody straightened. "We have a guest. Isaiah and Addie wanted to talk to him in the yard, but he should be in shortly."

Jonah perked up. "Oh, yeah!" He bolted back out the door.

"Who is it?" Ella asked, standing.

"The new pastor. He's making the rounds, visiting different ranchers today."

Lydia shot to her feet. Maybe she could escape through the back door. "Thank you for having me, Ella. I'll be going now."

"You're leaving?" Cody said, a wrinkle appearing between his brows. "I thought you were staying for supper."

"Well, I..."

She got no farther. Samuel came into the room, hat in hand and a friendly smile on his face. When he saw Lydia, he stopped dead in his tracks.

Time froze as their eyes locked.

~

Samuel stood in silent shock. The last person he'd expected to see in the Brooks' living room was Lydia. Recovering his manners, he stepped forward. "Hi, Lyd...uh, Mrs. Jefferson. Mrs. Brooks."

Mrs. Brooks glanced between him and Lydia before producing a hesitant smile. "Pastor Allen. How nice to see you again. Would you like some tea?"

"No, thanks, ma'am. I'm just going around introducing myself to folks in this area. Your husband here offered to show me around the ranch, but we wanted to greet you first."

"That's thoughtful," Mrs. Brooks said. "Thank you for coming."

"Of course." Samuel grinned. "Cody said he'd show me how to rope a bull sometime."

A snort came from Lydia's direction. His eyes followed the sound, taking in the smirk on her face. "What? You don't think I can do it?"

Her mask settled back in place. "I'm sure you can do whatever you set your mind to."

Now why did those words feel like an insult? Samuel scratched his neck. Before he could formulate a response, Lydia turned to Mrs. Brooks. "Thanks for the tea, Ella. I should be getting back to town."

"I'll walk you out," Mrs. Brooks replied.

The two women headed for the door. Cody watched them go. He hummed thoughtfully before turning to Samuel. "Am I off, or is there tension between you and Lydia?"

Samuel stifled a sigh. He caught a glimpse of Lydia through the window. She stood with her arms crossed and head down, listening to something Mrs. Brooks said. He tore his gaze away. "We used to be engaged."

Cody stared at him. After blinking a few times, he whistled low. "Well, I'll be. I'm guessing it didn't end on good terms."

"I don't know why it ended." Samuel stuck his hands into his pockets. "Everything seemed to be good. I asked her to marry me right before leaving for seminary. We exchanged letters for a few months, and then they stopped coming from her. When my parents came to see me, they said she and her family up and left town. I never knew what happened to her." He glanced out the window again. "I still don't." His tone hardened. "Though it seems she married my childhood best friend after disappearing." That stung more than it should.

Cody put a hand on his shoulder. "There must be more to the story. I've known Lydia for a little while now, and she doesn't seem the type to just abandon ship."

"That's just it. She's not. But she won't talk to me. In fact, I get the sense she can't stand the sight of me."

"Yeah. I caught that." Cody nodded toward the door. "You're a preacher. Your line of work is all about forgiveness and grace, right?"

"It is."

"Seems to me the first step toward reconciliation is breaking down those barriers. It probably won't be done in a day, but maybe you can start by giving her space. That might be what she needs most. I imagine you both felt shock seeing the other again."

Samuel scoffed. "That's putting it mildly. She appeared in my life again as suddenly as she disappeared from it."

"Give her some time, Samuel. Get to know this town and the people in it. Maybe Lydia will soften toward you as she gets used to you being around."

Samuel eyed his new friend. His lips turned up in a smile. "You're a wise man, Cody Brooks. I think you have the philosopher in you."

"More like, I have a wife and a sister. Both of whom have taught me a lot about women." Cody shook his head. "Not that I'll ever understand them."

Mrs. Brooks came back inside, her children surrounding her. She shooed the little ones onto the rug, where the baby had just woken up from her nap.

Cody lifted Rosie into his arms. "Hey, little darlin'."

"I need to start supper," Mrs. Brooks said. She turned to Samuel. "Are you sure I can't offer you any tea?"

He smiled. "No, ma'am. But thank you."

She nodded. Samuel expected that she'd head for the kitchen, but she stood a few moments staring at him until he felt uncomfortable under her intense gaze. He shuffled his feet. Mrs. Brooks blinked, then turned and left the room.

If Cody noticed the strange exchange, he didn't say anything. Most likely, his attention was wrapped up in his daughter. A pang smote Samuel's chest. What would it be like to hold a child of his own? A product of the love between man and wife?

Lydia's face came to mind. For a brief second, Samuel let himself imagine her with a baby in her arms, a smile on her lips as she held their child out to him. He closed his eyes, willing the vision away. It did no good to dwell on something that would never happen.

"Would you like to hold her?"

Samuel coughed, shaking away the lingering dream. "What?"

"Rosie. Do you want to hold her?" Cody held his little girl toward Samuel.

Samuel recognized the gesture of trust. He smiled and opened his arms. "I'd love to."

CHAPTER 5

"*A*ll right, young lady, what's going on?"

Lydia peered over her shoulder. Her mother-in-law stood, hands on hips, eying her as she stirred their vegetable soup at the stove. Lydia strove for a calm tone. "It was a long day."

Dorothy's eyes softened. "And a hard week, at that." Sadness touched her face. No doubt, she was thinking of Frank and Charlotte. Their loss had pained her just as much as it hurt Lydia. Dorothy released a sigh, then shook her head. "I'll set the table."

Thankful that she didn't have to explain her turbulent emotions, Lydia added some pepper to the pot and gave it another stir.

"So are you going to tell me what's really going on?"

Mid-reach for the ladle, Lydia paused. Dorothy Jefferson could sniff out trouble a mile away. Apparently, her vague response hadn't worked. Dodging her question now would only lead to more questions.

Scooping the soup into bowls, Lydia forced herself to speak. "You heard about the new preacher?"

"Of course. Everyone's talking about him. According to the Holt girls, he's mighty handsome." Dorothy sidled up to Lydia, a sly grin on her lips. "You know, it wouldn't hurt if..."

"It's Samuel Allen." The words escaped in a rush.

Dorothy's mouth fell open, matchmaking scheme dropped as suddenly as it began. "Oh...my."

Lydia jerked her head once in a sharp nod. She brought the bowls to the table. After they said a blessing, she cut some thick slices of bread to accompany the soup. The silence between them stretched so long, Lydia fidgeted. "Say something, Mother."

"Hmm?" Dorothy glanced up, blinking. "I'm sorry, dear girl. Just thinking." Another minute passed. With a plunk, Dorothy put her spoon down and faced Lydia. "Have you forgiven him?"

"Wh-what?" Lydia dropped her own spoon. Soup splashed over the side of her bowl. She wiped it with a napkin, avoiding Dorothy's gaze.

"You heard me." Her mother-in-law's voice was gentle. "Have you forgiven Samuel?"

Lydia's throat tightened. She squeezed the napkin between her palms, fighting tears. "I don't know if I can," she whispered. "Not after what he did."

Dorothy took her hand. "He was nineteen, Lydia. It doesn't excuse his actions, but he might have panicked when he heard you were pregnant. The prospect of fatherhood either makes a man run or grow up. In Samuel's case, he ran. But that was seven years ago. He may regret what he did. He might have changed his mind."

Lydia dabbed her tears. "Changed his mind?"

"Have you ever considered that he could have regretted his choice and come home to find you?"

Her world seemed to tilt on its axis. "No." That wasn't possible. Was it?

Dorothy's voice gentled even more, barely over a whisper.

"If he'd come back, he had no way of finding you. We packed up your family overnight and left. No one even knew about you and Frank since you married in a different town. If Samuel wanted to find you, he'd have no clue where to begin."

I'm not the one who disappeared without a word.

Samuel's words from the schoolhouse rammed into her with surprising force. He'd acted as though she owed *him* an explanation. Even so...

"He abandoned me, Mother. He abandoned *Charlotte*." Hot tears filled her eyes. "Even if he did change his mind, he still wasn't there when we needed him most. He knew my reputation would be shattered, and he didn't come back to make it right."

"I know, honey." Dorothy lifted a hand to Lydia's cheek. "Forgiveness doesn't come easily. But even if Samuel isn't sorry for what he did, you owe it to yourself to forgive him. It's only going to eat at you more and more until bitterness is your constant companion. I don't want that for you. Charlotte wouldn't want that for you either."

Words choked her. Lydia shook her head. "I don't know, Mother."

"Just try, darling girl." With a gentle pat, Dorothy lowered her hand and stood. "I'll do the dishes. Why don't you relax? I know you've had a hard week. More so now that your past has come calling."

Lydia rose. She planted a kiss on Dorothy's cheek. "What would I do without you?"

"I haven't a clue." Dorothy chuckled. "Now skedaddle."

The small clapboard house they lived in didn't provide much room to truly skedaddle. The downstairs boasted a kitchen, dining table, and some space for a sofa, a few end tables, and a pretty upholstered chair. The stairs near the sofa led up to two bedrooms that were only big enough for a bed, dresser, and bedside table each. Lydia didn't mind. She had plenty of reasons to be thankful. Having a home was one of those reasons. Frank might have left them a comfortable windfall after his death, thanks to his job as a banker, but money went faster than Lydia liked. They were blessed to have a home in town, not to mention her job, which provided a small but steady income.

She sat on the sofa and reached for the Bible sitting on the end table. Flipping it open, she began to read.

Judge not, and you will not be judged; condemn not, and you will not be condemned; forgive, and you will be forgiven.

The words from the Gospel of Luke made her mouth drop open. She stared at the page, the words staring back. Lydia sucked in a breath and quickly flipped to a new page.

Bear with each other and forgive one another if any of you has a grievance against someone. Forgive as the Lord forgave you.

Apparently, Colossians was in agreement with Luke. She sent a sigh heavenward. "I get it, Lord. You want me to forgive." She sighed again, closing the Bible. "But how do I do so? How do I let go of the past when it still hurts so much?"

Nothing audible came to her. But a silent peace spread through her soul. Lydia sat with it, eyes closed, amazed that such a feeling could coincide with the anxious churning in her gut. She'd simply have to take things one day at a time, one encounter with Samuel at a time. She didn't plan on seeking him out. But if they happened to meet, she could be cordial. Maybe with time, the anger would dissipate.

Lydia drew in a long breath. "I choose to forgive, Lord. Please help me to be kind when I see him." She huffed. "Because I still want to smack him."

～

*J*itters pulsed through Samuel while he greeted the parishioners coming through the door Sunday morning. He'd presided over many church services through the years under John Rivers, but this felt different. This was his parish, his flock.

He didn't want to let them down.

Travis came up the steps with Cassie. Connor slept in his arms. Travis greeted Samuel with a grin. "It's mighty nice having a pastor here in Harmony Springs. Knowing that we'll have regular church services now is a blessing."

Cassie tossed back her blond curls, an easy smile on her lips. "It's good to see you again, Samuel. I trust you're settling in fine?"

"Yes, ma'am. I thank you for the meals you've provided over the past few days. They've been a lifesaver."

She chuckled with a wave of her hand. "I'm glad you enjoyed them. We need our pastor at his best." Giving his arm a pat, she nodded at him and made her way into the church.

Travis clapped him on the back. "You'll do great. See you inside."

As soon as the Doyles disappeared through the door, a soft, feminine voice drifted up to him. "Good morning, Pastor Allen."

He whipped around. Lydia stood with Dorothy Jefferson, hands clasped in front of her. Something he couldn't read sparked in her eyes, but she had a pleasant look on her face. Not exactly a smile, but not a frown either.

That was progress.

Hope flurried in his chest. "Good morning, Lyd—uh, Mrs. Jefferson." He turned to her mother-in-law, a woman he hadn't seen since he was nineteen. "And...Mrs. Jefferson."

The older woman bustled up the steps and enveloped him in a hug. "Gracious, Samuel, you can call me Dorothy, just as you did back home." She set him back, studying his face. "My goodness, you've turned into a man."

He chuckled. "Seven years will do that, ma'am. But you haven't aged a day."

"Still the charmer, I see." She laughed. "I'm looking forward to your sermon, young man. You and Frank talked for hours on end when you were boys. I imagine that gift for gab translated to preaching?"

His collar felt tight. Samuel tugged at it, his cheeks a bit warm. "I hope so."

"Well, you'll have to come over for supper some evening. How's Friday?"

Samuel caught sight of Lydia. She'd quietly climbed the steps and stood a pace behind Dorothy. Her lips pressed in a tight line. His hope evaporated. "Thanks for the offer, but I don't think..."

"We'd be happy to have you come."

His jaw fell open and he stared at Lydia.

She lifted her chin, her brows arching up. "Mother plans to make her beef stew."

Samuel's mouth watered. Dorothy had been famous for her beef stew back home. It was one of his favorite meals. His gaze bounced between the two women, still uncertain. Lydia held his gaze when their eyes met again. He couldn't read her. His heart ached hearing her call Dorothy "mother," hammering home the fact that she'd married Frank. But considering she'd told him to leave her alone the last time he saw her, this felt like an olive branch.

"Thanks for inviting me. I'll be there."

"Wonderful," Dorothy said. "We'll expect you at six o'clock." She clapped once and headed into the church.

Lydia took a step forward, then hesitated. She twisted her fingers around a handkerchief and avoided his gaze. Samuel forced himself to remain quiet, waiting for her to speak. Finally, she met his eyes.

"Did you ever try to find me?"

Her voice was so low, he hardly heard her. But his heart slammed into his ribs as he realized what she asked.

"Yes, Lydi. I looked for you."

She inhaled sharply. He reached out, but Lydia stepped away. His hand lowered slowly back to his side. Her behavior confused him. Was she still angry? Or was something else holding her back? Why had she asked that question?

"I..." She cleared her throat. One hand fluttered to her heart, and she finally met his gaze. "I'll see you Friday."

Samuel released a breath. He nodded in response. Lydia went inside, and he took a minute to compose himself. Thankfully, no other parishioners lined the yard. It was time for him to begin the service, but he gripped the porch railing and inhaled deeply.

One thing was for certain. Lydia Jefferson could still rattle him like no other.

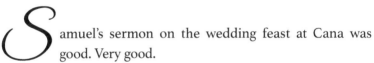

Samuel's sermon on the wedding feast at Cana was good. Very good.

Lydia shook her head, a slight smile tugging at her lips. Of course it was. Dorothy was right—he'd always had a gift for speaking. Samuel made friends wherever he went, well-liked and respected by others. Lydia had marveled at his charisma time and again throughout their youth. Watching him now, surrounded by parishioners in the yard, seeing his interactions with them as they enjoyed the welcome potluck lunch and hearing his ready laugh, it was clear nothing changed in that regard.

That didn't do much to calm the storm she felt inside. She

didn't understand how he so cruelly turned her and Charlotte aside.

But he had searched for her. When?

When Dorothy suggested that morning they invite Samuel for supper on Friday, Lydia initially balked. She wasn't ready to entertain the man in her own home. But Dorothy reminded her that charity extended even to one's enemies. That softened her enough to agree. When Samuel hesitated after Dorothy invited him, Lydia knew it was because of her recent actions toward him. Convincing him to come hadn't been easy for her, but that peace from earlier spread through her when she succeeded.

Along with a familiar zip through her stomach, one that signaled attraction.

Oh, no. That particular feeling had no place in her life anymore, not toward him. Never toward him. She might be willing to forgive, to be cordial, but falling for him again? Absolutely not.

"Mrs. Jefferson!" Ruby came running toward her, arms extended.

Lydia swept her in a hug. "Hello, sweet girl. Did you enjoy services today?"

"Uh-huh. Grandma says the new pastor is talented." Her nose scrunched. "Whatever that means."

Lydia smiled. "It means he has a gift. A calling."

"Like you being a teacher?"

Warmth flowed through her heart. "Exactly." She'd initially picked up teaching because she thought it would help bring in money for her family. But it turned out to be something she loved dearly.

"What do you think of Pastor Allen, Mrs. Jefferson?"

Ruby beamed up at her with wide, expectant eyes, but they were interrupted by a deep, male voice behind them. "Yeah, Mrs. Jefferson, what do you think?"

She straightened, gripping Ruby's hand in hers as she

turned to face Samuel. His blue-green eyes sparkled with mirth, a challenge resting in them. Lydia's heart responded, tugged toward him, much as it had been in their youth.

Feelings were deceptive.

Shoring up her defenses, Lydia produced a tight smile. "Pastor Allen, have you met Ruby?"

His gaze fell to the child. "Hello, Ruby. How are…"

Stopping midsentence, he stared. His face went white.

A shot of concern went through Lydia. "Samuel?"

He blinked.

Ruby moved forward, peering up at him. "Are you all right?"

"I…I think so." Samuel bent down, a shaky smile forming. "Sorry about that. You look so much like your…mother." His eyes flicked up to Lydia before he brought them back to Ruby.

He thought Ruby was hers. Lydia swallowed. Would he make the connection that their daughter indeed would have been at Ruby's age now?

The little girl nodded with a serious air. "That's what Grandma always says. She also says I could be Mrs. Jefferson's twin."

Confusion blanketed Samuel's face. "But…I thought…" He cleared his throat. "Isn't Mrs. Jefferson your mother?"

Ruby shook her head. "My mama died with my papa when I was littler." She frowned. "I don't really remember them anymore."

"I'm sorry to hear that." Samuel took the girl's hands. "But I'm sure whoever is watching you now is doing a great job."

"My grandma." Ruby nodded toward Pearl, who was talking with Dorothy. "But she gets sick a lot. I think she's scared something might happen to her."

Pain squeezed Lydia's chest. She put a hand on Ruby's shoulder. "I thought she was getting better."

"I don't know. She coughs a lot."

Samuel rose. "Do you think she'd like me to visit sometimes?"

Ruby's eyes lit up. "Yeah, she would. I heard her telling Isaiah's mama that she wanted to ask you to check on us. Would you, Pastor Allen?"

"I'd love to. But I want to talk to your grandma first."

"Okay." Ruby tugged him away. "C'mon, let's go."

Samuel's gaze lingered on Lydia even as he started in Pearl's direction. He raised a hand in farewell, then turned his attention to Ruby. They made it to Pearl. The little girl performed introductions before darting off to play with Alice and Isaiah.

Lydia exhaled hard. Samuel's reaction to Ruby, thinking she was hers, spoke volumes. He looked like he'd seen a ghost. What went through his head in those moments? Did he regret leaving her and Charlotte to themselves? Or was he relieved to have never found them?

She had so many questions, but would knowing the answers set her free?

Or break her completely?

CHAPTER 6

Samuel sat beside Pearl in her small cabin on Wednesday. Ruby was right—her grandma happily accepted his company. He suspected her time on earth was short and she wanted spiritual companionship before going to her eternal home. Though he'd counseled a few people before who were nearing death, Pearl was by far the most peaceful about the fact.

"I know the good Lord has a place for me," she said, a faint smile on her lips. Her gaze traveled to Ruby, who played in a corner with some dolls. Pearl lowered her voice. "My only regret is leaving that sweet child alone."

"Where will she go?" Samuel asked.

Pearl coughed, the sound deep in her lungs. Samuel jumped up to pour her a cup of water. After the elderly woman took a drink, she sighed. "Thanks, young man. As for my Ruby, Lydia Jefferson promised to take her in when I go."

Lydia? Samuel blinked. "You want a single woman to raise her?"

Pearl's eyes twinkled despite the cloudiness marring her gaze. "Oh, I have faith there will someday be a man to step in as

Ruby's new papa. I've had many conversations with the Lord about it. I want my baby girl to have two loving parents. She's been without that for too long." She eyed him. "You're single, right?"

The urge to tug his collar was almost too much to resist. Even so, heat spread over his neck. "Uh...yes...but—"

"Hmm. I thought so." Pearl sipped another bit of water. "Do you like children, Pastor?"

How in the world had this conversation turned to him? This time, Samuel did pull on the neckline of his shirt. "I do, ma'am, but—"

"But nothing. It's an innocent question."

The glee on her face told him it was anything but innocent. He shook his head. "Pearl, are you playing matchmaker?"

"Ain't no playing about it. My Ruby needs a good father, and as far as I can tell, you'd be a good candidate. Why don't you ask Mrs. Jefferson on a proper date?"

He choked on air. Coughing, his head whipped back and forth. "I can't do that."

"Why not?"

Not willing to air his history with Lydia to a near stranger, Samuel smiled ruefully. "I just moved to town. My focus now is settling in and getting to know my parishioners. There's no time for courting."

Pearl snorted. It led to another coughing fit. She waved away the water he offered her. "Hogwash," she huffed once she caught her breath. "Haven't you learned yet that God's timing differs from ours? Maybe He doesn't want you doing this alone."

She was a tenacious one—he'd give her that. Samuel patted her hand. "Your desire to see Ruby with a mother and father is commendable, Pearl. But it doesn't mean I'm the one to be that father."

Pearl harrumphed. "Who said this had anything to do with Ruby?"

His brow furrowed. He tilted his head to the left. "Isn't that what brought this whole conversation about?"

"Maybe it started that way, but the more I think of it, it would make sense even if Ruby's future wasn't at stake." She stared at him, and Samuel got the distinct impression she looked into his very soul. He squirmed in the chair. Pearl's lips tipped up. "Yes," she murmured, still eying him. "There's something about you and Mrs. Jefferson. I can't put my finger on it, but I have a feeling you're meant to be together."

Samuel's mouth fell open. "Ma'am, with all due respect, you just met me." Never mind the fact that his heart leapt at the thought of being Lydia's again. This time for good. She might have been somewhat cordial to him yesterday, but it was clear as day she didn't trust him. Though he still couldn't figure out why.

Shame flickered as he remembered how they'd crossed a boundary his last night in Aspen Grove. Fine...he could think of why she didn't trust him. He'd taken her innocence when he'd been responsible for protecting it. A sigh escaped. No wonder she despised him.

Pearl's pat on his hand jerked him back to attention. Her eyes drooped, but she still wore a smile. "Don't be put out, Pastor. I'm an old, old woman who's seen much over the years. What will be will be." With that cryptic statement, she held out her hand. "Help me lie down, please. I need a nap."

Samuel carefully pulled Pearl to her feet. The walk to the bed didn't take long. He made sure she was situated, then went to stoke the fire. December was nearly upon them. The chill in the air hinted at winter's imminent arrival. Pearl needed to stay warm. The last thing she needed was to get worse. Samuel found another blanket and spread it over the already-sleeping woman. He stepped back, watching the slight rise and fall of the blankets. "Lord," he whispered. "Please, bring her comfort."

A small hand slipped into his. Ruby gazed up at him, her hazel eyes luminescent. "She sleeps a lot," the little girl said in a low voice. She tugged him toward the table in the corner. "Would you like some bread and jam?"

He had to get back to town. Mrs. Holt cornered him after services Sunday and issued an invitation for supper this evening. If he didn't leave soon, he'd be late. But a quiet interior nudge told him Ruby needed him, needed reassurance in the uncertainty she faced.

Mrs. Holt and her daughters could wait.

Samuel took the seat Ruby offered. She opened a container and lifted out slices of bread, setting them on a couple of well-worn plates. He stood. "Would you like some help?"

She shook her head, black curls bouncing. "You're the guest."

He slowly lowered himself back down. While Ruby prepared refreshments, he wondered how a child so young knew what to do. She couldn't be more than five or six. Even so, she possessed a maturity he hadn't seen in children twice her age. Whatever she'd experienced in her young life, it made her grow up fast.

Too fast.

She brought the plates to the table. "Here you go. Grandma and I made the jam after picking berries this summer. It's blackberry. There are lots of blackberry bushes around here." She took a big bite of her bread, leaving a smear of purple-black jam across her face. "Isn't it yummy?"

Samuel chuckled. He pointed to his own face. Ruby began licking away the jam, but her eyes remained on him in expectation. He took a bite and chewed slowly. "Mmm. Very good. You and your grandma did a great job."

"Thanks."

She ate another giant bite. Samuel watched her, something pulling at his heart. Her mass of black hair, the shade of hazel in her eyes, her various expressions...all reminded him of Lydia.

When he'd first seen the child on Sunday, he was rendered mute. He'd been certain she was Lydia's daughter. Though he hadn't seen any of Frank in the girl, because she was Lydia's miniature, he assumed they were related. To find out they weren't had also been a shock.

That brought more questions to mind. Lydia always wanted a passel of children, but she had no child with her at church. Had she and Frank been unable to have a baby? Though the thought of her with his former best friend rankled, a rush of sadness passed through him. Lydia was meant to be a mother. The fact that she hadn't had that chance hurt his heart.

What would have happened if he'd stayed in Aspen Grove? If he'd married her as he should have instead of going to seminary? Perhaps they'd have kids of their own—kids who resembled Ruby.

The child in question stared at him, a frown on her face. "Pastor Allen, are you all right?"

That jarred him out of his thoughts. He nodded. "I'm fine, Ruby." After another bite of bread and jam, a thought came to him. "Pastor Allen sounds kind of stuffy, huh?"

She giggled with a nod.

Samuel tapped his cheek, giving her a big smile. "Well then, why don't you call me 'Pastor Samuel' instead? I think that sounds better."

"Okay, Pastor Samuel." Ruby finished her bread. She sat back in her chair.

A sudden coughing fit came from the bed. Samuel rose at once, hurrying to Pearl's side. The woman didn't wake. He found a second pillow to put under her head. One of his doctor friends once said elevating the head could help with a cough.

Pearl's soon eased, though glimmers of pain remained on her face even in sleep.

His chest burned. How much time did she have left?

Ruby sniffled from the table. Samuel glanced her way. Large tears rolled down the girl's cheeks. Her eyes remained locked on her grandma. He went back to the table, kneeling in front of Ruby. Before he could say anything, she launched herself at him, her arms going around his neck and holding on tight.

"She's...gonna...leave...me...too," Ruby sobbed. "Isn't she?"

If his heart hurt before, it was nothing compared to the sensation he felt now in the face of a child's helpless grief. He wrapped his arms around her in return. There was nothing he could say, nothing that would comfort the little girl.

All he could do was be there.

~

On the evening Samuel was to join them for supper, a howling windstorm blew through town. The final day of November proved to be a frigid one. Lydia stoked the fire in the small living space while Dorothy stirred the stew. Savory aromas wafted through the house—tender beef, earthy carrots and potatoes, and a hint of Dorothy's secret ingredients. Sugar and red wine. Neither item was easy to come by, but the saloon owner parted with a bottle of Chardonnay for a surprisingly low price. Lydia half suspected the man had a soft spot for her mother-in-law. Not that Dorothy noticed. She hadn't noticed a man since her husband passed over a decade ago.

Three raps sounded in quick succession at the door. Lydia's stomach swooped low. She took her time getting to her feet, resisting the urge to smooth her dress. What a strange mix of trepidation and anticipation rolling in her gut. Lydia couldn't decide which felt stronger. She pushed to her feet, willing her stomach to stop flipping.

Pulling the door open, she drew in a deep breath. Samuel gave her a tentative smile. "Hello, Mrs. Jefferson."

Offer forgiveness. Lydia motioned him in. "You can call me Lydia, Samuel. I made a bigger fuss over my title than was warranted."

He stepped over the threshold. His blue-green eyes bored into hers. "Are you sure?"

"I'm sure."

"All right...Lydia." His gaze raked her face, leaving the room feeling quite hot despite the door being open.

Dorothy bustled over while Lydia shut the door. The warmth on her face radiated like a lamp. "Samuel, I'm so glad you could make it."

"Thanks for the invitation, Dorothy." He sniffed the air, a smile spreading over his face. "It smells delicious. But that comes as no surprise."

"Oh, you." She swatted his arm, a pleased smile on her lips before she headed for the stove. "Everything's ready. I'll just ladle up the stew and we'll eat. Please, have a seat."

Samuel pulled out a chair, then turned to Lydia with an air of expectation. She knew immediately what he wanted. Biting her lip, she sank into the seat as he pushed it in behind her. "Thank you."

The words sounded so formal. Samuel either didn't notice or was too polite to comment. He took the seat beside her just as Dorothy brought two steaming bowls of stew to the table. She went back for the third. "Samuel, would you mind saying grace?"

"Not at all."

Dorothy sat with the third bowl of stew. She held out her hands, one to Lydia and one to Samuel. Lydia stared for a moment, her heart dropping again. They always joined hands for grace, but that meant she had to hold Samuel's hand. Something she'd done plenty of in her youth. But now?

His gaze flashed between her and Dorothy before he extended his hand to her mother-in-law. Then, ever so slowly, he held his other hand up toward Lydia. She paused a moment, then slipped her hand into his.

Lydia didn't hear a word of his prayer. She was too focused on the way his warm, rough palm felt against hers, bringing her back to their teen years. Back to a time that was good, full of innocence and first love.

She blinked back tears. It would do no good to cry in front of Samuel and Dorothy.

With an *amen*, Samuel released her hand, allowing her to breathe again. They tucked into their food. Dorothy asked Samuel about his time in seminary. He launched into a long explanation that let Lydia study him without fear of being caught. It was obvious he enjoyed his years of formation, that he carried a passion for ministry. His eyes sparkled and his face remained animated while he talked. Dorothy asked questions that furthered the conversation. Lydia ate her stew, listening, but couldn't help wondering what life would have been like if he'd just come home sooner. If he'd come as soon as he knew she was in trouble, her reputation wouldn't have been at risk. Instead, she'd had no choice but to marry someone else.

"Enough about me," Samuel said with a laugh. He sopped up some stew with his bread. His gaze turned to Lydia. "How are your parents? Are they here too?"

Sadness washed over her. How she wished they could be. "No. They died of cholera on our way to the Dakotas."

That had been another severe blow.

Samuel's spoon clattered back into its bowl. His mouth worked for a moment before he sighed. "I'm sorry to hear that. They were good people."

Lydia acknowledged his statement with a nod. What else could she say? Her parents loved Samuel. They'd been as devastated as her when he refused to do the right thing.

An awkward silence persisted. Finally, Samuel spoke. "Will you tell me about you and Frank?"

Her heart all but stopped. Forcing an even tone, she met his gaze. "What do you want to know?"

"When did you get married?"

Lydia shot a panicked look at Dorothy. The older woman gave her a small nod. As calmly as she could manage, Lydia said, "About five months after you left."

Hurt etched itself onto Samuel's face. Silence permeated the room for several long, awkward moments. When he spoke, his voice sounded raw. "Why?"

Lydia closed her eyes. Was he really so obtuse? "You know why."

Another stretch of silence lengthened. Finally, he sighed. "Your reputation?"

Dorothy took Lydia's hand while responding to Samuel. "You know Frank and I moved to the Dakotas after my husband's death to be near my daughter. We came through Aspen Grove to visit an old friend a couple months after you left for seminary. When he found out what had happened and that Lydia's reputation was on the line, he offered to marry her. We left soon after. They were married on the way back to our Dakota home."

"I see." Samuel clenched his fist, his Adam's apple bobbing. He released a long breath. His gaze turned to Lydia. "When my parents said you had disappeared, I wanted to leave seminary. I wanted to find you. Father talked me out of it. He said no one knew where you'd gone, that it would be a wild goose chase." His gaze speared her, raw grief apparent. "I'm sorry to say I listened to him. It was only later that I sent out inquiries, trying to see if I could locate you." He reached out a hand. "Please forgive me, Lydi. I should have been there for you."

She let out a breath of her own. His nickname for her never failed to make her insides flutter. A feeling she had no business experiencing now. "I forgive you, Samuel." She pressed her hand to his briefly, then slid it back to her lap. "But I can't say I trust you."

He closed his eyes. "I deserve that."

Dorothy stood. "There's something I need to fetch from my room. I'll be back shortly."

Lydia watched her go, but when she returned her gaze to Samuel, his attention was on her.

He leaned forward. "Was he good to you? Did he..." Swallowing, he clenched his spoon. "Did he do what I couldn't?"

"Yes." That she could say without pretense. Frank had been good to her, and their friendship had only grown over the years of their marriage. "He was a good husband and a better father."

Samuel blinked. "F-father? You had children?"

Lydia shook her head. "Just our daughter."

Our daughter, meaning hers and Samuel's. Not that she would spell it out. Samuel could figure that on his own.

He blinked a few more times. His eyes narrowed the slightest bit before widening. "But...where is the child?"

Grief pulsed through her. "She died. Influenza took her and Frank from me days apart."

Samuel's hands covered hers. Sorrow shone in his eyes. "Lydi—I'm so sorry you had to go through that. I can't imagine the pain you've suffered."

Was his sadness for her alone? Or did he feel the pain that he'd also lost a child? Lydia couldn't bear to ask. She pulled her hands away as Dorothy came down the stairs.

Her mother-in-law sat beside Samuel, two photographs in her hands. "I thought you might like to see these."

He accepted the first one she offered. Lydia didn't have to ask what it was. She knew Dorothy only possessed a few pictures. Samuel likely held the family portrait they'd had done when Charlotte was three years old.

Samuel sucked in a breath. He stared at the picture again. "This is your daughter?"

"Yes."

"She looks just like you. Just like Ruby."

Lydia nodded. "She did."

When would referring to her little girl in the past tense cease to hurt?

"Here's the other," Dorothy said, sliding the second picture his way.

Samuel picked it up. An incredulous laugh burst from his mouth. "I remember this." He held the picture up to Lydia. "That was quite a day, wasn't it?"

She smiled as she took in the image of her sandwiched between Samuel and Frank, all three of them grinning at the camera, despite the photographer telling them to be serious. Ten-year-olds weren't the best at following directions—especially when the two boys insisted on teasing the whole time. Lydia chuckled, shaking her head. "How could I forget? You'd both just threatened to dump me in the lake."

Samuel grinned back. He turned his attention to Dorothy. "I can't believe you still have this."

"It's a good reminder of happy days." Dorothy produced a light smile. "Now, why don't we have dessert?"

Lydia rose. "I'll help."

Dorothy waved her down. "I've got it, dear. But thank you."

Lydia sank back down. As Dorothy bustled about, plating servings of pumpkin pie, Samuel placed one hand over Lydia's again. When her gaze met his, the solemnity there jolted her. He squeezed her hand. "I truly am sorry, Lydia. For everything." He lifted the picture of her family. "You lost so much."

Pressure built in her chest. She breathed deeply to tamp it down. It took a few seconds before she could speak. When she did, she produced a tiny smile. "It's in the past, Sam."

"But..."

She cut him off. "Can we leave it there? Please?"

He stared at her before giving a single nod. "If that's what you want."

"It is." At some point, she should probably ask him why he didn't come back to Aspen Grove when she told him she was pregnant. But did it truly matter now? Dorothy was likely right —he didn't want to give up his dream and made a dumb, youthful decision he clearly regretted. He'd searched for her. That had to be enough.

There was no point rehashing the past.

CHAPTER 7

The tentative peace between Lydia and Samuel continued into December. It helped that they didn't see each other often outside of church services. Lydia tried to push him from her mind during the week, but he crept into her thoughts more than she cared to admit.

Two weeks after their supper, Lydia did her best to focus on the lesson as class drew to an end. Just one week separated her students from their Christmas holiday, and their behavior matched the anticipation. Even students who normally listened well seemed to have caught the excitement and bounced around in their seats. Lydia chuckled. She was fighting a losing battle, but in the spirit of Christmas, she didn't mind.

Her gaze landed on Ruby. The little girl had been quiet all day, keeping to herself while the other students kept up a steady stream of chatter. Since the children were now working on Christmas cards for their families, she walked to her youngest student and knelt by her seat. "Ruby? Is everything okay?"

The girl turned teary hazel eyes her way. "Granny is sick," she said softly.

"Is she still coughing?"

Ruby's lip trembled. "It's worse. I saw her hanky. The coughs made it red."

Red? Lydia's heart thumped hard. If Pearl was coughing up blood, she needed a doctor. And the nearest doctor was twenty miles away in Elkhorn.

Ella had been bringing Ruby to school this week, commenting that Pearl hadn't felt well enough to leave the cabin. Cold fear sliced through Lydia. Were they about to lose her?

Ruby tugged at Lydia's sleeve. "Granny wants Pastor Samuel to come today. Can you take me to him after school?"

"Of course."

The little girl's face eased. "Thanks, Mrs. Jefferson."

If Pearl had asked to see Samuel...

Lydia clamped down the negative thoughts pummeling her brain. It did no good dwelling on what ifs. She'd see for herself how Pearl fared after school.

A howling sound came from outside. Lydia went to the window. Tree branches whipped in the wind. Clouds hung heavy and low in the sky, their dark color indicating snow. She shivered. Last winter had seen days like this—usually leading to a blizzard. But they'd not had snow yet this winter. Surely, the first snow wouldn't be a storm.

She hoped.

Lydia willed time to pass faster. Her concern for Pearl only increased with each tick of the clock. By the time school let out, her stomach churned with anxiety.

Parents milled about the yard, glancing at the sky and commenting on the frigid temperatures. Cody arrived for Isaiah and Ruby. Lydia hurried to meet him. "I'll take Ruby home today," she said. "Pearl isn't doing well and might need care."

"You sure?" Cody eyed the sky. "You might get trapped there on the mountain."

Hopefully not. Lydia lifted her hands. "I have to help. Ruby has been downcast all day. She needs me too."

"All right. I'll alert Travis to you heading up to the Calhoun place. He can check on things as well if needed."

"Thanks, Cody."

He tipped his hat in response.

Once he had Isaiah, Cody headed home. All the children had been picked up.

Breathing a sigh of relief, Lydia went inside to collect Ruby. "Come on, sweetie. Let's go see Pastor Samuel."

∾

Samuel sat at his desk, tapping a pen against the solid wood. He stared unseeing at the paper before him. His thoughts were consumed with Lydia, much as they had been since he came to Harmony Springs. Things were getting better. The two of them might not be at friendship yet, but he'd take what he got. While Samuel was thankful they were on speaking terms, several questions continued to float through his mind.

How had Lydia's reputation been at risk to the point she needed to marry? Had someone seen them leave the barn early that morning? Why hadn't she said anything to him? They'd written each other often enough, yet she never said a word to indicate trouble.

But clearly, she'd been in trouble. To the point that she married Frank.

He froze as a thought crept across his mind. Was it possible she'd been pregnant? That would explain her hasty marriage. Just as quickly, he dismissed the notion. Surely, she'd have told him if there'd been a baby. He told her he'd come home to marry her immediately if that happened.

No. She must have had another reason.

Samuel sighed and leaned back in his chair. His sermon sat half written in front of him. Maybe he should take a break. With thoughts of Lydia haunting him, he couldn't focus. And he needed to focus. John would be here tomorrow to see how things were going and offer encouragement and advice.

A sudden knock at the door caught his attention. Pushing back in his chair, Samuel stood and made his way to the front of the house. He opened the door to reveal the subject of his recent thoughts. "Lydia?"

She stood bundled in a coat and scarf. "Hi, Samuel. I'm taking Ruby home. She says her grandma is sick." Her voice lowered. "To the point she's coughing up blood."

Samuel's heart sunk. "How can I help?"

"Pearl asked if you would come."

"Of course." He reached for his coat. "I'll escort you."

"Thanks, Sam." Her smile seemed genuine, combined with relief.

Samuel shrugged into his coat. Only then did he see Ruby standing behind Lydia. "Hi, Ruby."

She waved, her hazel eyes dark with concern. "Are you going to help my grandma?"

"I'll do my best," he promised. Plunking a hat on his head, he held out his hand to Ruby. "Shall we?"

The walk to town didn't take long, but the silence that followed them spoke of anxiety and fear. They reached the stables and hitched up a buggy to take them the three miles to Pearl's home up the mountain. Samuel made sure his companions were well bundled with a blanket before driving the buggy out of the livery. He watched the clouds with growing trepidation. Wind blew around them. If it started to snow, they'd be dealing with a whiteout.

He prayed it didn't come to that.

~

A stench unlike anything Lydia smelled before welcomed them to the Calhoun cabin. Pearl lay curled in a ball, bloody handkerchief in hand. The fireplace held only ashes, no warming flames.

Ruby shrieked and ran to her grandma. "Granny!"

The old woman opened her eyes. "Ru..." She coughed long and deep. More red stained the already-soaked hanky.

Heart hammering with dread, Lydia dropped to her knees beside the bed. "Pearl. We're here."

Samuel knelt beside her as Pearl's gaze shifted to them. "It's time," she rasped.

Ruby's sobs filled the cabin. Lydia pulled the child to her while Samuel took Pearl's hand. They remained at her side for several long, painful hours, listening to her thready breaths grow shorter. Lydia offered her sips of water throughout, but after three hours, Pearl refused to drink.

In the fourth hour, Pearl reached a weak hand to Ruby's curls. "Goodbye, precious girl. I love you."

"I love you, Granny." Ruby kissed her grandma's cheek.

Pearl's gaze moved to Samuel and Lydia. "You two take care of my Ruby."

You two?

Lydia's heart stuttered, but she had no time to consider Pearl's words. With a long exhale, the older woman's body relaxed into the bed, and she closed her eyes for the last time.

Samuel pressed his fingers to her neck. His throat bobbed as he turned to Lydia and shook his head. Tears shimmered in his eyes. He murmured a prayer over Pearl's body. Lydia stood, backing away from the bed with Ruby in her arms. The little girl cried harder, burying her face in Lydia's shoulder.

Rustling sounds came from the bed. She looked over to see Samuel lifting a sheet to cover Pearl. Grief for Pearl, for Ruby, smote Lydia's heart. Judging from the way Ruby clung to her, the child hurt deeply. How could she not? She'd just lost the last family member she had.

As if reading her thoughts, Ruby choked out a question. "What's gonna happen to me?"

At least Lydia could reassure her about that. "You'll come live with me. I'll take care of you."

Ruby pulled back. Her watery gaze searched Lydia's. "You? You'll be my mama?"

"Do you want me to be your mama?"

Ruby nodded solemnly. Lydia hugged her close, joy pulsing through her. Maybe having a little girl in her home again would help heal the hurt in both their hearts. "Then, yes, sweetie, I'll be your mama."

Hope lit the girl's eyes, but grief pulled at her features. "Okay." She laid her head on Lydia's shoulder once more. Though she no longer sobbed, Ruby's tears soaked into her dress.

Samuel's hand came to rest on her other shoulder. Lydia faced him. Deep lines etched across his brow. "We should probably head out."

Her gaze went to Pearl's shrouded body. "Sam...we can't just leave her."

He motioned to the window. "If we don't go now, we'll be stuck here. I'll get some men tomorrow to help me dig a grave for her."

Ruby wailed as soon as the word *grave* left his mouth. Lydia stroked her hair, rocking her body side to side in what she hoped was a calming motion. "What do you mean, 'stuck'?"

He pointed out the window. Lydia's breath caught. Though it was dark, the eerie light provided by snow allowed her to see.

White flakes poured down in sheets, heavy and thick. He was right. If they didn't leave now, they'd be snowed in.

And their reputations would be shattered.

She gave him a shaky nod.

Samuel squeezed her shoulder. "I'll hitch up the buggy. Gather whatever you need for Ruby."

He strode into the steadily falling snow, closing the door behind him. Lydia asked Ruby for her help in getting clothes and dolls together. They swaddled the girl's possessions in a colorful blanket—"It was my mama's," Ruby said softly—and waited for Samuel at the door. He came in soon after, stomping the ground to release snow from his boots. "Ready, ladies?"

Lydia nodded. Samuel lifted Ruby and carried her to the buggy. Lydia followed, carefully stepping in the footprints Samuel left as he walked. Already, several inches of snow covered the ground. The wind picked up, and for a moment, Lydia could barely see two feet in front of her. The sudden burst calmed as fast as it rose, but warning bells sounded in her mind.

They had to get back. Fast.

She accepted Samuel's hand to help her into the buggy. No words passed between them, but he gave her fingers a slight squeeze before jumping in next to her. Lydia cradled Ruby close to her chest as the conveyance moved forward.

They went slowly, navigating the ever-deepening snow. Lydia had no idea how far they'd traveled in the blinding white. She held Ruby and prayed they would make it safely back home.

A loud crack reverberated around them. Before she could blink, a large branch crashed onto the buggy. It hit directly between the vehicle and the horse, breaking through the wood. Samuel lost hold of the reins. The horse whinnied in fright, then bolted, leaving them behind.

Lydia gasped. "We're stranded." She turned to Samuel in panic. "What are we going to do?"

"I...I don't know." He sounded just as upset as her.

The wind picked up again. Snow swirled around them. The merciless blizzard showed no signs of stopping anytime soon.

Samuel squinted into the snow. "Is that a cabin?"

Lydia glanced to the left. A small structure stood a stone's throw away. Relief flooded her. "There are several hunting cabins in these mountains. That must be one of them."

"Good. Let's go." He jumped from the buggy, then turned to reach for her. Lydia kept her hold on a quiet, shaking Ruby and leaned toward him. Samuel's hands encircled her waist. He lifted them easily and made sure her feet stood firmly on the ground before letting go. Even then, he gripped her hand in his as if afraid they'd get separated.

Which was a real concern. With as thick as the snow fell and the wind blowing it around, it was a miracle they'd even seen the cabin.

It took only a minute or two to reach their shelter, though it felt longer. Lydia's arms ached from carrying Ruby, but she didn't dare put the girl down until they were inside.

Samuel pushed open the door and glanced around the room. "It'll suffice."

They crowded inside. Though they were out of the wind, the cabin felt ice cold. A tiny table stood in one corner. Some logs rested against the fireplace. Ratty blankets were stacked against another wall. A few tins lined some shelves on the wall.

Sparse and uninviting.

They had to get warm, but as Lydia let Ruby down and Samuel got to work lighting a fire, she knew they were in trouble. The logs would only last so long, maybe an hour or two. It was unlikely that anyone would come looking for them this night. It was too dangerous.

"Mama, I'm hungry," Ruby whispered.

Joy and pain warred in Lydia's heart. Joy at the ready acceptance Ruby showed in calling her *mama*, and pain because she had nothing to offer the child for sustenance. "I know, sweetie. I wish I had food."

Samuel had a small fire going. He stood and rummaged through the tins on the shelves. "There's some tinned beans here. It's not much, but it'll give her something."

They heated the beans over a fire. Ruby ate slowly, her eyes drooping more with each bite. Samuel offered Lydia some, but her stomach felt too unsettled to eat. He watched her with concern in his eyes. She gave him a tired smile. "I'll be fine, Sam. Thanks."

"All right." He paused, his gaze flicking to Ruby, who was falling asleep in Lydia's arms. "We're going to have to spend the night here."

She sighed. "I realize that."

Samuel swallowed. He stared into the fire, then back at her. "That fire will be out in an hour. It's going to get cold."

Her eyes narrowed. "What aren't you saying?"

"The three of us will need to sleep in close proximity to stay warm."

Lydia's hand flew to her throat. "What?" She gulped. "How... close?"

"Body heat is the only way we're going to make it, Lydi. I'm sorry."

Her face flamed. She opened her mouth to argue, then clamped it shut. He was right. As much as she hated to admit it, it was the only way.

Samuel's expression was grim. She exhaled with a shake of her head. "Fine."

He studied her another minute before getting to his feet. "I'll make up a bed of sorts."

Lydia swallowed. Samuel spread out two blankets on the floor to shield them from the ground's cold bite. He took the remaining two blankets and shook them out. "Here. This one can go around you and Ruby. Then the last one will be sufficient for all three of us."

At least that would provide something of a barrier. Lydia wrapped herself and Ruby in the blanket, then lay on the makeshift bed. Samuel stoked the fire once more. He hesitated once he turned her way again. "I wish there was another way."

She forced words out. "It'll be fine."

It most certainly would not be fine, but maybe if she pretended it was, she'd feel better about this whole situation. As it stood, she could only imagine the backlash that would occur when people found out she and Samuel spent the night together in an abandoned cabin. Ruby would hardly be considered an appropriate chaperone.

Maybe, if they were fortunate, no one would find out.

Samuel lowered himself to the ground. Lydia kept a tight hold on Ruby, sharing her warmth with the girl. When Samuel's body pressed into hers, she bit back a stunned gasp. The blanket settled over the three of them before his arm went around both her and Ruby. Nestled against him, her back to his stomach, Lydia reminded herself to breathe.

This is for survival.

She closed her eyes and tried to ignore the fact that she was once more in Samuel Allen's arms.

CHAPTER 8

*C*old. So, so cold.

Samuel woke with a groan. Why was his room this blasted freezing? And what happened to his bed? It was rock hard.

He opened his eyes, ready to investigate, then stilled. A mass of black curls tickled his nose. The smell of vanilla with a hint of lavender seeped into his senses. His arms were curled around something soft and...

Samuel sucked in a sharp breath. Lydia. Ruby. The blizzard, the broken branch, being forced to seek shelter in the cabin. All three of them huddling together out of sheer necessity to keep warm.

Lydia's back expanded and contracted against his chest. At least she slept peacefully. Ruby snuggled closer to her and murmured. Samuel tucked a bit of the girl's hair behind her ear. For now, sleep let her forget her loss.

A strange sound caught his ear. Frowning, Samuel strained to listen. It almost sounded like heavy boot steps outside. Was it possible...?

The door to the cabin swung open. Travis burst inside,

followed closely by two men from town. Their names escaped Samuel. All three came to an abrupt halt and stared at him.

Travis recovered first. "Thank God. When we saw the broken buggy, we feared the worst."

Lydia stirred against Samuel. She turned into him, her eyes fluttering open. "Sam?"

The sweet, sleep-roughened rasp to her voice made fireworks explode in his stomach. His arm tightened around her in response. All at once, he realized just how their situation might appear. Alone in a cabin, Lydia waking up in his arms. Heat crept up his neck. Never mind the fact that Ruby lay there with them. If news of this got out, they'd be in deep trouble.

He cleared his throat and pushed back the blanket covering him. "Good morning, Lydia. We've been rescued."

Confusion clouded her hazel eyes. She blinked, then glanced toward the door. When she saw the men, she gasped. "Oh!"

Samuel released his hold on her and Ruby. Lydia in turn burrowed deeper under the blankets, hugging the child to her chest. Her grip woke Ruby, who yawned and gave Lydia a sleepy smile. "Mornin', Mama." Her eyes then turned to Samuel. "Hi, Papa."

His heart rammed against his chest. The sweet, childlike trust Ruby exhibited warmed him thoroughly. On the other hand...why had she called him that? It didn't sound good, considering how they were found. In any other circumstance, he'd be thrilled. Judging from their three visitors, however, he was in for some questions.

One of the men behind Travis coughed. The other stared with gaping mouth.

Travis's brows inched higher. "Did you two get hitched without telling anyone?"

Samuel scrambled to his feet, moving to block Lydia and Ruby from sight. "No. We got caught in the blizzard on our way back from Pearl's. A branch cut between the horse and buggy. Thankfully, this cabin provided shelter."

Travis nodded. "The horse came back into town on its own. That's what alerted us to the fact that something was wrong. We couldn't leave until first light, though, not with all the snow out there."

The man with the gaping mouth stepped around Travis. Samuel finally recognized him. Mr. Holt. Father of the tittering young women who seemed obsessed with making Samuel belong to the family. Permanently.

He shifted from foot to foot. Of all the people in town...

"You were here all night?" Mr. Holt's gaze shifted behind Samuel. "With her?"

Lydia pushed up. Her eyes snapped with indignation. "It was survival, Mr. Holt. Pure and simple."

The man had the decency to look abashed. But he didn't stop there. "Why'd the girl call you mama and papa?"

Samuel's hackles raised at Mr. Holt's pointed gaze. "Ruby just lost her grandma, sir. She's had a rough time of it. Lydia is now her guardian."

Mr. Holt eyed him. "Lydia, is it?"

Realizing his mistake, Samuel clenched his jaw. "Mrs. Jefferson. For all intents and purposes, she is Ruby's mama now."

"And calling you papa?"

The other man spoke, a man Samuel still didn't recognize. Samuel drew in a breath as he prayed for patience. Why was this what the men were stuck on? They'd just passed a freezing night in an abandoned cabin. They were fortunate to be alive. He fought against the urge to grind his teeth.

Thankfully, Travis intervened. "I don't think these questions are helpful right now." His gaze found Samuel's. "Pearl died?"

His throat tightened, the fight draining away. "Yeah. Last night. She needs burial."

Travis nodded. Sorrow etched lines on his face. "I'm right

sorry to hear that. We'll start digging a place for her on her land as soon as the snow melts a bit. She in her cabin?"

"Yes. I wrapped her as best I could."

"Good man." Travis clamped a hand on his shoulder. "I'm glad you were there when she passed." His gaze moved to Lydia. "You, too, ma'am."

Samuel turned around. He offered Lydia his hand, pulling her to her feet when she accepted. He then did the same for Ruby. The little girl hid behind Lydia's skirts, eying the strangers with distrust. He couldn't blame her.

"Well, let's get you all home," Travis said, motioning toward the door. "It's going to be slow going, especially with riding all three horses double, but we'll walk at times if needed."

Lydia hung back as the other men exited the cabin, whispering to each other. Samuel took her hand. "It'll be all right, Lydi."

She clutched his hand tight. "I have a bad feeling about this, Sam."

Travis stepped toward them. "Lydia, I'll talk to them, ask them to keep this quiet."

A small cry escaped her. "If you had to organize a search party, most of town knows we were missing, don't they?"

Travis hesitated before shaking his head. "I wouldn't say most."

"But enough people are aware Samuel and I were lost together. Overnight." She shuddered.

Samuel pulled her a little closer, offering what support he could.

Travis's brows quirked, his gaze bouncing between them.

Ruby frowned at the adults with confusion on her face. "What's wrong?"

Smoothing the hair from the girl's brow, Lydia produced a smile. "Hopefully nothing, sweetie."

~

*N*othing, indeed.

Lydia tried to calm herself with long breaths, but the ride home only increased her nerves. She held tight to Travis as his horse picked its way through the inches-deep snow. Mr. Holt and Mr. Greyson kept sending glances her way. She couldn't determine what they were thinking, but their expressions didn't inspire confidence.

Her heart thudded with conflicting emotions. Fear that her reputation wouldn't survive this. The strange peace she'd felt waking up warm and held tight by her former love. Mortification at being caught in Samuel's arms, no matter the circumstances. Relief that they'd made it through the night alive.

Over it all, though, Ruby's sweet, little-girl trust in her, the quick willingness to accept her as a mother, made everything else worthwhile. Come what may, they had each other. They had Dorothy.

They'd be fine.

We'll be fine, right, Lord? She glanced up at the sky. *It feels like You're giving me a second chance at being a mother. Help me to do right by Ruby.*

Her gaze found Samuel's. He rode behind Mr. Greyson, flashing her a smile when he caught her watching him. His easy confidence had always calmed the turmoil in her heart. Now, however, it only served as a reminder that their situation was dire. Was he unaffected by this whole thing?

When they finally made it to town, Lydia breathed easier. That is, until curious faces appeared at shop windows, peering out at the rescue party trudging down Main Street. Travis led them down an alley to Lydia's home. After pulling his horse to a stop, he helped her down. Samuel jumped to the ground and proceeded to help Ruby from Mr. Holt's horse.

"Do you want us to take you home, Samuel?" Travis asked.

Samuel shook his head. "I can walk. Thanks, Travis."

"All right. We'll head out, then."

Lydia took a step forward. "Thank you for everything. It's a relief to no longer be trapped in that cabin."

"My pleasure, ma'am." Travis tipped his hat with a smile. He spurred his horse around and started off.

Mr. Holt and Mr. Greyson followed suit, though neither said goodbye. Unease swept through Lydia's stomach when Mr. Holt glanced back, his gaze locking with hers. She couldn't name the emotion simmering in his eyes, but it sent shivers up her spine.

"Come on," Samuel said, taking her hand. "Let's get you inside."

Without thinking, Lydia pulled away. "I appreciate your help, Samuel, but we can't be touching in such a familiar manner."

He blinked, then grinned. "Why not?"

So many reasons. Not the least of which being their history. She only shrugged and took Ruby's hand. Summoning a smile for the child, she started for the porch. "Are you ready to see your new home?"

Ruby nodded. The door flew open before they reached the top step.

Dorothy rushed outside, enveloping Lydia in an embrace. "Oh, my dear girl. I feared the worst when you didn't come home yesterday." She pulled back, cupping Lydia's face in her hands. "Are you all right? What happened?"

A rush of emotion clogged Lydia's throat. She cleared it before speaking. "It's a long story."

Dorothy's gaze fell on Samuel, then Ruby. Surprise flashed over her face. She blinked, then waved them all in. "Come inside. I'll make some hot cocoa."

Ruby perked up. "Cocoa?"

"Yes, dear. I even have some peppermint sticks we can put in the mugs."

The door shut behind them, but Samuel paused in the entryway.

Lydia tilted her head. "Are you coming?"

Weariness lined his forehead. He shook his head. "I'll give you time with your family."

"No!" Ruby's cry startled them all. The little girl flung herself at Samuel, clinging to his legs. "You're my papa now. You can't leave."

Heavy silence permeated the room. Dorothy's gaze swung from Ruby to Samuel to Lydia and back again.

Samuel rubbed the back of his neck, ears reddening. "Ruby," he said, kneeling before the girl, "why do you think I'm your papa?"

"Because Granny said so."

Lydia's mouth fell open.

Surprise crossed Samuel's face. He glanced up at Lydia, then down at Ruby. "What did your granny say, exactly?"

"That you and Mama belong together and that you would be a good father for me." Ruby pulled back, hands going to her hips. "You were there. She said it to you. Granny didn't think I could hear her, but I did." She wrapped her little arms around his neck. "So you'll stay, right?"

Lydia felt frozen to the spot. Pearl had said such things? To Samuel? Mortification swelled for the second time that day. Once upon a time, those words would have delighted her. But now? After everything that had passed between them? Their friendship was tentative at best. It would take time for trust to build again. Lydia wasn't entirely sure she wanted to be friends with Samuel, not like before.

Not when her heart could so easily get crushed a second time.

She put her hands on Ruby's shoulders. "Sweetie, Pastor Samuel and I are not married. He can't be your papa."

Ruby shook her head. She held tighter to Samuel. "Then marry him."

Oh, gracious. Lydia's stomach swooped. A vice-like grip took a stranglehold on her throat. All she could do in response was squeak.

Samuel stared at her for a few moments. Something shone in his eyes, something she couldn't read but nevertheless sent sparks shooting through her veins. After what felt like an eternity, he turned back to Ruby. "There are lots of things that have to be right for two people to get married, Ruby. It can't just happen."

"But Granny said..."

He gently cut her off. "I know. She meant well. Your granny loved you very much and wanted you to have a mama and a papa. Right now, though, you have a mama who will take very good care of you. Maybe someday she will get married and give you a papa."

"But I want you for a papa." Ruby's lips set in a stubborn line, one Lydia had seen on Pearl from time to time. There was no arguing with the woman when she got that look.

Dorothy cleared her throat. "Perhaps this can be a discussion for another time. Right now, Ruby, would you like to help me with the cocoa?"

Ruby hesitated. She clung to Samuel. "Will I see you soon?"

He gave her a hug. The tenderness on his face and the gentle way he held the child poked holes in the wall around Lydia's heart. Would this have been how he was with Charlotte? Tears welled in her eyes. She turned around, swiping her cheeks with the palm of her hand.

"Yes, Ruby, you'll see me soon. I promise."

I promise.

An unpleasant feeling churned in Lydia's stomach. He'd said the exact same thing to her years ago. Though he might have regretted it later, he hadn't come when she needed him most. Her muscles tightened and her head snapped up. "Ruby, say goodbye to Pastor Samuel. He needs to be getting home."

Samuel glanced up at her, confusion written on his face. She raised her brow. "You have a visitor coming, do you not?"

Alarm registered on his face. He gave Ruby one more hug before springing upright. "I forgot about that."

Thankful for the excuse to see him out, Lydia led him to the door while Ruby joined Dorothy in the kitchen.

Samuel paused and faced her. "Lydia, is something wrong?"

Forgive.

Lydia inhaled slowly, pushing down the anger that had taken her captive. She blew out her breath and found a smile. "It's nothing. I think everything that happened yesterday and today have caught up with me."

His blue-green eyes remained on her.

Lydia swallowed. He always could see into her very soul. She opened the door. "I'll see you later."

He stayed where he was, lifting one hand to cup her elbow. "It will be all right, Lydia."

"I hope so."

Samuel opened his mouth, but no words came out. Eventually, he shut it and gave her a nod. "See you at church on Sunday?"

"We'll be there."

He searched her eyes one more time, then headed into the wintry street.

CHAPTER 9

*J*ohn River's train was due any moment. Samuel stood on the platform, bundled in his coat as he waited for his mentor to arrive. He'd spent the day finishing his sermon and readying the house for his guest. After a harrowing twenty-four hours, he was ready to talk with John.

A long whistle sounded. The train came chugging around a bend. Five minutes later, it pulled into the station and passengers disembarked.

Samuel stood on his toes, his gaze sweeping the small crowd. A familiar head of white hair caught his attention. Grinning, Samuel waved his hand in the air. "John!"

A matching smile filled his mentor's face. He strode with long steps until he was close enough to wrap Samuel in a hug. "Samuel, good to see you." He pulled away, his brown eyes twinkling. "Seems this town suits you."

"It does." Samuel reached for the man's bag. "Let me get that for you."

John chuckled. "I won't say no. I'm not as young as I used to be." He arched his back, hands pressed to his hips.

Samuel nodded toward the street. "Shall we?"

"Certainly. I want to hear all about how you're settling in."

"Well..."

He got no farther than that when a woman's shrill voice came from several shops away. "Pastor Allen! Yoo-hoo!"

Mrs. Holt. Samuel suppressed a sigh. "John, are you up for meeting a few of my parishioners right away?"

John wore a grin. "Of course, of course. Lead the way."

As Mrs. Holt and Francine came down the steps of the mercantile, Samuel pasted on a smile of his own. "Good afternoon, ladies. May I present..."

"Pastor Allen," Mrs. Holt interrupted. "I've heard the most distressing news from my husband." She leaned closer, though her volume didn't diminish. "Did you really stay in a cabin overnight with Mrs. Jefferson? Alone?"

Several people stopped and stared. John's brows rose. Francine wore a deep frown, arms crossed over her stomach. An uncomfortable heat burned Samuel's chest. Mr. Holt must have ignored Travis's directive to keep quiet.

"Ah...not alone, exactly."

Good grief. He sounded guilty as sin.

Samuel cleared his throat and tried again. "That is to say, we got stranded in the blizzard on our way to town. We had no choice but to take shelter. And we weren't alone. Ruby Calhoun was with us."

Mrs. Holt sniffed. "A *child* is hardly a proper chaperone, Pastor Allen." She tapped her foot. "My husband also said you were...*holding*...Mrs. Jefferson in a rather compromising manner when they found you."

Samuel stiffened. He would not rise to her bait. He would not...

"One must wonder if Mrs. Jefferson's reputation should remain intact."

Anger flared hard and fast. Samuel glared at the woman. "What exactly are you implying, ma'am?"

She didn't seem intimidated by his flash of temper. If anything, it goaded her on. She plopped her hands on her hips, looking around at the crowd gathering near them with a gleam in her eyes. "I'm implying, sir, that two unmarried people spent the night together in the same bed. Our pastor and teacher, no less! What message does that send to your flock, I wonder? What lesson would that teach the students of this town?"

"Nothing happened." Samuel ground out the words. "Lydia is blameless in this. What would you have had us do? Freeze to death in that cabin? There was no firewood and no way of keeping warm through the night on our own. We did what we had to do to survive. All *three* of us."

Mrs. Holt harrumphed. "Lydia, is it? I didn't realize you were on a first-name basis with the schoolteacher."

Blast it all. He'd done that earlier, raising Mr. Holt's suspicions. Not that he felt the need to hide his friendship with Lydia, but it only added fuel to the fire that was quickly blazing out of control.

John put a hand on his arm. "Samuel, we should probably go."

Mrs. Holt drew herself up. "You are supposed to be above reproach, Pastor Allen. I expect you'll do the decent thing to uphold Mrs. Jefferson's reputation. Otherwise, she won't have a job come Monday."

Dread slammed into him. "What do you mean, she won't have a job?"

"I met with the other members of the school board." The woman appeared far too smug. "There are strict rules on teacher conduct. Mrs. Jefferson broke several of those rules. Out past town curfew, alone with a man, spending the night with said man...shall I go on?"

Samuel gritted his teeth. "There was no choice."

She shrugged a slender shoulder. "Rules are rules, sir."

Tossing her hair, she held out a hand to her daughter. "Come along, Francine."

The young woman grimaced, giving Samuel an apologetic wave, but she followed her mother without a word. The townsfolk who witnessed the exchange whispered among themselves.

Samuel couldn't see straight. He gripped the handle of John's bag, his thoughts consumed with Lydia. Would she really be out of a job because of something beyond their control?

John put a hand on his shoulder. "Are you all right?"

"No." Samuel exhaled, his body drooping. "This is going to devastate Lydia." He released a bitter laugh. "And I'm at fault. Again."

His mentor frowned. "Again?"

Samuel glanced around. There was still too much attention fixed on them. "Let's walk. I'll explain on the way."

And he did just that. By the time they reached Samuel's house, John knew of his history with Lydia along with the events that led to them bunking down in the cabin. The older man shook his head as he sank onto Samuel's sofa, eyes wide. "That is quite a story, son. What an ironic turn of events."

Samuel sat across from him in a chair. "Ironic?"

"Seven years ago, you engaged in actions that did ruin your Lydia's reputation. This time, nothing untoward happened, but the result is the same." He leaned forward, resting his elbows on his knees. "Why didn't you marry her then? It would have been the honorable thing to do."

Samuel hung his head. "I know. I took the coward's way, convincing myself that no one would find out, that we could pretend nothing happened until I finished seminary and could marry her then. I've regretted it every day since."

John hummed softly, studying Samuel with narrowed eyes. Silence stretched between them. That was John's way. He took time to think things through rather than spout platitudes or assurances that everything would work out. Samuel sank into his cushion, sapped of energy after revealing his mistakes of the past. Even so, the typical shame didn't hound him. John had a way of listening without judgment.

Finally, his mentor spoke. "You were young, Samuel. You regret what you did, and the past is in the past. But now, you have a choice to make. I know this current situation isn't anyone's fault. You did what you had to do to live another day. That was good and noble. You saved both Lydia and Ruby." His eyes softened. "Now what do you plan to do? Lydia doesn't deserve to take the fall for this. You hurt her once. If you do so again, you'll never recover her trust."

Samuel's heart squeezed tight. He closed his eyes, fists clenched. "The only way to save her reputation would be to marry her."

"Yes."

His throat bobbed. "I love her, John. I never stopped loving her. But she has so much anger locked inside. She's trying to forgive me for the past, but there's still pain there. And she doesn't want to talk about it, even though there's so much I have to ask."

John nodded. "She had more to lose then, and she did lose it. Somehow, her reputation suffered from your actions while you remained untouched. That would be enough to make a person bitter. If you do marry her, remember that her heart is wounded. She needs to be gently wooed. Show her that you are trustworthy by your daily words and actions. Let her know you love her—not just in word, but in deed. It won't be easy, especially if she's resistant to you."

"What if she never loves me back? Or trusts me?" The very thought sent fear racing through him.

John responded with a firm calm. "Then you lay down your life for her, anyway."

~

*L*ater that evening, just as the sun made its descent in the western sky, someone knocked at the door. Lydia stopped kneading the bread dough, blinking. They weren't expecting anyone.

Dorothy went to answer.

Ruby sidled up to Lydia, clutching her skirt. "Who's here?"

"I don't know, sweetie." Lydia wiped her hands on her apron. "We'll find out in a moment."

"Mr. Farrow." Dorothy's surprised voice carried to the kitchen. "Please, come in."

"Thank you, ma'am." The head of the school board entered the house. He took off his hat, holding it loosely between his hands.

Prickles of nervous anticipation rolled over Lydia. She inclined her head in greeting. "Mr. Farrow. What brings you here this evening?"

The man wouldn't meet her eyes. He shuffled to the sofa, where Dorothy invited him to sit. He motioned for Lydia to join him.

Dorothy met her gaze. "Ruby and I will finish the bread."

She nodded, her tongue glued to the roof of her mouth. Lydia sank into a chair and raised her chin. Whatever this was about, she'd meet it with dignity. "How can I help you, sir?"

"Mrs. Jefferson, first of all, please know this wasn't my idea."

She blinked. Mr. Farrow finally raised his gaze to hers, a sad grimace on his face. "Mrs. Holt called together an emergency meeting of the school board this afternoon. She believes you broke several rules from the teacher code of conduct."

Icy fear sliced through her. "Mr. Farrow, nothing happened between me and Pastor Allen. I promise."

"I believe you." He released a weary sigh, rubbing his forehead with one hand. "Unfortunately, I'm the only one on the school board who does. The other three outvoted me."

Lydia had a sinking feeling she knew what he meant, but she forced herself to ask the question, anyway. "Outvoted you on what?"

"Because of a breach of contract, your employment at the school is terminated immediately."

The man shuffled, misery on his face, but Lydia couldn't help a flare of anger. "I didn't do anything wrong." The anger gave way to panic as her gaze landed on Dorothy and Ruby. "Mr. Farrow, I have a daughter to care for now. I need that job."

Surprise flashed in his eyes. "A daughter?"

"Pearl Calhoun passed yesterday. She wanted me to take care of Ruby in her stead." But she couldn't do that without a means of support.

Mr. Farrow's shoulders slumped. "I'm afraid your chances of being hired elsewhere are rather slim with the rumors floating around. Even if you're innocent, people will believe what they'll believe."

Hands shaking, Lydia buried them in her lap. Her panic intensified, stomach churning, heart thumping, eyes watering. "Please, sir, is there any way I can continue in my position?"

"There is one..." He didn't seem inclined to continue. Lydia bit her lip, summoning as much patience as she could. Finally, he let out a breath and went on. "If you marry Pastor Allen, yes. You can keep your job."

He might as well have taken a knife to her gut. All the air whooshed from her lungs, and she couldn't control the horrified expression that filled her face. Her only options were to marry Samuel or lose her job?

Which would be worse?

"Mama can marry Pastor Samuel?"

Ruby's hopeful voice sounded at her left. Lydia blinked at Mr. Farrow twice before looking at her new daughter. Ruby's eyes were alight, her hands clasped in front of her with delight. "Please, Mama. I want him to be my papa."

What was it about Samuel that made Ruby so insistent on him being a part of her life? And not just part of her life—an integral one. Lydia's feelings around Samuel were already confusing. To think of marriage was too overwhelming.

Three firm knocks pounded on the door. Desperate for an escape from the current conversation, Lydia jumped up. "I'll get it." She walked faster than necessary and opened the door. Her stomach dropped with her jaw.

Speak of the devil.

"Samuel."

Of course, it was him. It seemed her tumultuous emotions would get no rest today.

He shifted from foot to foot. "Hi, Lydia. Can we talk?"

No.

She felt trapped. The last thing she wanted to do was have a conversation with him, not when her head spun in a million directions. But what choice did she have?

Ruby squealed before Lydia could respond. She bounded over, a grin on her face. "Hi, Pastor Samuel."

An answering smile grew on his lips. He crouched down, embracing the girl as she leapt into his arms. "Hi, Ruby."

Lydia closed her eyes. Her heart thudded against her ribs. Ruby deserved this. She deserved a man who would love her as only a father could. And she deserved to be taken care of. Without a job, Lydia couldn't do that, not on her own.

Swallowing hard, she opened her eyes. Determination pulsed inside. She could do this. For Ruby.

The little girl still had her arms wrapped around Samuel. He said something quiet to her, then tapped her nose before standing. "I need to talk to your mama for a bit, if that's all right."

"Sure. You gotta get married. Mr. Fallow said so."

He blinked. Lydia flushed and hurried to grab her coat from a nearby peg. "Why don't we walk while we talk?"

"That's fine." He peered over her shoulder. Lydia followed his gaze. Mr. Farrow watched them, suspicion in his eyes. When she turned back to Samuel, he rested a hand on her upper arm. "You have company. Am I interrupting?"

"No." Lydia dropped a soft kiss on Ruby's head, then turned to Dorothy. "I'll be back soon, Mother."

Dorothy waved a hand, having taken up Lydia's place at the bread bowl. "Take your time, dear. There's no rush."

Not sure what to make of that comment, Lydia bade Mr. Farrow farewell and slipped out the door, shutting it behind her. Cold air nipped her face, and she shivered. As she buttoned her coat, she spoke to Samuel. "Where are we going?"

He plunged his hands into his pockets. Uncertainty clouded his face for a moment. "The church?"

She nodded her agreement. They walked in silence for a few minutes. Memories flitted through her mind, of walks much like this in their younger years, when no words were necessary to fill the space between them. Then, it was comfortable. Now, the weight of expectations pressed down on them.

Snow crunched loudly under their shoes. Samuel darted glances at her on occasion, but each time she thought he might say something, his mouth snapped shut and his eyes focused forward. The entire trip to the church passed without a single word spoken between them.

He held the door for her when they entered the sacred space. Lydia moved to the front pew and sank into it while Samuel lit a few lanterns. Soon enough, he dropped to the seat beside her. He wasn't close enough to be touching her, but she felt his presence acutely, nonetheless.

Finally, he exhaled out a long breath. "I am so sorry, Lydi. Truly. I didn't think this would blow up on us."

She didn't have to ask what he meant. Tears stung her eyes.

"Mr. Fallow came by to tell me the school board decided I no longer have a job. Not unless..."

Samuel's gaze met hers. "Not unless we marry."

The tears slipped from her eyes. "Yes."

He reached out, cupping her cheeks while rubbing the moisture away with his thumbs. "I came to see you with the intention of asking you to be my wife."

Her heart skittered, then plunged. She pulled back. His hands dropped back to his lap, though his eyes remained on her. "Sam, we're barely back to speaking terms after being apart for so long. We can't even claim true friendship anymore. How are we supposed to live as man and wife?"

He sighed, leaning back into the pew. "Lydia, I should have married you seven years ago. It was wrong of me to leave you to your shattered reputation then. I won't make the same mistake now." After a moment's hesitation, he pushed on. "I admit to having quite a few questions still bothering me, things I think we need to hash out if we want to make this marriage an agreeable one."

Her spine stiffened. "I don't want to talk about the past. We said we'd leave it behind us."

"We can't, Lydi." His soft voice sent tingles up and down her spine. Unwelcome butterflies joined the tingles as he took her hand. "We have to talk about it. It's part of both of us. We can't let it fester."

Why did it feel like defeat to admit he was right? Lydia pressed her lips together. As much as she dreaded the thought, she didn't want bitterness to be their norm. "Fine. But not until after the Christmas season. We'll have enough to worry about, and I want Ruby to have as happy a Christmas as possible."

"That sounds reasonable." The hint of a smile tipped his lips. "See, we're already working through things. That's a good sign, right?"

Despite herself, Lydia chuckled. She shook her head. "I suppose it's better than constant arguing."

His eyes darkened, and his grip on her hand tightened. For several long moments, his gaze pierced hers. Slowly, one hand lifted to her hair. His fingers grazed a stray curl, and he tucked it behind her ear.

Lydia's breath caught. She was suddenly transported back to their carefree teenage years, when love was easy and her whole life felt wrapped up in this man. She'd once been eager to marry him. A moment like this would have sent her into a world of joy.

Then she'd spent years harboring anger and resentment toward him. She now was caught somewhere in the middle, no longer wanting to keep herself locked in the prison of unforgiveness, but also unable to trust him the way she once had.

Samuel's voice broke into the quiet. "I wanted to ask you here for a reason, Lydia. There's a lot we'll have to sort through if we marry. We will need God's grace to make this work." A wry smile tugged at his mouth. "I want to do this right, in His eyes and in yours." He slid from the pew, getting down on one knee. "Lydia, if you'll have me, I promise to be a good husband to you and a good father to Ruby. Will you marry me?"

Her gaze swung to the cross hanging over the altar. All her life, she'd wanted to marry for love. She thought she had that with Samuel years ago, but she ended up married to Frank instead, a marriage of convenience. Now, she was faced with another marriage that only promised security. She and Samuel might have been in love once, but that was a long time ago. Lydia held no illusions that love would grow again. That ship had sailed.

What do I do, Lord?

Ruby's sweet face filled her mind. And her decision was made. With a little sigh of resignation, she nodded. "Yes, Sam. I'll marry you."

CHAPTER 10

*R*ushes of relief washed over Samuel at Lydia's softly spoken words. She didn't seem happy about their upcoming nuptials, but at least she didn't look sick over it.

Too much, anyway.

He pressed a gentle kiss to her forehead as he got to his feet. "Do you want to marry immediately so you can be with your students this final week before the holidays, or should we wait until next term?"

Lydia shook her head. "I need to be there for the children. Maybe..." She chewed on her bottom lip.

Samuel's attention fell to her mouth. An intense desire to kiss her flooded him, but he resisted. He might still be in love with her, and they might be getting married, but any blatant physical affection from him would likely be unwelcome.

Oh, Lord, help me to be temperate where Lydia is concerned. Please.

"Maybe we should marry immediately." Her throat convulsed. She wrapped her arms around her midsection. "Your pastor friend can do that, right?"

That wouldn't be a problem. John was fully on board with a marriage between Samuel and Lydia. He nodded.

Lydia drew herself straighter, chin raising. "After church tomorrow, then?"

"How about before church?"

She blinked. "Before?"

"Yeah. Then I can introduce you as my wife. We don't need to make a bigger deal of it than that. It'll shut down any argument for you not remaining at the school."

Lydia's shoulders slumped. "You realize this is just going to make the rumors appear valid?"

He took her hand. The anguish on her face tore at him. "No matter what we do, the rumors will persist. At least this way, your reputation will be restored."

She eyed him. "As will yours."

"Lydia, I don't pretend that this affects me as much as it does you. No one came for my job like they did yours." He frowned. "At least, not yet."

"They might still. Or would, if we didn't marry. Your office is one that requires exemplary behavior, even the appearance of such behavior."

"You're right. Though with us getting married, I guess we'll never know." He pressed her hand gently between his, then let go. "Why don't you head home and get some rest? We'll sort everything out in the morning."

Her response was a jerky nod. Was she trembling?

He took a step closer, capturing both of her hands. "Hey. It'll be all right."

Her hazel eyes swam with tears. She just looked at him without saying a word. A single tear slipped from her eye, making a trail down her cheek. Air whooshed from Samuel's lungs. With one step forward, he gathered her into his arms and held her close.

So much for no physical affection.

She remained stiff for several long, painful moments. Just as Samuel was about to accept the fact that she wouldn't take comfort from him, a harsh cry escaped her lips. She sank into him, her hands raising to his chest and balling the fabric of his shirt in her fists. Heavy sobs shook her. Tears wet his chest. Samuel ran his hands over her back, resting his chin on top of her head as she cried.

Minutes later, her grip relaxed. Lydia sniffed a few times and pulled back. Her cheeks reddened like twin apples, and she wouldn't meet his gaze.

Samuel pulled a handkerchief from his pocket. "Don't be embarrassed, Lydi. This situation would be enough to make anyone cry." He wiped the tears from her face.

"I don't see you crying," she mumbled.

Samuel hooked a finger under her chin and tipped it up. She finally met his gaze. He swiped once more with the handkerchief, then gave her a smile. "I'll take care of you. I promise."

Something flickered in her eyes. She pulled back, crossing her arms. "Pretty words, Sam. But I'll need proof of that."

Right. She didn't trust him. He'd do well to remember that as he tried to woo her heart. "You'll get proof."

Lydia stared at the floor. A black curl bounced against her cheek, begging him to tuck it behind her ear. Before he could do so, she spoke. "What time should I be here tomorrow?"

"Church service is at ten o'clock. How does nine sound?"

She nodded, then turned to go. Samuel hurried after her. There was no way he'd let her walk home alone in the dark, no matter how safe Harmony Springs seemed.

The walk back to her house was as quiet as the walk to the church had been. When they reached her front door, Samuel pushed it open for her. "I'll see you tomorrow."

Her gaze lifted to his. She sighed softly, shaking her head.

"Goodnight, Sam." Without another word, she slipped inside and shut the door.

He walked down the steps, his gait slow. Tomorrow, their lives would change. They'd be where they should have been years ago. He blew out a breath and gazed up at the starry sky.

In a little over twelve hours, he'd be a married man.

~

*L*ydia smoothed the material of her prettiest dress. A deep rose color, it boasted lace at the sleeves and neckline, with matching lace trim along the full skirt. No one would mistake it for a wedding dress, but it was the best she could do on short notice. She felt confident when she wore this dress, and she desperately needed confidence for the day to come.

Reaching for a pin, she secured a final lock of hair and checked her reflection in the small mirror above her dresser. It would suffice.

Ruby flew into the room. "Today Pastor Samuel is going to become my papa," she exclaimed, clapping her little hands.

Lydia couldn't help but smile at the girl's enthusiasm. She bent down, holding out her arms. Ruby stepped into them with an ease that thawed the fear in Lydia's heart. No matter what, she had her daughter. And at least someone was happy about this upcoming marriage.

Dorothy came into the room. She halted almost at once. "Oh, my dear girl." Tears welled in her eyes. "You are stunning."

Lydia rose, Ruby's hand in hers. "Thank you, Mother."

"I have a gift for you and Samuel. A little token, really." Dorothy slipped a hand into her pocket and pulled out a small folded piece of cloth.

Lydia accepted the offering. She opened the cloth and gasped. Her gaze flew up to her mother-in-law. "Your rings?"

"Yes." With a fond smile, Dorothy ran a finger around each one. "Clive and I had a wonderful marriage. After he died, I couldn't bring myself to part with either of our rings. I've kept them safe all these years. But now they can see the light of day with you and Samuel."

Lydia shook her head, covering the rings once more. "I can't take these, Mother. They're yours."

"Nonsense. Considering my marriage started much like yours, it felt only right that you have them."

Confusion took over. Lydia blinked at Dorothy. "What do you mean, your marriage started like mine? I thought you and Clive were a love match."

Dorothy laughed, shaking her head. "Oh, no, dear. Have I never told you our story?"

Apparently not. All Lydia knew was she'd never seen two people more in love than Clive and Dorothy Jefferson. She shook her head, speechless.

"Let's sit." Dorothy motioned to the bed. They sat on it while Ruby went for one of her dolls.

"When I was eighteen years old, Clive moved to Aspen Grove. We did not see eye to eye when we first met. I thought he was too arrogant, and he thought I was immature." She chuckled softly. "We were both right. Each of us had a stubborn streak a mile wide. One day, I went to the forest to gather berries. A storm blew up so fast, I had to take shelter in a nearby cabin. Only, when I got there, Clive was already sheltering too. The storm was too intense for either of us to do anything but hunker down. We ended up falling asleep, and the next thing we knew, the mayor and pastor found us. It didn't take long for word to spread. I faced a ruined reputation, and for once, Clive did the honorable thing and proposed marriage."

Lydia's mouth hung open. "I had no idea."

"The beginning of our marriage was difficult. There were

times I thought we'd drive each other crazy. Or worse." Dorothy laughed. "I can't pinpoint what changed, but over time, we grew to respect one another. Respect turned to admiration, and admiration turned to love. By the time Jessica and Frank came along, we were deeply in love and remained so until his death." She patted Lydia's hand. "So you see, you're in a similar situation. These rings will be a sign of your commitment to Samuel and his to you. Please, take them. Let it be my wedding gift."

How could she refuse? Lydia hugged Dorothy. "Thank you."

"Anything for my girl." Dorothy smiled, wiping away a tear. She rewrapped the rings and placed them in her pocket. "I'll keep them safe until the ceremony. Speaking of which, it's about time we go."

Lydia gulped. "I don't think I'm ready for this."

"You are." Dorothy pulled her up. "You're strong, Lydia. And you used to love Samuel with all your heart. Maybe you'll find love again."

Doubtful. There was too much history between them, too much sorrow. Lydia pasted on a smile. "Maybe."

Dorothy chuckled. "You don't believe you can, but just wait. That boy is still crazy about you. I can tell."

Warmth stuttered through her veins, followed closely by a chill. Lydia swallowed. Before she could say anything, Dorothy linked arms with her.

"Come on. Let's get you married to your childhood sweetheart."

Lydia allowed herself to be pulled from the room. Ruby skipped along behind, chattering about Samuel being her new papa. The whole way to the church, Lydia tried to puzzle out why Dorothy seemed so happy about this turn of events. She knew her history with Samuel. And now her mother-in-law would be by herself in her house.

"Are you sure you'll be fine living alone, Mother?"

"Don't you worry about me," Dorothy replied without hesitation. "As for being alone..."

"What?"

"Well, I received a letter from Jessica yesterday. She's entering the final month of her pregnancy and wants me to be there when the baby comes. I think she's nervous about being a first-time mother and could use the help, especially after struggling for so long to conceive." She gave Lydia a little smile. "I was thinking of going to visit for a few months."

"A few...months?"

"If you can handle me being away."

It had been years since Dorothy saw her youngest child. Jessica was a few years older than Frank, and she'd married and moved to the Dakota Territory with her husband several years before Frank and Lydia married. It made sense that she would want her mother around when she had a baby. But still...

"It's a long trip to the Dakota Territory. Are you sure you'd be fine traveling by yourself?"

"Train travel makes it easy. It's not as though I'll be going by covered wagon." Dorothy chuckled. "It'll be fine, Lydia. I just want to be sure you'll be fine."

Settling into life with Samuel would not be easy. Raising a daughter with him would be challenging as well. But she had friends here. She wouldn't be alone.

"Yes, Mother, I'll be fine. You should go see Jessica."

Relief crossed Dorothy's face. "Thank you, dear girl. I hate to leave you, but—"

"But Jessica needs you."

Times like this made Lydia miss her own mother. If her parents hadn't died in that cholera outbreak, would they be here in Harmony Springs with her? She didn't begrudge Dorothy the time to see her daughter. But she would miss her mother-in-law dearly.

The church came into sight, and all other thoughts fled

Lydia's mind. Dread seized her. She was about to tie her life to the man she'd been angry at for the past seven years.

What could possibly go wrong?

~

Samuel paced at the front of the church. John stood calmly by the altar, Travis at his side. Samuel had asked his friend to act as a witness. Cassie was coming as well, but she'd said she needed to run a quick errand before joining them. Hopefully, she arrived soon. It was two minutes past nine o'clock.

And his bride wasn't here yet either.

"Maybe she changed her mind." He tugged at his tie, nerves getting the better of him.

Travis clapped a hand on his shoulder. "I'm sure she'll be here soon."

The church doors opened. Cassie breezed in, Connor in her arms, followed closely by the Brooks family. Before Samuel could ask, Cassie smiled. "Lydia and Ella are close friends. She'd want her here."

"Hey," piped in a little voice. Samuel's eyes fell on Jonah. The boy had his hands on his hips, as mutinous as a five-year-old could be. "Auntie Lydia wants us here too."

Cassie grinned, pressing a kiss to Jonah's head. "Which is exactly why you're also here."

Mollified, the little boy smiled.

The door burst open. Ruby rushed in, out of breath and grinning. "Pastor Samuel!" She ran forward, launching herself into his arms.

Samuel chuckled, relishing the show of affection and innocence. If only Lydia would be so excited to see him. But he doubted that would ever be the case.

"Mama's almost here! My new granny said I should let you

know so we can have a..." Her brow scrunched before she lit up. "A proper wedding."

Cassie patted Samuel on the arm and leaned close as Ruby scampered toward a pew. "I knew you wouldn't be single long." She winked before sitting beside Ella.

As if they'd had a choice in getting married.

Samuel bit back a sigh. It was kind of their friends to make this seem like a somewhat normal wedding ceremony. But it wasn't. This was damage control, plain and simple.

For a third time, the door opened. Dorothy came in with Lydia. Samuel's breath caught when he beheld his bride. Forced marriage notwithstanding, she was stunning. Her gaze met his, and her chin tilted up. A smile tugged at his lips. She'd always had fire in her soul. They might not have much choice, but she was going to face this with her head held high.

Dorothy walked her down the aisle. As they drew closer, various emotions played over Lydia's face. She held his gaze, but her lips trembled. Dorothy handed her off. Samuel took her hands, silently vowing to do whatever it took to make her feel at home with him.

Lydia's gaze wandered over his shoulder. She smiled at their gathered friends. When she looked back at him, some strength returned to her eyes. He squeezed her hand and smiled. Her lips turned up slightly in return.

John opened the prayer books in his hands. "Are you ready?"

"Define ready," Lydia muttered under her breath.

Samuel bit his lips to keep from laughing. He gave her hands another squeeze. "It'll be all right, Lydi."

At her skeptical expression, he shrugged and smiled again. He'd just have to prove it to her.

"Dearly beloved, we are gathered today to witness the union of Samuel Allen and Lydia Jefferson. Marriage is a sacred bond, one that joins two people for life."

Lydia's sharp inhale and her sudden death grip on his fingers told him how nervous she was. He ran his thumbs gently over the backs of her hands, keeping his gaze glued on hers, willing her to calm. After a few moments, her breathing resumed a normal pace.

"Now for the vows." John turned to him. "Do you, Samuel, take Lydia to be your wife, to have and to hold from this day forward, for better, for worse, for richer, for poorer, in sickness and in health, to love and to cherish, till death do you part, according to God's holy law?"

Everything that should have been years ago crashed into Samuel. If they'd married as originally planned, this would have been a joyous day. Lydia would be standing before him in a white dress, a church full of their friends and family, and they would both be bursting with happiness. Instead, they had few witnesses and his bride seemed ready to bolt. Even so, he couldn't deny that this was his heart's desire. He loved her, and he would spend the rest of his life living up to the vow he was about to make.

"I do."

Two simple words. Two words that would join him to Lydia for the rest of his life.

John went through the same litany for Lydia. Her hands grew clammy within Samuel's, but when it came time for her "I do," she said it with quiet determination.

With a smile, John shut his book. "I now pronounce you husband and wife." His smile turned to a grin. "Samuel, you may kiss your bride."

What?

Samuel stared at his mentor. That hadn't been part of the plan. Samuel specifically mentioned *not* having the traditional kiss as part of the ceremony last night. He didn't want to frighten Lydia any more than she already was. Yet John smiled back at him with an innocent expression.

As innocent as a snake.

What was it with matchmakers in this town?

Samuel returned his gaze to his bride. Lydia's hazel eyes went wide. Her gaze dropped to his lips before shooting back up to his eyes. Something like a mask settled over her face, blocking him from reading her expression.

No, he couldn't do it. Not now.

He leaned forward and brushed a kiss over her cheek.

Their audience clapped, but a little voice rose over it. "No, no! That's wrong."

Everyone's eyes turned to Isaiah. He sat shaking his head. "You're supposed to kiss like my mama and papa. Here." He pointed to his lips.

Ella blushed while Cody chuckled. Samuel bit back a smile of his own. Even Lydia's eyes danced with amusement, though her cheeks turned a dark shade of rose, matching her dress.

"Isaiah, not everyone likes to kiss in front of others," Ella whispered to her son.

But Isaiah only doubled down. "But they're married! Why wouldn't they want a real kiss?"

Samuel opened his mouth to respond to the boy, but Lydia stopped him with a hand on his chest. "Go ahead."

His gaze flew to her. "What?"

"It's just a wedding kiss," she whispered. "I can handle it."

He didn't want her to handle it—he wanted her to enjoy it. But that was probably asking too much. Lydia wore an expression of steely resolve. She lifted her chin and waited.

Samuel hesitated a brief moment before bending to press his lips to hers. He lingered only a second or two, but it was enough to send bolts of lightning coursing through his body. Eyes closed, he pulled back a few inches. Good grief, if a simple kiss could rattle him this much, he was in trouble.

"That's better," Isaiah declared, sounding far too satisfied.

Samuel opened his eyes to find Lydia gazing at him with...

sadness? resignation?...in hers. His heart plummeted, remembering the uphill battle before him. His wife didn't love him. She didn't trust him. They'd only married to save her reputation. But that didn't mean love and trust couldn't grow. And Samuel was determined to see it happen.

No matter how long it might take.

CHAPTER 11

*L*ydia stared up at Samuel's home. Just a mile from the church, on the outskirts of town, it sat two stories high, brick-colored with white trim. Whomever had maintained the home before Samuel got to town had done a good job.

She took tentative steps into the foyer, Ruby's hand held tight in hers. Samuel had helped pack up her and Ruby's belongings after church services. Cody and Ella helped them move everything in their wagon. Cassie provided a casserole for supper so they didn't have to worry about cooking. Pastor Rivers took himself to the hotel in town, saying the new family needed time to settle in.

She would have preferred he stay. Then there would be a buffer between her and her new...husband.

How long would it take to get used to thinking of Samuel that way?

Ruby tugged her hand. "Where do we put our things?"

Samuel came through the door, valises in hand. He smiled at the child. "Would you like to see your room?"

"My own room?" Ruby's eyes widened.

"Yep. It's upstairs."

He led the way. Lydia trailed behind them, trepidation growing. The house wasn't large. Much like in the home she'd shared with Dorothy, there was a parlor and a kitchen with a small space for a dining table between the two rooms. A fireplace sat in the parlor, along with a settee, a few small tables, and a large cushy chair. There were stairs off the parlor leading up to the second level. There couldn't be more than two bedrooms. Did that mean...would she and Samuel...?

She closed her eyes, pausing on the stairs. Of course, they would share a room. They were married, after all. And if she dared suggest she share a room with Ruby instead, people were bound to find out. Children talked. She'd learned that early on as a teacher. Which would lead to questions she didn't want to answer.

Her lips tingled. She pressed her fingers there, remembering Samuel's kiss at the church. It had been nothing like his kisses in the past. This one was soft, almost unsure, but her stomach zipped and jumped at the short contact.

Not a good sign.

Lydia had every intention of protecting her heart. It had been shattered twice. She couldn't let it break again.

"Here we are." Samuel's cheerful voice came from the hall.

Lydia scurried up the remaining stairs in time to see Ruby dart through a doorway.

Samuel chuckled. He took a step forward, then hesitated. His head swung around, and their gazes collided.

Lydia summoned a smile. "It's a nice house, Sam."

"Thanks." He poked his head into the bedroom. "Ruby, I'm going to show your mama her room, okay?"

"Okay, Papa."

The sweet way Ruby spoke to Samuel had tears springing to Lydia's eyes. They could have had this so much sooner. They could have been man and wife, working together to raise Charlotte. If only…

She shut the thought down. It did no good dwelling on the past. Her anger was liable to rise if she did, and she was so tired of being angry.

Samuel motioned to a door straight across from Ruby's. "Want to see?"

His tone seemed almost shy, nervous. It softened Lydia. She moved toward him. "Sure."

He led her into the room. She took in the surprisingly clean quarters. The bed was bigger than she expected, neatly made with a simple blue quilt. In the corner stood a wooden wardrobe. A small table with a washbasin and pitcher sat next to a large window, and at the foot of the bed was a wooden chest.

"I hope…you don't mind…"

Samuel rarely fumbled his words. Lydia turned to him, brows raised. "Don't mind what? Being married to you or sharing this room with you?"

His cheeks flushed. "Uh…both, I suppose." A little cough escaped him. "And sharing the bed—are you all right with that?"

Lydia crossed her arms. "I think I can handle it. It's not as though we haven't shared sleeping space before. Twice, in fact. One of which led to this entire situation."

He flinched. "Right."

She'd never seen him look quite this flustered. He appeared ready to rush from the room. Instead, he stepped forward, his hands landing on her shoulders. Intense blue-green eyes met hers. "Lydia, I won't do anything that would make you uncomfortable." His gaze darted at the bed. "I won't…take anything… you aren't willing to give. Not again." He swallowed and dropped his gaze.

Did he think himself solely at fault for that night so long

ago? Despite her own rising embarrassment, Lydia spoke softly. "You've never forced anything from me, Sam. I didn't think you'd start now."

His hands tightened on her shoulders, his expression intensifying. "If I hadn't insisted you stay..."

She put a finger over his lips. "We're not talking about the past, remember?"

"Not now, at least." His gaze didn't waver. "But after Christmas, Lydia—we need to talk. About everything."

Anxiety clawed. She drew in a breath to loosen its hold. "When the time comes."

"Mama, Papa, come see the pretty birds!"

The tension broke. Samuel let his hands drop to his sides, a wry laugh leaving his lips. "We've been summoned by our daughter."

Lydia's breath hitched as they strode to Ruby's room. *Our daughter.* The way he said it, so natural and easy...the way he was with Ruby, going right to the little girl and kneeling beside her at the window...the way he listened, all his attention on her...

Lydia's heart squeezed. Already, he was a good father. But once again, her mind whispered what could have been.

"Mama, come see. They're so blue."

For a brief moment, Lydia froze. It wasn't Ruby's voice she heard—it was Charlotte's. Her little girl loved blue jays, exclaiming over them any time one flitted close to the house. Now Ruby stood, face pressed to the window, excited over the same bird. Lydia peered outside. A pair of blue jays huddled on a branch near the window. They twittered for a few moments before taking flight. Lydia watched them go. To her surprise, instead of sadness, gratitude welled in her heart.

Thank You, Lord, for those sweet years with my girl. I don't know why You took her so soon—but I'm glad You let me have her for a time. And thank You for a new daughter to ease the ache of Charlotte's loss.

Ruby leaned into her, a grin on her face. "Weren't they pretty, Mama?"

Lydia smiled, brushing back some of Ruby's hair. "Yes, sweetheart. Very pretty."

A prickling sensation brushed over her neck. She glanced at Samuel. His eyes focused on her, warmth in his expression. As Ruby went back to the window, he leaned closer. "You were meant to be a mother, Lydi."

Her heart swooped and air stuck in her throat. Oh, no. No, no, no. He should *not* be able to take her breath away with a simple compliment. She stood on shaky legs. "I think...I'm going to unpack my things."

He blinked at her but nodded. "Would you like some help?"

"No, I've got it. Thank you."

She needed space. Samuel was being entirely too sweet about their whole situation, almost as if he was happy to be married to her.

Which was ridiculous. He couldn't be any happier about this than she was. Their lives had been turned upside down in a matter of hours. It wasn't what either of them wanted.

Lydia scurried out of the room, but she felt his gaze follow her. She leaned against the wall in the hallway, taking deep breaths to steady her heart. A sinking sensation made her stomach rock hard. It would be all too easy to fall for Samuel again if he continued acting like this. And she couldn't afford to let herself open like that. Not again.

Closing her eyes, she huffed a sigh. She'd just have to be careful and guard her heart. With a resolute nod, she pushed off the wall and walked into her room.

*S*amuel sat in Cassie's Café with John. Three days had passed since he and Lydia married. Three days since she'd thrown herself into the final week with her students, going to school early and arriving home late as she prepared for the Christmas holidays. He hadn't seen as much of her as he thought he would. Not yet. In two days, though, she'd be on break and they would be in forced proximity for almost a month.

To his surprise—and suspicion—John hadn't yet brought up Samuel's marriage. They were nearly finished with lunch, and their entire conversation had revolved around ministry and pastoring a small community. His mentor would only be in town until Saturday. He would leave on the same train as Dorothy as they both traveled back east to the Dakota Territory. At least he could be sure Saturday's supper would distract from his tension with Lydia.

He couldn't figure out his wife. She was pleasant and affable most of the time, but she seemed to withdraw whenever he tried to take their conversation deeper. Samuel was getting tired of surface-level small talk.

"So...how's your wife?"

And there it was.

Samuel eyed John over the rim of his coffee mug. "As well as can be expected, I suppose."

"Which means what, exactly?"

"We're civil to one another. Ruby has been an excellent buffer. If Lydia and I agree on anything, it's that Ruby is our first priority."

So much so that Lydia hadn't yet slept beside him. Their first night as a family, before Samuel and Lydia retired for the evening, Ruby woke frightened and crying after a nightmare. From what they'd been able to gather, she'd dreamt about her grandma's death. Lydia opted to sleep in their little girl's room to soothe her fears. As Ruby's nightmares recurred each night this week, his wife continued to sleep in the other room.

Which was fine with him. As far as he was concerned, sleeping beside her would be a special form of torture. And penance. So close, but unable to hold her.

John studied him. Just when Samuel started to fidget under the man's intense gaze, John chuckled. "You've got it bad, my friend."

Samuel sipped his coffee again, avoiding John's eyes. "We already established that."

"Yes, but I didn't realize how much you loved her." John leaned forward. "What's your plan to woo her?"

"Honestly? I don't know. I'm not sure I can come up with a good plan until I know exactly why she's been so upset with me all these years. That's a wall between us, and she said we can't talk about it until the new year."

"That shouldn't make a difference in your efforts to court her. You already have a long history together. Use that to find ways that show you care. If you just sit around and do nothing, she'll never learn to love and trust you again."

Samuel leaned back. "You have a point." He drummed his fingers against the table. "I just don't know where to start."

"What's her favorite dessert?"

"Cinnamon jumbles."

John tilted his head, brow furrowing. "What's that?"

"It's a cookie. Lydia loves cinnamon in her desserts, but those cookies are special to her. Her mother always made them for her birthday."

With a smile, John leaned forward, his eyes over Samuel's shoulder. "Then I suppose you should find out if Mrs. Doyle makes them."

Cassie came to a stop at their table. "Find out if Mrs. Doyle makes what?"

John grinned at her. "Samuel was just wondering if you

made cinnamon jumbles." He lowered his voice to a conspiratorial whisper. "They are the new Mrs. Allen's favorite."

Eyes lighting up, Cassie hopped in place. "Bringing your wife her favorite treat? How romantic!" Her lips turned down, but just as quickly, they formed a smile again. "I don't have any made now, but I can get some ready within the hour. Will that suffice?"

Lydia wouldn't be home for a while. Samuel nodded. "That'll do just fine, Cassie. Thanks." Another idea occurred to him. "Actually, can I order supper for my family as well? Lydia's been working long hours, and I don't want her to worry about cooking tonight."

Cassie grinned. "If Lydia's not in love with you before spring, I'll be shocked." She refilled their coffee. "I can make up a basket with our supper special and have it ready when the cookies are done."

Samuel smiled. "That sounds perfect. You're the best."

"Don't you forget it." She winked and headed back to the kitchen.

John smiled, satisfaction written on his face. "Perfect first steps."

Uncertainty nagged Samuel. "Are you sure? She's going to know I'm trying to gain her affection."

"There's nothing wrong with that. Just make sure you let her know it's because you care, not because you want anything from her."

Samuel frowned. "Aren't I doing this because I want her to love me back?"

"Partly. But the main reason should be simply to show her she's loved. Yes, her falling in love with you would be ideal, and that's what I'll be praying for. But she needs to know that your love is unconditional, Samuel. Can you show her that, regardless of how she treats you?"

Slowly swirling the coffee in his mug, Samuel considered

the question. He stared at the dark liquid as he contemplated his answer. "I'd like to think I can. But if I face rejection, I might shut down."

"Fight that urge, Samuel. That's the last thing either you or Lydia need. Once she feels safe, I think she'll open up. But that requires you remaining open too."

Samuel pushed out a breath and chuckled. "You don't ask much, do you?"

John's lips tugged upward. "If forty years of marriage taught me anything, it's that love is a choice, one you make every single day. It's not always easy, that's for sure. But then, Christ loves us even when we're unlovable. He asks us to do the same with others."

"Good point." Samuel plunked his mug on the table. "All right, I'll give it my best. I'll show Lydia my love in word and deed." He grinned. "And I know just the place to start."

"Oh?" John's brows rose. "Other than dinner and dessert tonight?"

Samuel stood, draining his coffee in one long swallow. "Yep. Want to come with me to the mercantile? I know just the thing to order for Lydia's Christmas gift."

CHAPTER 12

*L*ydia sat on the edge of Ruby's bed, watching her little girl sleep. For the first time since they moved into Samuel's house, Ruby slept peacefully. That meant Lydia needed to work up the courage to go to her own room.

The room she shared with her husband.

She gulped. Despite the freezing temperatures outside, Lydia felt much too warm. She was beginning to suspect Samuel had some lingering feelings for her.

Just today, when she returned home from work, he'd had supper on the table waiting for them, courtesy of Cassie's Café. After they ate, he surprised her with cinnamon jumbles. She'd stared in disbelief at her favorite cookie. Samuel put a couple on her plate before making a pot of tea to go with it, shooing her to the parlor to relax after her workday. He hadn't even let her clean up the kitchen. Instead, he took it on himself.

What was his motive?

Lydia bit down on her bottom lip. There was no use delaying the inevitable. She pressed a kiss to Ruby's forehead, then pushed up from the bed and walked on unsteady legs to her own room.

Samuel sat in bed, his Bible open on his lap. He glanced up when she entered the room. Surprise shone from his eyes. "Ruby's asleep?"

"Yes."

Lydia fiddled with the ties of her robe. The nightgown she wore beneath was modest, but taking off the robe in front of Samuel felt like too much. Especially when his blue-green eyes watched her with something soft shimmering in the depths. She swallowed and crossed her arms over her stomach.

Samuel dropped his gaze to the Bible and shifted slightly to the side. He didn't say anything, but Lydia knew he'd done it to make her more comfortable. Blast it all, he was being sweet again. She quickly untied her robe and draped it over the bedpost, then shimmied under the covers, tempted to cover her head with the heavy quilt.

A deep chuckle came from Samuel's side of the bed. "I won't bite, Lydi." Amusement colored his words.

Lydia snorted, the sound unladylike. She didn't care. Burying her face in the pillow seemed a good option, so she nestled deep into the soft bit of cloth and feathers.

He moved, making the bed creak and groan. She pulled her head out slightly from its hiding place in time to see Samuel blow out the candle on his bedside table. The room plunged into darkness.

Lydia breathed easier and relaxed back into her pillow. But as soon as she felt the warmth from Samuel's body spreading to her, as she listened to his even breaths, butterflies began a rapid dance inside of her.

"This is strange, isn't it?" Samuel's voice pitched deeper than normal, though it was close to a whisper.

Strange was putting it mildly. "Yes."

He rolled to his side, facing her. Though she could barely see his outline in the dark, she felt the intensity of his gaze on hers. What thoughts were going through his mind? Lydia's cheeks heated as the silence stretched on. Maybe she should pretend to be asleep...

"Why did you and Dorothy come to Harmony Springs?"

His question startled her. "Oh...it's nothing major. Dorothy's husband was born here. His parents moved to Aspen Grove when he was still a baby. I think Mother wanted a connection to him after...after we lost everything in the Dakota Territory."

"Then why not go back to Aspen Grove after he died? That's where they met and fell in love, after all."

Lydia's face burned. She closed her eyes even though he couldn't see her. The Bible said the truth would set one free. Would that be the case now? She let out a long breath. "It was because of me."

"You?" A question sat in his tone.

She sighed. "I couldn't handle the idea of going back. Not when..." Oh dear. How to admit this out loud?

It turned out she didn't have to. Samuel released a sigh of his own. "Not when you would be faced with memories of me."

"Yes." Yet in a twist of irony, coming to Harmony Springs had reunited her with Samuel. Far more than she'd ever thought possible.

"I'm sorry, Lydia." Pain laced his words. "I'm sorry I left all those years ago without marrying you. I'm sorry another man had to step in to save your reputation when I should have." He exhaled long and slow. "You and Frank...did you have a good marriage?"

"He and I were friends. We were comfortable together and formed an affectionate bond. That's more than a lot of people can say. So yes, we had a good marriage."

"Did you love him?"

"Of course, I loved him. I loved him since we were children."

A small huff escaped Samuel. "That's not what I meant and

you know it." The pause that followed left Lydia holding her breath. "Were you in love with him?"

With a small shake of her head, she burrowed deeper into the bed. "No. Neither was he in love with me. Friendship was all we were capable of giving one another."

Another pause. Another minute pregnant with things unspoken.

When Samuel's hand found her shoulder, Lydia jumped. "Is that all we have to look forward to? Friendship in marriage?"

The vulnerability in his voice made her brow arch. She almost pointed out that theirs was just as convenient of a marriage as hers with Frank had been, but something stopped her. Instead, she pressed her lips together and fought for the right words. "I think we're already at a kind of friendship, don't you think?"

His hand slipped from her shoulder, leaving it cold. He chuckled, but it sounded rough. "Not nearly like the friendship we once had."

A shudder passed through her body. "Sam, we've been in the same town a matter of weeks. We barely started speaking again when we were forced to marry. Everything is happening so fast."

"I know." He sounded weary. "I just hope…"

When he left the sentence dangling, Lydia leaned closer. "You hope what?"

"Nothing. At least—nothing I can speak of now."

Before she could ask him what he meant, Samuel tugged the quilt snug over her shoulders. "Get some rest, sweetheart. Morning will be here all too soon."

She froze, eyes wide. "Wh-what did you call me?"

"Huh?"

Was that genuine confusion in his voice? Lydia bit her lip. Maybe he hadn't realized he used the endearment he had when they were young and in love. It wasn't his fault her heart flipped at hearing *sweetheart*. It also wasn't his fault her emotions were all over the place, refusing to settle on any one feeling. "Never mind."

He rose up on his elbow. "Lydia..."

"Goodnight, Samuel."

When he remained propped up, Lydia shut her eyes, willing her heart to slow its rapid beat. After another minute, Samuel lowered himself back to the bed.

"Goodnight, Lydi."

~

*T*hree days later, at the train station, Samuel gave John a hug. A few people milled about, the cold weather keeping many indoors, but Samuel and Lydia wouldn't miss sending John and Dorothy off. Ruby had said her goodbyes the night prior before going to Alice's for a sleepover. "It's been good having you here. Safe journey."

His mentor smiled. "Thanks. It'll be nice to have a traveling companion much of the way." He glanced at Dorothy, who had Lydia enveloped in an embrace. "Dorothy is a delightful lady. What are the odds we'd be traveling to the same town to visit family and friends? It's almost providential."

Samuel's brows went up. He blinked, staring between the two. Dorothy caught John's eye. She blushed like a schoolgirl and ducked her head. John chuckled softly while Samuel gaped.

"Is there something going on, John?"

"We've agreed to a correspondence once she's back here and I'm in Chicago. After that, we'll see."

Judging from the besotted smile on John's face, correspondence wouldn't be the end of this new friendship. He clapped his mentor on the shoulder. "You both deserve happiness. I hope this works out."

John turned to him with a serious expression. "I could say the same for you and Lydia." He leaned closer. "Remember, keep wooing her."

"I plan to." Regardless of the fact that he was still scared to fail.

Dorothy bustled over, hugging Samuel. "You be good to my girl while I'm gone, you hear me?"

"Yes, ma'am."

She pulled back and studied him. A smile spread over her lips. "Yes, I do believe you will be." Dorothy leaned closer. "I always thought there was more to your story."

What?

Before he could ask what she meant, the train whistle blew. John picked up Dorothy's luggage along with his own. They said their goodbyes, then disappeared onto the train.

Lydia sniffed beside him. Samuel turned, his stomach dropping at the tears in her eyes. He looped an arm around her waist without thinking. Her body stiffened. Realizing his mistake, Samuel almost released her, but she turned into him and relaxed, leaning her head on his shoulder.

"I'm going to miss her." Voice sad, Lydia kept her eyes on the train even as it slowly pulled away from the station.

Samuel squeezed her a little closer. "All this change must feel overwhelming."

She half laughed, half snorted. "You think?"

His lips tugged up in a smile. Her spunk was still intact. Good. He chuckled and led her down the boardwalk. People hurried by, bundled in their coats. They passed the livery, and Samuel pointed down the street. "Would you like to stop at Cassie's? I heard she has cinnamon jumbles on her main menu now."

"Does she?" Lydia's brow hiked. "Would you have anything to do with that change?"

He shrugged. "It's Christmastime. Apparently, cinnamon is a popular seasonal flavor."

"Mm-hmm." They walked a few moments in silence, then Lydia pulled to a stop. She slipped from his grasp and faced him. "You didn't answer my question."

"Caught that, did you?" He chuckled. He slipped his hands into his pockets, uncertainty swirling in his gut. "Yes, I did ask Cassie to keep them in stock."

His wife stared at him. Samuel shifted his weight as her hazel eyes remained on him. "Was I wrong to do so?"

She blinked a couple times before shaking her head. "No. It's...sweet." Her gaze dropped. "But I don't understand. Why did you do it?"

"Because you like them."

Lydia's brows drew together, and her gaze swung back up to his. Her mouth opened and closed twice. Clearing her throat, she stepped closer to him. "You asked Cassie to put cinnamon jumbles on the menu because I like them?"

Hadn't he just said that? "Yes."

She didn't seem convinced. "Are you sure it wasn't because you feel guilty over everything that's happened between us?"

Samuel sighed. He offered his arm. Lydia accepted it after a brief hesitation. He started walking again, heading for the café. "Lydi, I do feel guilty for hurting you. I'm sad that freak circumstances led to this marriage. But that's not why I asked Cassie to keep the cookies. You and I have been friends, we've been in love, and now we're married. I know they're your favorite. I just..." He shrugged and kept his gaze ahead. "I just wanted to do something nice to show you I care."

It was on the tip of his tongue to tell her he still loved her, but that could prove disastrous. He kept that thought to himself.

For now. Someday, he'd have to declare his feelings. But only when Lydia showed she'd be open to them.

He felt her gaze on him, but he kept his own eyes forward. Let her process his words at her own pace. Maybe she'd realize this marriage could be one full of love rather than simply an escape from ruin.

Just before they reached the café, Lydia once again pulled him to a stop. His heart lurched at the tears gathered over her lashes. "Lydia, are you...?"

She put her fingers over his lips. "Sam. Thank you."

Her hand fell away right after her thanks, but the warmth remained. A smile stretched across his face. "You're welcome."

She gave him an answering smile.

Samuel held open the café door for her, and together they walked to the display counter. Cassie beamed at them from behind it. "Well, if it's not two of my favorite people." She gave Samuel a knowing look. "Cinnamon jumbles to go?"

His cheeks heated, but he nodded. "Yes, please." He turned to his wife. "Is there anything else you'd like? Maybe something for Ruby?"

Lydia perused the selection of treats. Samuel crossed his arms over his chest, content to wait.

"Pastor Allen. A word, if you don't mind."

He froze. That voice, high and sharp, put him in mind of a hunter sighting prey. Stifling a sigh, he turned and forced a polite smile. "Mrs. Holt. How can I help you?"

She sat at a table, nose in the air, and pointed to the chair across from her. "Have a seat."

Trying not to bristle, Samuel put a hand on Lydia's back. "I'll return shortly."

Her gaze flickered between him and Mrs. Holt. She nodded and turned back to the display. Samuel walked to Mrs. Holt's table, sitting only to avoid appearing rude.

The woman didn't make him wait. "I'm surprised you decided to wed Mrs. Jefferson," she said without preamble.

Her tone stiffened his spine. "It's Mrs. Allen."

"Yes, yes." Mrs. Holt waved a hand. "But what I don't understand is *why* you married her."

"Don't you?" Samuel asked, his tone dry. "I don't recall being given much choice, thanks to you and your school board."

"Perhaps we were a bit hasty." Mrs. Holt cleared her throat, fiddling with her napkin. "An annulment could..."

"Absolutely not." Samuel stood. Fire burned in his chest. He planted his hands on the table and leaned forward. "An annulment would only further ruin Lydia's reputation. And in case you weren't aware, marriage is a sacrament, not to be taken lightly. I made vows before God and man, and I intend to keep them." He pushed up, giving the woman a final glare. "Good day to you, ma'am."

Spinning around, he nearly ran into Lydia. Her wide eyes and pale face told him she'd overheard at least part of the conversation. Taking her arm, he steered her toward the door. Only when they were outside, away from prying eyes, did he stop and face her. "Are you all right?"

Color splotched her cheeks. "I can't say it was pleasant hearing Mrs. Holt suggest you abandon your vows so carelessly, but I am glad you stood your ground."

"Oh?" He chucked her gently under the chin. "You could have been free of me."

She huffed. "As you stated so clearly, that would ruin me further." A shy smile pulled at her lips. "But thank you again. For defending me."

"Anytime." Samuel motioned to the paper bag in her hands. "Did you get everything you needed?"

"I did. Cinnamon jumbles for myself, snickerdoodles for Ruby...and a slice of chocolate cake for you."

His mouth dropped open. Heat swirled in his stomach at the tenderness in her eyes, aimed at him. Chocolate cake was his favorite dessert. He laughed softly. "You remembered?"

She reached for his hand, giving it a light squeeze. "I remember everything, Sam."

CHAPTER 13

*F*our days before Christmas, Samuel stood at the stove making pancakes when Ruby came bounding down the stairs. She held a book clutched to her chest. "Papa, did you know some people have trees for Christmas? Look!" Opening the book, she displayed a picture.

He crouched down and grinned. "Yes. My parents and I cut down a Christmas tree every year when I was a boy. We made decorations and put candles on the tree to make it pretty like this." He tapped the picture in Ruby's book. "It was my favorite tradition."

Her eyes grew large. She bounced on her toes, hope lighting in her eyes. "Can we get a tree to decorate?"

Visions of finding a tree with his new daughter made Samuel's heart light. His gaze landed on an open corner of the room. "Sure. What do you think about putting the tree right there?" He pointed.

"Yeah!" Ruby pumped her fists in the air. Joy shone from her little face. "Can we go now?"

Chuckling, Samuel shook his head. "Not before breakfast. You need to eat first."

"Okay."

Ruby plopped onto her chair and clasped her hands. "I'm ready to eat."

"All right."

As Samuel plated some pancakes, Lydia came down the stairs. She had on a warm dress and shawl, but her long hair hung over her shoulder in a braid rather than pinned up in its usual style. He stopped in his tracks, plate in hand, and stared.

Lydia blushed. Her gaze dropped. "Good morning."

Samuel couldn't think of a single coherent thing to say. Thankfully, Ruby saved him from responding.

"Mama! Papa said we could get a Christmas tree today. Will you come too?"

Lydia blinked. Her eyes shot up and met Samuel's. "A Christmas tree?" A smile formed on her lips. "Oh, that sounds wonderful. We'll have to stop by the mercantile and see if there's anything to decorate with."

Finally getting his feet to move, Samuel placed the plate in front of Ruby. He turned to Lydia. "Would you like some pancakes?"

"Yes, please."

She smiled at him, then moved into the kitchen as well. As he poured more batter, she began making coffee.

Longing clutched his heart. Here they were, carrying out the simplest of tasks as a married couple, and it was more than he could have dreamed of after her disappearance. But he wanted even more. He wished he had the right to pull her into his arms and kiss her good morning. Words of love bubbled up inside, begging for release, but he pushed them away. He couldn't tell her now. She'd only retreat into herself once more.

Be content with the present.

The words from a sermon John gave over a year ago flitted through Samuel's mind. Yes, he would be content. But that didn't mean he couldn't continue his pursuit of his wife.

He leaned closer to her, one hand coming to rest lightly on her waist. "You look lovely this morning."

She glanced at him over her shoulder. Color poured into her cheeks. Touching her braid, she returned her attention to pouring coffee. "I feel rather like a schoolgirl. My pins seem to have disappeared." Her gaze fell on their daughter. A smile played on her lips. "I think our girl wanted to be grown up today."

"Yeah! Now my hair is like Mama's." Ruby giggled.

Samuel turned. Sure enough, Ruby's hair featured pins he hadn't noticed until now. "You definitely look like your mama."

Ruby's grin stretched wide.

Samuel chuckled and leaned toward Lydia. "I think your braid is lovely. You seem more..." He tilted his head, searching for the right word. "Relaxed."

Lydia shook her head, her blush deepening. She twisted the end of her braid and handed him a mug of coffee. "That's probably because classes are on holiday for Christmas."

"Either way," he leaned closer, "you're beautiful."

She inhaled a soft breath, her gaze never leaving his. Her throat bobbed with a swallow. The magnetism pulsing between them prompted Samuel to move closer. Their connection lasted a few seconds longer until Lydia sniffed, her brow wrinkling. "The pancakes are burning."

Samuel whirled around. Grabbing the spatula, he flipped the three cakes. He breathed a sigh of relief. The round disks were dark brown but not black. "Should still be edible. I'll take these." After plating them, he poured the remaining batter onto the pan. A couple minutes later, he sat at the table, putting one plate in front of Lydia and the other on his placemat.

"Hurry, Mama, Papa. We need to get a tree!" Ruby grabbed her plate and put it in the sink. "I'll get on my coat and hat and mittens." She ran for the stairs, calling over her shoulder. "I'll get yours out too."

"How does she have so much energy?" Samuel asked.

"Children have a surprising store of that." Lydia took another bite of her pancakes. "These are good, Sam. Thanks for making breakfast."

"Happy to."

They ate for a few minutes. Questions burned in Samuel's mind, until finally he couldn't keep quiet. "Was Charlotte as energetic as Ruby?"

The fork froze halfway to Lydia's mouth. She gaped at him. The heavy silence was too strong. He opened his mouth to apologize, but Lydia spoke first.

"Yes. She had endless energy." A soft expression crossed her face. She put her fork down. "Charlotte used to get up before dawn and run around the house singing. She always wanted to help out once we started the day. One of her favorite things was animals. She'd feed the newborn calves and lambs with me, then we'd pick berries. She had so much joy, so much life." Tears filled her eyes. She blinked rapidly, dashing a hand across her cheeks. "I miss her so much. It physically hurts."

Samuel slipped his hand over hers.

Lydia pressed a napkin to her eyes. She sniffed before her watery gaze met his. "You would have loved her."

Though the comment struck him as odd, Samuel smiled. "I'm sure I would have. Especially since she sounds so much like her mama."

Lydia laughed, the sound a little broken. "What do you mean?"

"The desire to help others, having joy in life. That's you, Lydi. It always was."

For almost a minute, Lydia stared at her plate. Finally, she shook her head. "I'm afraid I lost my joy a long time ago."

"You can find it again."

"Maybe in some ways. But I don't think I'll ever be that carefree girl again. Too much has changed."

Samuel brought her hand to his lips. He pressed a gentle kiss to her knuckles. Lydia gasped and tried to pull her hand back. Samuel didn't let go. He held her gaze as he lowered their hands back to the table. "Lydia, life hasn't turned out the way you hoped or planned. But I truly believe there's still joy to be found. Maybe..." The words stuck in his throat. With a deep breath, he plunged on. "Maybe you can find new joy. With me and Ruby. I want to make you happy, if you'll let me."

She stared at him, her hazel eyes misting once more. "I don't know, Sam."

"We've been given a second chance, Lydia. Not many people get that. Maybe it'll lead to joy." He pressed her fingers gently before letting go. "Just think about it."

"A second chance? Is that what you think this is?" She raised her brow, sitting back in her chair. "We were forced into this. It's hardly a second chance."

"I'm choosing to believe that's exactly what this is. Second chances come in many different packages. Ours is unconventional, but maybe it's the only way we could be together again." He smirked. "I doubt you'd ever have allowed me to call on you otherwise."

Her chin lifted. "No, indeed."

"My point exactly."

"You wouldn't have come calling, anyway."

Was that vulnerability in her eyes? Samuel stood, his palms against the table. "Believe me, Lydi, if I thought you were open to it, I would have jumped at the chance to win back your heart." He winked, whisking their plates to the sink. "In fact, I plan to do just that."

The bold words rolled off his tongue before he had a chance to think about them.

Lydia's jaw dropped and her eyes widened. She clutched her coffee mug to her chest. "Sam..."

He couldn't take it back now. Besides, that was his plan. She might as well know. He grinned and walked toward her. Slipping one finger under her chin, he pushed up to close her mouth. "Careful, sweetheart. We don't need you catching flies."

~

*T*he woods held such beauty in winter. Lydia took a deep breath of the crisp, cold air. It felt good walking through the trees, listening to Ruby's excited chatter and Samuel's happy responses as they searched for the perfect tree. She answered when spoken to, but her mind kept straying to Samuel's words at breakfast.

He planned to win her heart.

The traitorous organ thumped hard at the thought. At first, she'd wondered if that was something he decided this morning. He'd had his share of spur-of-the-moment decisions before. But on further reflection, she realized everything he'd done since their wedding indicated his care.

She couldn't decide how she felt about that.

For so long, they had planned to spend their lives together before. Her heart had been his completely, her love for him unbreakable. Or so she thought. His betrayal hurt more than she'd believed possible, and anger took the place of love. But now...

Her gaze settled on the two members of her new family as Samuel swooped Ruby up into his arms. Their daughter laughed with delight. Samuel beamed, his love for Ruby clear, even after such a short time. His eyes, bright with exercise and laughter, shone like stars. Lydia's breath hitched. It was a sight to behold.

Maybe you never stopped loving him, not really.

She stiffened. No. Her anger might be melting away, but that did not mean she'd fall back into his arms and declare her undying love. There was still too much she needed to know, too much she was afraid to ask. Until she could trust him again, she wouldn't risk her heart.

No matter how charming and sweet he might be.

Liar. Your heart is already at risk.

She shushed the inner voice and stomped forward. A distraction would help. She gathered some loose snow into a ball and straightened, a grin slipping free. Samuel twirled Ruby before setting her on the ground. As soon as he started walking again, Lydia let the snowball fly.

It hit him square in the back.

Samuel yelped and spun around. The shock on his face had laughter springing from Lydia's mouth. She braced her hands on her knees, trying to bring her mirth under control.

"Snowball fight!" Ruby yelled. She hurried over to Lydia. "Get Papa."

The two of them scooped up more snow.

Samuel planted his hands on his hips. "Hey, two against one isn't fair."

"Too bad." Lydia lobbed another ball at him. This time, it hit his arm.

Samuel's face broke into a grin. "All right, you asked for it." He ducked behind a tree. Moments later, he flung three snowballs in a row toward them. All fell harmlessly to the ground.

Ruby's nose wrinkled. "Papa doesn't have good aim."

"I heard that," Samuel called from his hideout.

Lydia bent down. "You go around that way, and I'll go the other way. We'll both get him at the same time."

Ruby's sweet giggles accompanied their snowball making. Once they each had several in hand, they hurried toward the tree. Samuel bent on his knees, focused on making his own arsenal. Lydia yelled, "Now!", and she and Ruby pummeled him with snow. Samuel laughed, ducking to avoid what he could, but his coat dripped white. He stood, sending a look at

Ruby that had her shrieking with laughter and hurrying to Lydia's side.

"Retribution is in order." Samuel took large, deliberate steps toward them.

Ruby peeked around Lydia. "You can't get us."

"Hmm, we'll see."

He lunged without warning and grabbed Lydia about the waist. Hoisting her into his arms bridal style, he grinned in triumph. "I got the captain."

Lydia wiggled, her laughter making her attempts at escape futile even as she locked her arms around his neck for support. "Sam! Put me down."

"No can do. This is a matter of honor, ma'am. Now, let's see." He hummed thoughtfully, glancing around the woods. "Ruby, where can we find a heap of snow to dump your mama in?"

"What? No!" Lydia stopped struggling. She batted her lashes at him. "Please, kind sir, let me go."

"I don't think so." His eyes sparkled with mischief. "You started this, after all. It's only fair that you take your punishment for that barrage of snowballs."

"What if I promise to behave for the rest of this trip?"

"Nope."

"Papa, here's a good place," Ruby called, dancing around a copse of trees.

Lydia smothered another laugh. "I thought you were on my side, Ruby."

"I can be on both sides."

Samuel chuckled under his breath. "She's got good logic there, sweetheart."

Her stomach swooped at his endearment. Their eyes locked. The rest of the world fell away, and it was just the two of them. Samuel's eyes smoldered. His gaze fell to her lips before jerking back up to her eyes. Lydia leaned closer, her heart crowding out the warning in her mind.

"What're you two doing?"

Ruby walked closer, eyes brimming with curiosity. Samuel's hands tightened on Lydia. He cleared his throat and turned to their daughter. "Nothing, honey. I think you're right—that's the perfect place to cover your mama with snow." He winked at Lydia and moved nearer to the snow bank Ruby pointed out. "Ready for your snow bath?"

"Snow ba—"

With a swoosh, he let her tumble into the soft pile of snow. Lydia sank into its depths. Ruby climbed in after her, giggling the whole while.

Samuel stood by, triumph in his eyes. "I think I win."

Lydia tried to sift through the powdery snow. "I didn't concede." Ruby snuggled into her lap, making movement difficult.

Samuel chuckled and held out a hand. "C'mon. I'll pull you out."

She shot him a mock glare. "I don't think so. That would admit defeat."

"Would that be so bad?" His mouth twitched as if he smothered a smile.

Lydia huffed. She wrapped her arms around Ruby and spoke into the girl's ear. "Maybe we should stay here and wait for your papa to find the right tree, hmm?"

Ruby wiggled out of her lap. "No! We have to find the tree together. Help, Papa." She reached out a hand to Samuel, who lifted her from the snow with ease. Ruby brushed herself off and skipped to a nearby tree. "This one is good. Just like the picture in Mama's book."

"That is perfect, Ruby," Samuel said. "Good eye. We'll cut it down if your mama agrees." He cocked a brow at Lydia. "Do you like it?"

The fir was full and green and not too tall for their house. Lydia smiled. "Good job, Ruby. That's our tree."

"Yay! Can I help cut it down?"

Samuel tilted his head. "I suppose that'd be fine, as long as you are very careful and follow my directions."

"I will, Papa."

"Good."

Samuel crouched in front of Lydia. "Well? Would you like me to help you out?"

"No, thank you." She gave him an innocent smile, her hands working at some snow beneath her. "I think I've got it."

"If you're sure—"

Lydia burst from the drift and flung a snowball straight at his chest. His surprised gasp made her grin. "Ha. I win."

She started for Ruby, but Samuel's arms encircled her from behind and trapped her against his chest. Warmth crept through her, starting at her back and spreading through all her limbs.

He pressed his cheek to hers and whispered softly in her ear. "As long as I win your love in the end, sweetheart."

CHAPTER 14

*J*t had been too long since Samuel decorated a Christmas tree. Not since he was in his teens. But now, surrounded by cranberry garland and candles and assorted ornaments from the mercantile, he wondered why he stopped the tradition as an adult.

Then again, most of the joy now was watching Ruby's excitement as they decorated. Her face glowed with happiness as she selected ornaments to place on the lower branches. Little-girl giggles surrounded him and Lydia.

His wife pulled gingerbread cookies from the oven. The heady scent of cinnamon, cloves, and ginger filled the house.

Samuel's mouth watered. He wandered toward Lydia and peered over her shoulder. "Are those ready to be eaten?"

She chuckled, shooing him away. "You know perfectly well they aren't iced yet. You'll just have to be patient."

He produced an exaggerated frown. Reaching around Lydia, he snatched a hot cookie from the pan. "Ouch!"

Lydia rolled her eyes. "Honestly, Samuel. You're as impatient as a child. It's better with icing."

Bouncing the cookie from hand to hand while it cooled, he

grinned. "Not necessarily. Haven't you ever eaten a gingerbread cookie straight from the oven?" He hitched a brow, his grin growing. "And don't you try to deny it. I've got plenty memories of us stealing cookies off the sheet straight from the oven."

"It's not stealing if your mother allowed it." She seemed to be fighting a smile of her own.

Samuel broke his cookie in half. "Here. You have the first taste."

He slipped the bit of cookie between her lips before popping the other half into his mouth. His eyes slipped shut as flavor burst on his tongue. "Oh, that's good."

"Mmm. I'll say." Lydia reached for another cookie, pressing it into his hand. "Now go give our girl this one."

Our girl. Sweeter words couldn't be spoken. The fact that she easily acknowledged their shared parenthood of Ruby made his heart swell with joy. It happened faster than he anticipated too. He'd expected more of a struggle from Lydia as they settled into life together. While she remained largely guarded, her heart didn't seem stone hard where he was concerned. Samuel counted that a victory, and it gave him hope for the future.

It had been a risk telling her he planned to win her love. But he didn't regret it. If anything, having his intentions in the open served to make things less awkward between them.

He tapped her nose and handed the cookie back. "You should be the one to share it with Ruby. After all, you made them." Grabbing her hand, he led her back to the tree.

Ruby jumped up and down between them. "I put more garland on."

The bottom half of the tree sported lots of red cranberries sewn on a length of string. Samuel chuckled, eying the top half. "I suppose your mama and I should make the rest of the tree match, huh?"

"Yeah." Ruby caught sight of the cookie in Lydia's hand. "Oooh, is that for me?"

"It is." Lydia handed the gingerbread to her. "I hope you like it. This is your papa's favorite cookie."

"Really?" Ruby gazed at Samuel with a grin. "Then it's my favorite too."

He laughed, ruffling her hair. "You haven't tried it yet, silly girl."

Ruby took a large bite. Around her mouthful, she spoke. "Yep. My favorite." She shoveled the remaining piece in her mouth and smacked her lips. "Yummy. Now can we finish the tree?"

"Of course, honey." Samuel grabbed the garland. "Should I toss it around or be careful?"

"Toss it!"

He grinned and threw his hand in the air. The garland landed on the uppermost branches in a tangle of red.

Ruby fisted some and threw it onto the tree. "Fun! Mama, you try."

"Oh, I don't know." Lydia peered at the garland as if it might bite. "This isn't exactly typical tree decorating."

Samuel snorted. "Typical? C'mon, Lydi, have some fun." He wrapped the garland around her head. "There. What do you think, Ruby? Does Mama match the tree?"

Ruby's giggles filled the room while Lydia stared at him, mouth open. Her lips curved into a smile, and she grabbed her own handful of red. "Fine. I'll play along." Instead of wrapping it around the tree, she threw the strand at Samuel and Ruby. It hung around their shoulders in haphazard fashion. "Now we all match the tree."

Laughing, Samuel dropped to the floor. "This is by far the most fun I've had decorating a tree."

Ruby snuggled into his lap while Lydia removed the garland from all of them and arranged it around the tree. His wife wore a content smile. When their eyes met, a jolt went through Samuel.

Lydia lowered herself to the floor beside him and Ruby, her hand just inches from his. "What do you think, Ruby? Was this a good tree decorating experience?"

"Oh, yes." Ruby nodded. She gazed up at the tree. "It's so pretty." Despite her words, the smile slipped from the child's face. Tears welled in her eyes, and she sniffed a couple times.

Lydia moved closer, alarm on her face. Her hand brushed Samuel's as she spoke. "Ruby, sweetie, what's wrong?"

Tears trickled down Ruby's cheeks. "Granny isn't here."

It was the first show of grief outside of her nightmares that their daughter expressed. No doubt, the sense of loss was more than a six-year-old could comprehend. He hugged her close, words failing him.

But they didn't fail Lydia. His wife slipped an arm around Ruby's back. "I know it hurts, Ruby, and that's all right. It's okay to cry, and it's okay to miss your granny."

"I...want...Granny," Ruby sobbed. She clutched Lydia's hand and buried her face in Samuel's chest.

His own heart tore in response to her sadness. He held her close, rocking back and forth. His gaze collided with Lydia's. The pain in his wife's eyes made him bold—he reached one arm around her back, drawing her close to him and Ruby. Lydia nestled her head against his shoulder. Though his heart leapt at her small display of trust, he kept his gaze on the little girl grieving between them.

After several minutes, Ruby's sobs quieted. Samuel rubbed her back. When Ruby finally lifted her head, he wiped the tears from her cheeks. His daughter turned around, snuggling her back into his chest and staring at the cranberry-covered tree.

"Do you think Granny would have liked our tree?"

"Yes."

Ruby let out a small breath. "Good." She turned her head to look at Lydia. "Mama, can we have some more gingerbread?"

"Of course." Lydia squeezed Ruby's hand, then let go and pushed herself up. "Let me ice them and make some cocoa to go with them."

A tiny smile lit Ruby's face. "Thanks, Mama."

As Lydia headed for the kitchen, Samuel smoothed Ruby's mussed hair. "Do you want to put on more ornaments?"

"No, thank you. Can we just sit here and admire the tree?" Ruby gazed up at him with wide eyes. "Maybe you can read 'The Night Before Christmas'?"

"Sure, honey."

The book lay on an end table mere feet away. Samuel lifted it from its spot, opening it and placing it in front of Ruby. "'T'was the night before Christmas, when all through the house, not a creature was stirring, not even a mouse...'"

∼

*E*arly Christmas Eve morning, Lydia stood at the kitchen window, taking in the snowy vista. It had been a few days since Ruby's rush of grief. Since then, her nightmares began again, and she had a few more crying bouts when she looked at the tree. Otherwise, she seemed happy and upbeat. Samuel worried about Ruby's swings in emotions, but Lydia knew how grief worked. She assured him their daughter's outbursts were normal.

A warm hand pressed against her lower back. She glanced over her shoulder to see her husband. His face had been scrubbed clean, any traces of overnight beard growth shaven. He wore a blue shirt that made his eyes look especially bright. Her stomach fluttered. "Good morning, Samuel."

"Morning, Lydia." He took a step back, shoving his hands

into his pockets. "I plan to head to the church to work on my Christmas sermon. Is that all right?"

She ignored the tingle that still danced over her spine where his hand had been. Better to pretend he didn't affect her so easily. Nodding, she slipped to the bread box. "I'll pack you a lunch."

He rested his hand over hers, stalling her movement. Their gazes met. Lydia had to remind herself to breathe. Samuel took a step closer. "Don't worry about it," he said. "I'll be home before lunch."

"All...right."

Drat. Her words sounded breathy and soft. Judging from the smile spreading over Samuel's face, he knew his touch rattled her. She tugged her hand out from under his and moved a couple paces away. "Ruby and I are going into town this morning to do some final Christmas shopping. She wants to get you a gift."

"She doesn't have to do that."

"Perhaps not, but she's insistent."

His eyes sparkled. "What about you? Did you get me something?"

Her stomach fluttered. Dropping her gaze, she shrugged. "Perhaps."

Samuel's chuckle tickled her ears. He leaned closer, trapping her against the counter with an arm on either side of her waist. "What is it?"

"I said 'perhaps.'" She pressed back as much as possible. Not that it created more space between them.

"If you didn't, I'd accept a Christmas kiss." Samuel's eyes glinted with danger. His gaze fell to her mouth and lingered there before finally roaming back up to her eyes.

Lydia's breath caught. She rested her hand against his chest with the intention of pushing him back. But her body refused to cooperate. Instead, her fingers toyed with the soft fabric of his shirt. Her throat suddenly tightened. "I did get you something," she whispered.

Samuel's gaze remained fixed on hers. He leaned even closer. Only inches separated them. "I'd still take a kiss, if you're willing to give it."

Her heart thumped so hard, could Samuel hear it? Or feel it, considering how close they stood? He waited, and she knew without a doubt that he'd only kiss her if she gave him the okay.

Never had she felt so torn. Part of her wanted to throw her reservations to the wind and let him love her. Another part of her retreated behind impregnable walls, unwilling to let go of the hurt she still felt over his past abandonment.

Forgiveness was one thing. Trust was another.

Samuel reached up, cupping her cheek. Desire flared in his eyes. His thumb brushed her jaw. Still, he made no move to close the small distance between them.

His respectful patience made the decision for her. Lydia's hand slid from his chest to the back of his neck. Maybe she could let him in. She could make a deliberate choice to leave the past behind and start anew. Closing her eyes, she lifted her chin.

Samuel's soft intake of breath was followed by an exhale that warmed her mouth. Any moment now, she'd feel the familiar, heady sensation of his lips on hers...

"Mama, I'm ready to go."

They jerked apart. Lydia's cheeks flamed as she turned to see Ruby standing on the bottom step of the stairs, curiosity on her face. Smoothing her skirt, Lydia produced a bright smile. "All right, sweetie. I'll get your coat."

She skirted around Samuel. "I hope your sermon writing goes well." *And I hope that interrupted kiss doesn't make things awkward between us.*

He chuckled. "Thanks, Lydi. You and Ruby have fun."

"Bye, Papa." Ruby hurried over and wrapping her arms around his waist.

Lydia took the opportunity to get coats for her and Ruby. By the time her daughter came to the front door, Lydia had her own coat on and helped Ruby with hers. They walked out the door hand in hand, their boots crunching in the snow.

In town, Ruby selected a variety of hard candies for Samuel's Christmas gift. While Mr. Peterson wrapped them in a pretty box, Lydia scanned the shelves. She had gotten Samuel a small gift—a handkerchief—but something urged her to find a more meaningful item. Her gaze landed on a beautifully bound copy of *A Christmas Carol*. Samuel loved Charles Dickens. She'd never understood the fascination, thinking his stories were far too depressing, but this one was reputed to be more hopeful. She ran a hand over the leather cover. Had Samuel already read it? It wasn't in his small collection of books. Perhaps it would be new to him.

Mr. Peterson came up beside her. "That's the final copy of that novel. People seem to like it."

"I'll take it. Can you wrap it for me?"

The older man nodded with a smile. He carried the book to the checkout counter. "A gift for the pastor?"

"Yes. He loves Dickens."

"Can't say I blame him. His stories keep ya spellbound."

She chuckled. "You sound like Samuel."

Mr. Peterson paused. His keen gray eyes studied her. "Are ya happy, ma'am? In your new marriage, I mean?"

Not sure how to respond, Lydia cleared her throat. She didn't know Mr. Peterson well, yet something about him spoke of trustworthiness. Even so, she dropped her gaze as she answered. "The circumstances surrounding our marriage were not ideal, but Samuel has been good to me. I think, in time, happiness is possible."

Mr. Peterson tutted. He finished wrapping the book and

handed it to her. "Maybe it's none of my business, but I didn't agree with the school board's decision. Survival is mighty difficult in blizzards. You and the pastor saved each other and that sweet little girl." He nodded at Ruby, who was spinning circles in the middle of the store. "You deserve a happy Christmas." He held up a finger, his eyes lighting up. "One moment."

He hurried to the back of the store.

Lydia held a hand out to Ruby. "You about ready to go home, sweetie?"

Ruby stopped spinning and skipped up to her. "Yes, Mama."

Mr. Peterson returned. He held a small package wrapped in foil paper. Handing it to Lydia, he grinned. "This is my Christmas gift to your family. Chocolate imported from Europe. We don't get this in often, but my son unloaded a shipment this morning. Merry Christmas. I hope it brings you some cheer."

Lydia gasped. "Oh, no, we can't possibly accept such a gift." She'd seen what chocolate cost when the store had it in stock. It wasn't cheap.

"As I said, it's a gift. I wish your little family nothin' but joy."

"Th-thank you."

Lydia stared at the wrapped package in her hands, Mr. Peterson's words repeating in her mind. *Nothing but joy.*

Her heart skipped a beat. What would it be like to experience a life of joy, despite the circumstances that brought her family together? They'd all seen their share of grief.

Was a life of joy still possible?

CHAPTER 15

Christmas morning had always been Samuel's favorite part of the year. Now that he had a family, especially a daughter, it felt even more magical. After the church service, they returned home to eat cinnamon rolls and open presents. Excitement and nerves rolled through him at the thought of watching Lydia open his gift to her.

Their little family gathered around the tree. Ruby bounced with joy, her eyes on the presents. Lydia brought mugs of cocoa into the room and set them on the small table beside the sofa. "You ready to open your gifts, Ruby?"

"Yes, Mama."

Samuel grinned. "Good." He grabbed the first present and handed it to Ruby. "Here you go."

With a delighted squeak, she tore into the package. A rag doll fell onto the floor. She scooped it up and hugged it to her chest. "Pretty dolly."

"You like it?" Lydia asked, a smile on her lips.

Ruby nodded. "Love it. Thanks, Mama."

"Two more." Samuel placed the packages in front of their

daughter, one green and one brown. "You choose which to open first."

Grabbing the brown gift, Ruby opened it to reveal an assortment of candies. She popped one in her mouth at once with a wide smile. The next package held some new hair ribbons in a variety of colors. Ruby *ooh*ed over the slips of fabric. Holding up a green one, she scooted onto the sofa and asked Lydia to tie it in her hair.

Samuel's heart swelled as he watched Lydia sweep Ruby's black hair into a low ponytail. He still couldn't believe what a gift he'd been given—a beautiful family, risen from the ashes of scandal. "Thank you, Lord," he murmured under his breath, gaze on his girls.

"Thanks for the presents." Ruby gathered them up. "I'm gonna put them in my room. My stuffed bear wants to meet the new dolly." Bounding toward the stairs, she giggled before taking the steps in quick bursts.

With a laugh, Lydia took a sip of cocoa. "I need some of her endless energy."

Her laugh made his heart stutter. Samuel drew in a long breath. "Would you like to open your gift now?"

She blinked at him, slowly setting the mug down. "You got me a gift?"

In response, he reached into the branches of the tree, pulling out a gold box. "Merry Christmas, Lydi."

Carefully, she opened the box. A gasp escaped her lips. She pulled out the locket resting inside. The delicate oval boasted tiny flowers and vines. It sparkled gold in the morning sunlight pouring through the window. "Sam, it's beautiful."

He took it from her, moving around the sofa to clasp it about her neck. "You always said you wanted one. I thought... maybe...it could be a symbol of our new beginning." With the locket fastened, he came back around and sat beside her.

She reached up, holding the necklace between her hands.

"It's perfect. Thank you." Her smile lit the room. "Now time for your present."

"You didn't have to—"

Lydia silenced him with a lift of her brows. Samuel smiled when she handed him the rectangular gift. "Might it be a book?"

She chuckled. "Open it and find out."

He unwrapped the paper, careful to keep it from ripping.

Lydia watched, amusement dancing in her eyes. "You know that's just going in the trash, right?"

Gasping in mock horror, Samuel put a dramatic hand to his heart. "What? It is?"

Lydia's laughter warmed him better than the fire flickering in the hearth. Making her laugh would never get old. Samuel gave her a cheeky grin before pulling the final bit of paper from the gift.

A square blue handkerchief met his gaze. He lifted it with a smile. "Very nice."

"There's more," Lydia said, nodding toward the package.

The other item was indeed a book. "*A Christmas Carol*! I've been wanting to read this."

"I thought you might." Lydia offered a little smile, peering up at him through her lashes. "Do you like it?"

He hadn't often seen her this shy. Samuel reached for her hand. "I love it. Thank you, sweetheart."

Her gaze lowered to their joined hands. With a soft inhale, she slipped her other hand over them. "Sam…"

"Mama, Papa! My dolly and bear are best friends now." Ruby skipped into the room, her toys in each hand.

Samuel chuckled under his breath. "She seems to interrupt us a lot."

Lydia's cheeks flushed pink. She pulled her hand away and turned her attention to their daughter. Samuel contented himself with watching them interact. Ruby's excitement shone bright, while Lydia *ooh*ed and *ahh*ed over the new "friendship" between doll and bear.

He couldn't imagine a better Christmas. Being here, with his new unlooked-for family, happiness permeated every fiber of his being. The only thing that could make it better would be a declaration of love from his wife.

Not that he expected that any time soon. But maybe, as he wooed her, she'd fall for him again.

A man could hope.

~

*N*ew Year's Eve arrived with frigid temperatures but little snow. Lydia sat in the Brooks' parlor with Ella and Cassie. The women chatted over cups of steaming cocoa while their husbands congregated in the kitchen with the children. Lydia held little Rosie, who lay sleeping in her arms. Rosie's sweet baby scent did funny things to Lydia's heart.

Things like make her want another baby. The desire curled through her so strongly, it was a physical ache. She breathed in deeply and banished the thought. There was no sense thinking such things when she and Samuel still hadn't found their former level of trust.

"Is everything all right, Lydia?"

Ella's soft question snapped her back to reality. Producing a smile, she nodded. "Of course."

"Really?" Cassie raised a brow. "Because your face says otherwise."

Drat. She forgot how easily her friends could read her. Lydia sighed. "I guess I'm wondering if Samuel and I will be able to work out our past."

Cassie tilted her head, confusion flashing over her face. "What past?"

Panic threatened for a moment. Lydia hadn't told Cassie

much about her history. She knew nothing about Samuel. The choice to trust another friend hovered before her. With a deep breath, she took the plunge.

When she finished her story, Cassie sat blinking. "You've been through a lot." Her nose scrunched. "What a strange turn of events that brought you and Pastor Allen to the same town. Not to mention being forced to marry." She leaned forward. "But you want to move past all that and start fresh?"

Lydia bit her lip. "I don't know if it's possible."

"So you haven't talked yet?" Ella asked.

"No. I asked him to wait until after the new year." Lydia cuddled Rosie closer. "We need to have that conversation. I'm just afraid of what it might reveal. Digging up the past will be painful." Her voice dropped as fear slammed into her gut. "He abandoned me and Charlotte. Maybe he regrets it now, but how do I know he won't abandon me again if things get hard?"

"That's a legitimate fear." Ella lowered her mug to the table and focused her gaze on Lydia. "You're both older and wiser now. The choices you made then aren't the same choices you'd make today. I know trust takes time to build, especially once it's been broken. The question is, are you willing to risk your heart and let Samuel in, even knowing that gives him the power to hurt you again?"

Was she? Lydia buried her face in Rosie's cheek, taking a moment to collect herself. "I don't know."

"Love is hard," Cassie said. "It means making the decision every day to love the person you vowed to cherish. Sometimes you won't feel it, but you can still choose it."

Wise words. "Putting love into action. That's good advice." Lydia's mind flitted through the various gestures Samuel had made over the course of their short marriage. "I think Samuel is trying to do that."

"Oh?" Ella leaned forward, a smile spreading over her face. "He's showing you love?"

Her heart warmed despite her reservations. "Yes. He's admitted he plans to win my love again, and I must admit that everything he's done since we married points to that."

"If he's trying, maybe he really has changed," Cassie said softly.

Men's laughter rang out while the squeals of children filled the air. Isaiah and Jonah burst into the parlor. Addie and Ruby soon followed, Connor toddling after them. Moments later, Cody, Travis, and Samuel lumbered into the room, arms raised and teeth bared.

What in the world?

Isaiah laughed so hard, he nearly lost his balance. "They're bears!"

"New year bears, to be exact." Samuel ambled closer, eliciting shrieks from the giggling children. "Very hungry new year bears."

He growled, lunging for Addie. The little girl screamed with delight and allowed herself to be caught. Samuel swung her up in the air, roaring loudly. The other kids vanished back into the kitchen, chased by Travis and Cody.

Addie wiggled. Samuel laughed and set her on her feet before prowling after her.

Ella leaned closer to Lydia. "Whatever his past choices, it seems you married a man who's good with children."

A lump formed in Lydia's throat. "He's always been that way. And he's incredible with Ruby."

So why had he left her when she became pregnant with Charlotte? It didn't make sense. Though she hadn't thought of it often, his actions then had been completely out of character. So out of character, she would have thought him to be someone else from his reaction.

If the news had come from anyone but his parents, she wouldn't have believed it.

Cassie reached out to cover Lydia's hand with hers. "Are you falling for him again?"

Heart jolting, Lydia inhaled a sharp breath. "No...I can't. Not until we clear the air. Besides, it's too fast."

"No?" Ella pursed her lips. "Are you sure, Lydia? Because the look in your eyes when Samuel played with Addie was something to behold."

The question haunted Lydia the rest of the night. She tried to ignore the fluttering in her stomach whenever her husband's gaze turned her way. On the ride home, he glanced at her several times, a question of his own lingering on his face. He held it in until they got home and tucked Ruby into bed.

When they were lying in their bed, lights out and warmed by the heavy flannel quilt, he finally spoke. "Something's on your mind, isn't it?"

It unnerved her that he could read her like this. She rolled to her side, facing him in the dark. "There is so much still unknown between us."

He lay quiet for a moment. "I've wanted to talk, Lydi. You know that."

The gentle rebuke didn't raise her hackles. Instead, she released a small sigh. "You're right. I wasn't ready. Too much happened too soon."

"And now?"

His voice held notes of hope. She knew he wanted their relationship to move forward, to grow into love. It couldn't until they hashed out their past. "I think I'm ready. But..."

He cupped her cheek with a gentle hand. "But it's going to hurt."

"Yes." Tears threatened to fall. "How could it not?"

A groan escaped his lips. "I was a fool. Nothing can make up for that. But I am so sorry for the pain I caused you. If I could go back and change what happened, I would." His thumb brushed her jawline, sending shivers up her spine. "Why don't we talk in the morning, after a good night's sleep?"

"All right."

He leaned forward, pressing a kiss to her forehead. "Goodnight, Lydia."

"Goodnight, Sam."

~

*T*he next morning, Lydia was a bundle of nerves. The looming conversation with her husband had her trembling.

Taking a deep breath, she fastened the locket he gave her around her neck. A glance at the bed showed Samuel still slept. She crept from the room, pulling the door shut behind her.

Ruby emerged from her own room. The little girl rubbed her eyes, a sleepy smile tugging at her lips when she saw Lydia. "Hi, Mama."

Lydia kissed the top of her daughter's head. "Good morning. Would you like some breakfast?"

"Yes, please. Can we have oatmeal?"

"Of course."

They enjoyed their meal together. Lydia covered a bowl to keep warm for Samuel, then washed the dishes. She glanced at the clock. He rarely slept this late. Maybe she should check on him.

"Ruby, can you...?"

Before she got the question out, the front door opened. Ruby clutched her skirts and spoke, voice confused. "Who are you?"

Alarmed, Lydia tucked Ruby behind her as she spun to face whoever had entered their home. Her jaw dropped, though her alarm remained for a different reason. Samuel's parents stood in the doorway. They stared at her with as much shock and confusion as she felt.

"Mr. and Mrs. Allen. What are you doing here?"

CHAPTER 16

*I*t perhaps wasn't the most polite thing she could have said, but she blamed the shock. Their stare-off continued until Mrs. Allen blinked and stepped forward. A few tendrils of dark-blond hair had escaped her bun, framing her oval face. She ran a hand down her burgundy traveling dress and gave Lydia a nervous smile. "Forgive me, my dear. I didn't expect to see you." She glanced around, brow furrowing. "I thought this was Samuel's home."

"It is."

The crease deepened. "Why are you in his house?"

"We're married. Didn't Samuel tell you?"

"M-married?" Mrs. Allen shrieked, one hand going to her chest. "No, he didn't mention that. But we haven't had a letter from him in a while. When did this...marriage...happen?"

Ruby peered out from behind Lydia. "Mama married Papa so I could have a daddy."

Both Allens stared at Ruby. Mrs. Allen blanched and swayed on her feet. Mr. Allen put an arm around his wife, guiding her to the sofa. The two of them whispered to each other.

Samuel had inherited his hair and eye color from his father. Even all these years later, it jarred Lydia to see how much alike the two men appeared, despite Mr. Allen being a couple decades older.

Lydia bit her lip. She took a step forward, clearing her throat to get their attention. "Did Samuel invite you here?"

"Of course he did." Indignation shone from Mrs. Allen's face, but it quickly faded. "Well, I suppose it's more accurate to say he extended an open invitation when he told us he was moving to this town. We wanted to surprise him for Christmas, but weather delayed our trip." She eyed Lydia and waved a hand at Ruby. "Though it seems we're the ones being surprised. Who's that young lady?"

Lydia took Ruby's hand and led her to a chair across from Mrs. Allen. "This is our daughter, Ruby." Might as well keep explanations simple for now. They could dive into the circumstances surrounding Ruby's adoption later, when Samuel woke up.

Mrs. Allen peered at Ruby, shaking her head. "She looks just like you."

"So you kept her, then?" Mr. Allen said, breaking his silence.

Cold swirled around her. Lydia frowned. "Kept her?"

"Samuel's baby. When you disappeared, we thought you were going to give birth in secret and give the child up for adoption."

The cold only increased. Lydia shivered, holding Ruby close. "Of course, I kept her. But this child isn't—"

"I suppose it's only right"—Mr. Allen continued as if she hadn't spoken—"that you and Samuel ended up together with your little girl. We never should have interfered in the first place."

Lydia's world came to a crashing halt. Before she could analyze those words and the implication behind them, heavy footsteps descended the stairs. Samuel appeared, wrapped in a robe, his face ashen. "Ma. Pa. What's going on? Interfered in what?"

His parents glanced at each other, his mother fiddling with a handkerchief. "Since you married Lydia, son, you must already know." Mrs. Allen glanced at Ruby. "I'm glad you had a chance to know your daughter despite our meddling."

He took another step closer, his face resembling a thundercloud. "*What* daughter? And what meddling?"

Lydia felt faint. Blood pounded in her head, and her hands shook. A horrible suspicion raced through her mind as she went to her husband. "Sam, did your parents give you a letter from me when they visited you in seminary?"

He frowned. "No. You sent a letter with them? Why not just mail it as you did the others?"

"I..." She swallowed, swaying slightly. Dots danced in her vision. Everything she'd believed about him—it was false? Lydia stared at her husband. "I thought...all this time...I was so angry..." She shook hard.

Samuel's angry expression changed to alarm. He caught her in his arms. "Easy, sweetheart. Let's get you back to the chair."

Lydia stared up at him. Her heart clenched in her chest. "You didn't know."

"Didn't know what?" He glanced from her to his parents and back again, easing her down onto her previous seat and kneeling beside her.

"About our...our baby girl. Charlotte."

His brow furrowed. "Ours? Lydia, what are you talking about? You said Charlotte was your daughter with Frank."

She shook her head. "No. Samuel, I married Frank *because* I was pregnant with Charlotte. Because I was told..." She glanced at the Allens, her throat tightening. "I was told you wanted nothing to do with me or the baby."

"*What?*"

Samuel shot to his feet. He paced, raking his hands through his hair.

No one said a word. The tension in the room was palpable. The Allens sat still as statues. Lydia remained in stunned silence. If Samuel hadn't known about the baby, then he hadn't abandoned her. He'd tried looking for her after she left Aspen Grove. No wonder he had been confused when they met again at the school.

She'd spent years blaming him for something he didn't do.

Tears streamed down her cheeks. Lydia buried her face in her hands. "I'm sorry, Sam. I'm so, so sorry."

"You have nothing to be sorry for."

She raised her face to see him glaring at his parents. Samuel crossed his arms. "What do you two have to say for yourselves? Because from what I'm gathering, you're the reason I missed out on knowing my daughter."

"Missed out?" Mrs. Allen pointed at Ruby. "But I thought..."

"She's our adopted daughter. A very recent event, in fact. Her grandmother died a few weeks ago and asked us to take her in. There is no blood relation between us and Ruby." His eyes softened momentarily as he smiled at Ruby. "But we love her like our own." He knelt in front of the wide-eyed child. "Honey, why don't you go upstairs and read a book? We'll call you down in a little bit."

Ruby's gaze darted around the room, resting on each adult for a couple seconds before she nodded. "All right, Papa."

He kissed her forehead and waited until she climbed the stairs. Then he whirled around to face his parents again. "Well?"

"Son, why don't you sit?" Mr. Allen said.

"I'd prefer to stand."

Mrs. Allen sighed. "We're sorry, Samuel. It was a bad decision on our part."

Through gritted teeth, Samuel ground out, "Start at the beginning."

"Lydia came to us four months after you left for seminary," his mother said. "She knew we were coming for a visit and confided in us about the baby. She gave us a letter and asked us to give it to you, saying it explained everything." Mrs. Allen hung her head.

Her husband took up the story. "We were disappointed things had gone so far between you two. But our primary concern at the time was your vocation, Samuel. We knew you'd leave seminary to marry Lydia if you knew about the baby. It would have ruined your dream of being a pastor. So we destroyed the letter. And when we came back, we told Lydia you didn't want the child."

Samuel went still as a stone. Anger radiated from him in waves. His fists clenched and unclenched. Lydia understood how he felt. How often had she experienced that very feeling toward him?

Unjustly, it turned out.

She reached for his hand. Samuel accepted it, clinging so hard, his knuckles turned white. He faced her, and Lydia's breath caught at the raw pain in his eyes. "All this time, you thought I didn't want you or Charlotte," he whispered brokenly. "No wonder you hated me."

Lydia stood, placing her free hand on his chest. "Sam..."

He stopped her with a finger against her lips, the gentle touch at odds with the anger flowing from his body. Samuel turned to his parents. His face took on the appearance of granite. "There's a hotel in town. Book a room. I need time to think about this."

His father helped Mrs. Allen to her feet. "We already did, son. We'll head there now. If you want to talk, you know where to find us."

Samuel jerked his head in a nod. His parents left, his

mother casting a sorrowful glance back before the door closed behind them. Once they were gone, Lydia's husband collapsed onto the sofa and sobbed.

⌇

*H*e'd never lost control of his emotions like this. Great, heaving sobs shook Samuel's body. His throat and lungs hurt, but it was nothing to the pain in his heart.

There was a daughter he'd never know, never hold, never love—all because of his parents' machinations. If he'd been told of Charlotte's existence, if he'd come back and married Lydia, would their child still be alive?

The sofa creaked beside him as his wife sat. She slipped an arm around his shoulder.

Samuel leaned into her, horror at all she'd had to endure sweeping over him. "Lydi..."

A moment later, she rested in his arms. Samuel wasn't sure which of them initiated the embrace, but he didn't care. He held her close and cried into her neck while her tears fell on his cheek.

They'd lost so much. Their future had been taken from them all those years ago, and he'd had no idea.

Minutes passed before Samuel regained control over his tears. He sat back, wiping his eyes. Lydia remained close. She slipped her hand in his and gave it a squeeze.

Samuel moved their joined hands to his lap. "We lost a child." Saying it out loud hurt more than he expected. Tears began to flow again.

"We did." Grief tinged Lydia's voice. "This must be a shock for you."

"For you too. You thought all this time I chose seminary over you and Charlotte."

"Yes." Lydia remained quiet for a moment, her eyes searching his. "It turns out my anger was wholly misplaced." She lowered her gaze. "I'm sorry for blaming you, Sam."

"You had no way of knowing. I'd have been angry if I was the one in your situation."

"Were you angry with me for disappearing?"

He blew out his breath. "Yes. I was so confused and disappointed. It hurt that you left Aspen Grove without a word. I figured you couldn't forgive me for what happened between us and wanted a new start somewhere else."

"We both made assumptions that weren't true." She sighed and leaned her head on his shoulder. "Does this answer the questions you had? The ones I wouldn't let you ask?"

He pressed a kiss to her forehead. "It does. I think we would have arrived at the truth ourselves once we did talk, and it might have hurt less than finding out like this." He rested his head against her soft hair.

"I agree. Hearing the truth from your parents..." She shook her head and fell quiet.

When he came out of his room earlier, his joy at hearing his parents' voices fizzled quickly as he caught their conversation with Lydia. He'd stood for a few moments in stupefied silence, trying to make sense of what they were saying. Pieces of the puzzle started to click in that moment. But it wasn't until he had the full story that Samuel realized the full implications.

Lydia had been alone and scared, carrying his child, and his parents twisted the knife in her vulnerability. No wonder she'd left. No wonder...

His eyes widened. "That's why you married Frank. It wasn't just your reputation—it was for our baby. You wanted Charlotte to have a father."

"Yes. I thought if you weren't going to be there, someone might as well be. Frank and I were good friends. He offered a solution to my problem, so I took it."

A new question bubbled up inside of him. He'd asked her before, but he needed to be sure. "Did you fall in love with him?"

Lydia's smile was sad. "No, Sam. Our marriage wasn't like that. We were friends and partners in raising Charlotte, but nothing more." She leaned against a cushion. "We even had separate bedrooms."

That explained the lack of other children. Samuel rubbed his thumb over her fingers. "It must have been difficult learning you'd be sharing a room with me, then."

A faint smile pulled at her lips. "That took some adjusting." She tugged her ear, looking down at her lap. Something more was on her mind.

"What it is, sweetheart?"

Her gaze flicked back up to his. She drew in a deep breath and released it in a long *whoosh.* "We were apart for seven years. Did you ever...court someone else?"

Was she jealous of the possibility? Warmth flooded his chest, dispelling a little of the sorrow. "No." He leaned forward, cupping her chin. "There was no one else for me, Lydi. I never stopped loving you."

Her breath hitched, her eyes trained on his. "Never?"

"Never."

Tears filled her eyes. She buried her face in his chest, her arms wrapping tightly around his waist. Samuel held her and closed his eyes. *Thanks for bringing us together again, Lord. These circumstances weren't ideal, but I'm grateful we're here. Please comfort us both as we process what my family did and try to find a way forward.*

His parents. Samuel exhaled slowly. They'd come all this way to spend time with him. But their betrayal all those years ago stung. Lydia had been wounded most, and now the pain must feel fresh. It certainly did for him.

He laughed suddenly, shaking his head.

Lydia startled. "What is it?"

"Just the irony of the fact that I'm mad at Ma and Pa, while my sermon this Sunday is all about forgiveness and second chances."

"Oh." She covered her mouth with her fingers, her eyes softening. "God knew what you'd be needing."

"Apparently, He has a sense of humor." Samuel shot a glance at the ceiling. "Noted, Lord."

Lydia chuckled.

Samuel reveled in the sound. If she could still laugh after such a shock, that boded well. "Lydia, how are you feeling right now?"

She pursed her lips. "I'm feeling so many things, I don't know where to begin." Her gaze flickered around the room before finally landing on him. "I'm horrified that I vilified you for so many years when you were innocent. I'm relieved that you didn't willfully abandon me and our little girl. I'm sad that you missed out on knowing her. As for your parents, I'm not sure what the full emotion is. I'm shocked and saddened that they'd do that to us, to their grandchild. But, surprisingly, I'm not angry."

His brow shot up. "You're not? I sure am."

Lydia ran a hand over his cheek. The light touch calmed his turmoil. "Sam, I've spent years being angry. I'm tired of anger. I was already growing tired of it in regard to you. While what your parents did was wrong, my heart feels sad that they missed out on what could have been too. Unlike you, though, it was their own choice. And I do understand wanting to protect your child at all costs—even if I'd like to think I would never stoop to that level."

Samuel raked a hand through his hair. "Their intentions might have been for my good, but it certainly wasn't good. I feel betrayed and robbed, Lydia. By my own parents. And I'll never know..." He choked on a sob. *I'll never know my little girl.*

Lydia rubbed a hand over his back. "Ruby is our daughter now. As you said, we've been given a second chance." She brushed her fingers under his eyes, drying his tears.

"You're right. I'm thankful for that." Samuel took her hand, bringing it to his lips for a light kiss. "I'm thankful for you too. Only God could have brought us back together." He smiled, kissing her hand again. "I meant what I said before. How we came to be with each other again isn't typical, but I intend to win your love."

Her soft intake of breath, combined with the shy surprise in her beautiful eyes, told him she wasn't as opposed to the idea as she might have been before. Hope lit inside—for them, for their little family, and their future.

At the very least, his parents' arrival had done some good— he and Lydia finally had the truth of their past revealed.

CHAPTER 17

*L*ydia stood in the kitchen, chopping vegetables for their supper. She glanced at Samuel as she worked. He'd offered to help, but she'd shooed him to the parlor, assuming he might need time to come to terms with what his parents had done. Now, she was rethinking that decision. Her husband sat slumped in a chair, staring into the fire.

What a strange New Year's Day this turned out to be.

She wondered at her lack of anger toward Mrs. and Mr. Allen. With answers finally reached, all she felt was relief. But Samuel had his world shaken.

She dumped the vegetables into the broth bubbling on the stove, an idea flitting through her mind. Lydia covered the pot and climbed the stairs to her room. She found what she wanted, then made her way to the parlor.

When she sat across from him, Samuel spoke. "Where's Ruby?"

"Ella came by about an hour ago, when you were out walking. She realized something was wrong and offered to take Ruby for the night."

He grunted in response. Lydia clutched the picture in her hands. "Sam..."

"Not yet, Lydi." His sigh filled the room. He patted the small space beside him. "Will you sit with me?"

She eyed the spot. "I'm not sure I'll fit."

He chuckled, the sound sad. "We'll make it work. Please?"

Ah, yes. Sam had always needed touch when he felt upset —a hug or a handhold in the past. Now, he wanted to hold her, and if that would help him feel better, she'd do it. Lydia slipped the picture into her pocket, then moved to his chair and burrowed into the sliver of space beside him. Samuel wrapped his arms around her, all but pulling her into his lap, and buried his face in her neck.

Lydia slid her arms around his neck. She leaned into him and rested her cheek against his hair. The motion, though familiar, felt foreign for a moment. Then Samuel sighed and pulled her closer, and her body relaxed.

How strange that she still had a lingering inability to trust him easily, even knowing that he'd not abandoned her and Charlotte.

His grief cut through her heart. She remembered the days she'd spent sobbing herself to sleep, wondering how life—how Samuel—could be so cruel. Now he felt the same emotions, but his found a home in his parents. Would he be able to forgive faster than she had? Or would this drive a wedge between him and his family?

"What am I going to do, Lydia?"

She blinked, moving back slightly. "What do you mean?"

A deep sigh left his lips. "My parents are here to see me, to get to know my new home, yet the last thing I want is to be around them. Not with what they did." His eyes flashed. "I'm a pastor. I preach mercy and forgiveness, but I don't know if I can show either."

She recognized the deep anger. It must be hard for him to

experience such emotions. While she'd seen him get angry in the past, it fizzled fast. Samuel was incapable of holding grudges. She'd never known anyone quicker to forgive. Would that be the case now?

Cupping his cheek, Lydia rested her forehead against his. "I know this is hard, and I'm not going to tell you that immediate forgiveness is possible. This is something you'll have to come to terms with." She rubbed his jawline with her thumb. "But I can tell you that living with anger and unforgiveness for years made me bitter. I don't want to see that happen to you, Sam. Your heart is too big. You have so much love to give. I believe you'll find a way to forgive your parents. It sounded as though they regret what they did."

He huffed. "Or they regret that the truth came out."

"Maybe."

She let her fingers slide into his hair, moving them with gentle strokes.

Samuel groaned and closed his eyes. "That's nice."

Continuing her ministrations, Lydia spoke softly. "Do you know what helped me begin to forgive you?"

"Hmm?"

"Knowing that you'd looked for me. That you regretted letting me go. It made all the difference. My anger started to dissipate, and my heart softened." She chuckled. "Then we had to get married—and your determination to love me has continued to destroy the walls I built against you."

Samuel's eyes flew open. He stared up at her. "Lydi..."

"I can't say I'm in love with you again. Not yet. I spent too long believing you couldn't be trusted. I know that's wrong now. But it might take my heart longer to process that than my brain. Even so...I want you to know I'm trying, Sam. I want to love you."

His breath hitched, his arms tightening around her. "That's more than I hoped for."

When his eyes dropped to her lips, Lydia's stomach twisted. The feeling wasn't entirely unpleasant. His gaze lifted back to hers. A question rested in the blue-green depths, reminding her he wouldn't kiss her unless she gave him a signal.

Maybe this was the perfect time to show some trust.

Lowering her head, Lydia pressed her lips to his. The kiss was soft and sweet, hopefully enough to let him know she'd be receptive to him. When she pulled back a second later, their gazes connected. The shock in Samuel's eyes gave way to wonder. He slid his hand behind her neck and pulled her closer. His lips claimed hers with a desperation she'd never felt from him.

A tiny seed of doubt tried to sprout, but Lydia shoved it away. She was done letting the past rule the present. Her body erupted with heat as her husband held her tighter and deepened the kiss. She'd forgotten that he kissed with such emotion and heart—just like he lived life. Surrendering to the feelings he provoked in her, Lydia melted into him and met his passion with her own.

After a while, Samuel slowed to tender, sweet kisses. His lips pressed against hers a final time, then he drew back. Lydia kept her eyes closed, joy and a hint of fear swirling inside. There was no going back to their safe daily routine after letting him in like that. The thought both thrilled and terrified her.

"Lydia."

She opened her eyes. Samuel gazed back at her with such tenderness, her breath caught. He smiled. "Thank you."

Shyness crept over her. She blushed and ducked her head.

Samuel chuckled, lifting her chin with a finger. "I've been wanting to do that for weeks." He tucked a lock of hair behind her ear. His gaze turned earnest. "But I want you to know that I will still do everything I can to woo your heart. That won't ever stop." He winked. "Even once you do fall in love with me."

"Samuel!"

"I mean it, Lydia. Showing you love is an endeavor I'll continue to my dying day. You're worth it."

Her heart swooped. This man...

"You've been so patient with me, even when you didn't know why I was angry with you."

"I should have married you before going to seminary." Samuel shook his head. "That would have been the honorable thing. Instead, I gambled on the fact that no one would find out." His face fell. "And we both lost."

Lydia reached into her pocket. "We did. In more ways than one." She pulled out the picture, the one with her and Charlotte. "Here."

Tears filled his eyes as he studied the image of his daughter. "She's beautiful." He gave her a watery smile. "Your miniature."

"Actually, she had some of your features. Her eyes were the exact shape as yours. And she had your dimples."

"Will you tell me about our daughter, Lydi?"

She smiled. "Happily. She might have looked like me, but she had your charisma and charm, your ability to make friends wherever she went. Sometimes it drove me crazy how many traits she inherited from you."

Her husband laughed. Lydia threaded her fingers through his. "One time, we visited Frank at his bank, and she had the customers laughing within minutes..."

~

The next morning, Samuel's heart pulled in two directions as he sat on the rear pew in the empty church. Lydia's stories the previous evening allowed him to know the daughter he never met. And the fact that he never met her sat like a stone in his stomach.

All because of his parents. Without their interference, he'd have married Lydia and welcomed Charlotte when she was born. She might even be alive today.

The stone sat heavier.

Samuel pressed a fist to his mouth to stifle his heaving breaths. He stared down at the sermon he was supposed to be writing. He'd picked it out last week, right after Christmas, with Lydia's help.

Be merciful as your Father is merciful.

He couldn't think of a single word to say. Not with anger churning inside like a furnace.

The sanctuary usually gave him a sense of calm and peace. It was why he came here this morning, hoping for some clarity over his parents. Instead, he might boil over.

He drew in a breath, then blew it out hard. *Lord, I know what You want from me. I know what Your word says. But I don't know if I can let this go.*

Three sharp knocks sounded at the door. Samuel got to his feet as Cody strode inside. The tall cowboy shook snow from his boots before proceeding forward. "Howdy, Pastor. I dropped Ruby off just now. Lydia said I could find you here."

"Good to see you, Cody. How can I help you?" The words sounded stiff, formal.

Cody's brows quirked. He looped his thumbs into his pockets. "From what I hear, it's me who can help you."

"Oh?"

Cody settled in one of the pews. "I'm not much of a talker, but I'm a mighty good listener." He folded his arms across his chest as if readying for a lengthy conversation.

Samuel sank into the pew beside Cody. "It's not a short story."

"My man Hank's overseeing the pastures today. I got time."

Like a flood, the story poured out of Samuel. He told Cody everything. His friend simply nodded or grunted, letting Samuel tell his tale. When he finished, Samuel slumped against the pew. "So you see, I've got a bit of a problem on my hands."

"No kidding." Cody thrummed his fingers against his knees. "I'm not sure what I'd do in your situation."

"If your parents did something like that, could you forgive them?"

Cody was silent for several long moments. A shadow passed over his face. "My parents died when I was ten. I think I'd be willing to forgive a lot if they could be in my life again." He crossed his arms. "Now let me ask you something. If your parents died today, how would you feel?"

Samuel jerked back. "I...I'd be devastated."

"Why?"

Why? Blinking, Samuel frowned. "Because they're my parents."

"And you love them?"

"Of course I do...oh." Samuel gave a wry chuckle. "I see where you're going."

"Good." Cody stood. "Forgiveness might take time. Lord knows I struggled to forgive myself for years after my parents died. Thought I could have done more to save them. Point is, not forgiving hurts you in the end. It hurts your relationship with God too." He pointed to the cross over the altar. "Considering what He did for us—dying to forgive our sins—I think we should take our example from Him."

Samuel's lips tipped up. He shook his head and got to his feet. "You ever consider being a preacher?"

Cody stepped back, hands raised. "Not my calling. Ranching's it for me."

Samuel rested his hands on his hips. He glanced at the cross, then back at Cody. "I'm still furious."

"You've got every right to be. Just don't let that anger turn into hatred or bitterness. You can't control the feeling of anger, but you can control how you act."

When Cody left, Samuel sat in the pew again, heaving a sigh. He bent forward and rested his elbows on his knees. "Lord, I'm gonna need Your help to offer forgiveness to my parents. This anger is stronger than any I've felt before." He sighed again. "I don't know what to do."

Forgive as you've been forgiven.

He raised his gaze. "I get it, Lord. But how?"

Do you know what helped me begin to forgive you? Knowing that you'd looked for me. That you regretted letting me go.

Lydia's words drifted through his mind. He let out a breath. His stomach churned, but logic wormed its way into his conscience. The sorrow on his parents' faces as they left last night spoke of regret. But was it regret over their choice seven years ago, or regret that they'd been caught?

Only one way to find out.

Samuel exhaled long and slow, then stood. He threw on his coat, folded up his partially written sermon and pocketed it, then left the church. His strides ate up the ground as he headed for the main street. Nerves unsettled his stomach, but he pushed through the door of the hotel and marched up to the front desk.

The receptionist smiled at him. "Howdy, Pastor."

"Hi, Nellie. I'm here to see Mr. and Mrs. Allen."

"Sure thing. I'll send someone up to get them." Her eyes narrowed, head tilting to the side. "You all right?"

Samuel scrubbed a hand over his face. "It's that obvious?"

"Afraid so." She pointed to the right. "There's a room over there with a basin and some clean cloths. Maybe some cold water on your face will help."

He chuckled. "I appreciate your bluntness. Thanks."

"While you're freshening up, I'll get the Allens." She paused. "Are they related to you?"

"My parents." The words almost choked him. His stomach

churned again. Samuel fisted a hand to his midsection, taking a deep breath. "They're visiting for a bit."

Nellie's face lit up. "How wonderful!"

"Yeah," he mumbled. "Great."

Ignoring her confused look, he bolted for the side room. He took a cloth from the pile and poured cold water over it, then pressed the cloth to his face. The cold cut deep, cooling his turbulent emotions. Samuel dried his face and inhaled until his lungs felt as though they would burst. He exhaled in a rush. Facing his reflection in the small mirror, he smiled grimly. "Here goes nothing."

He tossed the towels in the dirty bin, then exited the room to face his parents.

CHAPTER 18

*S*amuel paused halfway into the lobby. A strong desire to have Lydia at his side pulsed through him. He wasn't sure he could do this on his own.

Help me, Lord.

His parents stood by the reception desk. Pa locked eyes with him first. Anger surged. Samuel stopped walking, his hands clenching into fists.

Ma whirled around. Her hands went to her lips, large tears rolling down her cheeks. A stab of shock went through Samuel. He'd never seen his mother cry.

"Samuel," she whispered, taking hesitant steps toward him. It hit him suddenly that he'd not even had the chance to hug his parents before being walloped with the news of their betrayal. The way Ma stared at him, tears in her eyes, said she wanted to pull him into her arms.

He wasn't ready for that.

Pushing his hands into his pockets, Samuel raised his chin. "Can we talk?"

"Of course, son." His father motioned toward some chairs tucked into an alcove. "Will this suffice?"

Samuel nodded. The alcove provided a measure of privacy, for which he was grateful. He took a seat across from his parents. Interlocking his fingers together, he fought for words. Finally, he blurted out a single word. "Why?"

Pa heaved a sigh. "The simple answer is that we panicked. If it was known that you fathered a child out of wedlock, it would have ended your chance at being a pastor. We knew how much your chosen career meant to you. We just..." He stopped. "Well...not we. Your ma didn't want to deceive you or Lydia." He hung his head. "I convinced her it was for the best."

Samuel clenched his teeth. "Do you have any idea what I lost? First Lydia, then our daughter. She was raised by another man because they thought I didn't want her! And now..." His voice broke. "I'll never know Charlotte. Lydia and I lost seven years together. For what? My job and reputation?"

"It was wrong. If I could change things, I would." Pa looked him in the eye. "I've regretted my decision for years. It won't give back what you lost, but you have my deepest apologies."

Ma reached out her hand. Samuel couldn't bear the tears on her face, the entreaty in her eyes. He slowly placed his hand in hers. She squeezed it, bringing their hands to her heart. "We came here with the intention of telling you, Sam. The truth needed to come to light. Seeing Lydia and that sweet little girl..." She shook her head. "I thought our wrong had been righted. That God had given you a second chance with your family."

"He did." Samuel's throat felt raw. He stopped resisting the tears from falling. "Lydia and I are finding our way back to each other, and I love being a father to Ruby." Burying his face in his free hand, he gave in to his grief.

His mother's arms wrapped around him. Samuel leaned into her. As explosive and harsh as his anger had been, it melted away with his tears, leaving a hollow ache in his chest.

When he finally lifted tear-heavy eyes to his father, he whispered, "I forgive you, Pa."

Pa shook his head. "I don't know how it can be that easy, son. You've never been able to stay angry for long, but after what we did...what I did..."

"I'll admit when I came here, I was boiling over. But anger won't bring Charlotte back. It won't change the past. I don't want to waste precious time being upset with people I love when they're obviously repentant." A wry grin broke free. "Besides, if Lydia isn't upset with you, I can follow her example."

Surprise crossed his parents' faces. "She's not?" Ma asked.

"No. She said she was tired of being angry. I took the brunt of it."

Pa winced. "That's my fault."

His father's shoulders hunched. A frown marred his brow, and he stared at the floor. Samuel had seen that look many times over his career. Pa carried the weight of guilt like a millstone. Had he felt this way for the last seven years?

Samuel rested a hand on Pa's back. "You need to forgive yourself, Pa."

Pa jerked. His gaze jumped up to Samuel. "It's not that simple, son. I admire your ability to let things go quickly, but you didn't inherit that from me."

"Then pray for the grace to forgive." Samuel chuckled. "I've been doing little else since last night."

Ma clung to Pa's hand. "He's right, Paul. If Samuel and Lydia aren't holding on to anger, you shouldn't hold on to guilt. It's time to let it go."

Pa was silent for several heartbeats. He exhaled a weary sigh. "I don't know how."

"I know where to start." Samuel held out his hands. "Pray with me?"

His father hesitated before reaching out to accept Samuel's offer.

With a smile, Samuel bowed his head. "Dear Lord, thank You for bringing us to a place where healing is possible. Thank You for guiding Lydia and Charlotte to Frank and allowing them to have a good home as Jeffersons." His throat grew thick, and Samuel had to pause. Some emotion lingered—and probably would for some time. Focusing on the prayer, Samuel drew in a breath. "We all failed Lydia in different ways. Please forgive us for the parts we played. Thank You for bringing us back together and uniting our families. But now, Lord, my father needs Your mercy and grace. Help him to forgive himself, to let go of his guilt and sadness. He can't do it on his own, and he trusts in You. Bring healing, we beg You. In Jesus' holy name, amen."

Pa's face was wet with tears when the prayer ended. He gripped Samuel's hands and shook his head. "Thanks, son. I still don't know how to let go, but I feel some peace."

"Good." Samuel leaned forward. "Just take it one day at a time."

With a glance, silent communication passed between his parents.

Ma fiddled with her skirt. "We'd planned to stay a couple weeks. Considering everything that's happened, maybe we should cut our trip. You just got married and are raising a child."

"You're free to stay," Samuel said. "Our marriage was unexpected, but I'm sure having you around will be beneficial. You can get to know Lydia again, and you'll love Ruby. It'll be nice for her to know she has other grandparents."

His mother blinked. "Your marriage was unexpected?"

Oh. They didn't know the reason behind his quick wedding. He quickly went through the series of events that led to their marriage. When he finished, both parents' jaws hung low.

His father recovered first. "That's not what I expected."

Ma chimed in. "It sounds as though you were brought together despite your reservations toward each other. Only God could have worked that. It's a miracle. Your second chance at love."

"A second chance I'm grateful for."

The clock struck noon. Samuel stood. "I should get going. Lydia will be wondering where I am." He paused, then went with his gut. "Would you like to come back with me?"

His father clamped him on the shoulder, voice thick. "We'd love to."

~

*L*ydia glanced at the café menu with a smile. Cinnamon jumbles remained, a testament to Samuel's considerate request for her sake. Warmth spread through her. She peeked at her husband, who had his father and Ruby engaged in a story about a bear.

Was she falling in love with him? It was getting harder to separate past from present. Their love as teenagers had been strong and true, but whatever she felt now...it was familiar, yet different. Lydia couldn't put her finger on it, though things had shifted ever since the truth was revealed.

She brought her gaze back to the table to find Mrs. Allen watching her. Or Grace, as she'd insisted on being called.

Grace smiled. "It's so good to see you again, dear. I'm glad you and Samuel got married." She leaned closer, lowering her voice. "Despite how it started."

A flush sprang to Lydia's cheeks. "He told you about that?"

"He did. It might not have been a conventional way to marry, but you two were meant to be. It just took longer to get there." A shadow fell over her face. "Because of Paul and me."

From what Samuel told her, most of the fault lay with Paul,

but she could see how Grace would blame herself as well. Her new mother-in-law's mistake was one of omission. "What happened is in the past, Grace."

"Yes." Grace's gaze darted to Paul, who laughed at something Ruby said. "I just hope my husband will come to believe that."

"It might take him time, but I think he will."

When Samuel came home and announced that he had reconciled with his parents, joy had leapt in Lydia's heart. He'd taken her aside while Grace and Paul sat down with Ruby and told her how quickly his anger had faded—a fact he attributed to God's mercy—and that his father felt the burden of guilt over keeping them apart. Hopefully, Paul could release his heavy emotions. Lydia knew firsthand how they could tear a person apart.

When Sam first told her his anger faded, she'd felt a moment of jealousy over his easy forgiveness. While she spent years angry at him, he spent a day in anger before it passed. He'd guessed her thoughts and reminded her that he had the benefit of hearing their explanation right away, while she'd had to assume for years that he didn't want her. She grudgingly admitted that made a difference.

Even so, she was happy for Samuel. He couldn't hold on to grudges. It wasn't in his nature. Now, their families were united once more, and Ruby had the opportunity to know her grand-parents.

They seemed mutually taken with each other. Ruby sat between them, chatting happily, while Samuel and Lydia sat across from them. As Paul and Grace focused their attention on Ruby, Samuel stretched an arm around Lydia's shoulders, leaning close. "Maybe we can ask them to babysit while they're here, and I can take you on a proper date."

A zing shot through her stomach. Lydia pressed a hand there to calm the racing butterflies. "I'd like that."

His smile made her heart flip. "Good. I'll arrange something soon. Preferably before you start school on Monday." His fingers stroked lazily against her shoulder. "Are you ready to go back?"

"Yes. I've missed the children." She wrinkled her nose. "I'm not excited about my review by the school board, though."

"Review?" Samuel straightened. His smile disappeared, replaced by a frown. "In January?"

"Mrs. Holt claims three reviews a year are necessary. One in September, one in January, and one in June."

Her husband muttered under his breath. "That seems like a lot."

Lydia shrugged. "There's nothing I can do about it."

"Mrs. Holt already has a strike against you for being caught with me, and another because she's upset I married you instead of one of her daughters."

A giggle climbed her throat. "Yes—can you imagine being her son-in-law?"

Samuel shuddered. "No. And I will never have to find out." He tapped her nose. "You'll have to let me know how the review goes. If she's unjust toward you, I'll have a talk with her."

The fierce, protective look on his face made her melt. She kissed his cheek. "You're a good man, Samuel Allen."

"Eww!"

Ruby's squeal brought their attention across the table. Their daughter laughed. "I'm *never* kissing a boy. Ever."

Samuel leaned back, his arm still resting around Lydia. "Glad to hear that, sweetie. No boy will be worthy of you, anyway."

Paul chuckled, his blue-green eyes dancing with amusement. "I thought the same thing about you, son, that no girl would be worthy of you." He sobered and turned to Lydia. "I was wrong. So very wrong. I'm glad you're a part of the family, Lydia."

She recognized the peace offering. With a smile, she inclined her head. "I appreciate that, Paul." Her gaze swung to her husband. "It's not how we pictured this happening, but here we are."

"A happy, growing family," Samuel said, his thumb moving circles on her shoulder.

Grace lit up. "Oh, do you two plan on having more kids? That would be wonderful."

Lydia choked on her water. Coughing, she pressed a napkin to her mouth. Her face burned. She turned wide eyes toward Samuel.

His gaze softened. He spoke to his mother while gazing at Lydia. "I would love to."

Her lungs froze. Grace couldn't know the longing for a child had recently taken hold of Lydia. It wasn't a subject she'd dared mention to Samuel, not before they had their past cleared. Now it was. She had no reason not to trust him, to love him—except her heart still needed convincing after seven years of believing the worst.

The way Samuel looked at her melted a frozen section of her heart. His eyes lit with hope, gazing at her with such love, she almost felt it. Another chance to exercise trust presented itself. She took a deep breath, her gaze locked on Samuel's.

"I'd like that."

Surprise crossed his face, but it was replaced with a slow grin.

Flutters pulsed through her, and Lydia turned to Grace, her cheeks heating. "Eventually. Right now, our main concern is getting Ruby settled."

The little girl propped her chin on a closed fist. "If you have more kids, does that mean I'll have brothers and sisters?"

Plural of each? Oh, gracious. Lydia fanned her face with a napkin. "I don't know, Ruby."

"I want a brother first." Ruby's forehead wrinkled. "Wait, no,

I want a sister before a brother. Or can I have both at the same time?"

"Maybe, if your mama has twins." Grace's eyes twinkled. "There are twins on my side of the family, you know."

"Twins would be fine with me."

Samuel's whisper brushed warm air against her ear. Lydia shivered, pushing him gently. "*Eventually,* Sam. I'm not ready for..." She fumbled for words as her blush deepened.

His gaze turned serious. "There's no rush, Lydi. I'm just happy you're open to more children. Eventually." He lifted her hand, pressing a kiss to her wrist. "From what I remember, you wanted a whole passel of them when we were younger. Six, was it?"

She chuckled. "At least. There were times I thought ten would be fun."

"It would never be boring. Do you still like the idea of ten?"

The teasing glint in his eyes made her laugh. "I don't have an ideal anymore." She glanced at his parents. Seeing them engaged with Ruby again, she lowered her voice. "When I married Frank, I gave up on the thought of having more children. I made peace with the fact that Charlotte would be my only daughter. Now they're gone, and I have you and Ruby... and the possibility of other children. It's a big change. I just want to take things one day at a time. However many kids we're blessed with will be sufficient for me."

"Eventually, of course."

Lydia laughed. "Exactly." She blinked, biting her lower lip. "Are you all right with that?"

He lifted one hand to cup her cheek. "Lydia, I thought you were lost to me forever. No other woman caught my eye once you were gone. Now that we're together again, I'm content with whatever you want. Whether we have one child or ten, I'll be a happy man."

His words sent tendrils of heat through her stomach. Lydia

blinked back tears. How could she have doubted him for so long? He'd done nothing but prove that he was faithful and true. She leaned forward, pressing her lips to his cheek.

"Yuck," Ruby muttered. "They're kissing again."

CHAPTER 19

*S*amuel made good on his promise to take Lydia out for a proper date. When he asked his parents to watch Ruby, the exclamations of delight from both the child and the adults brought a glow to his heart. It took some creativity to make his plan come together, but hopefully, the effort would pay off and Lydia would enjoy the rather unconventional evening

She laughed when she saw the sleigh parked in front of the house. "Where did you find that?"

"The livery rents it out for a small fee. I thought it would be a fun way to get to our destination." He handed her up before jumping in beside her. Arranging the blankets, he smiled. "Comfortable?"

"Very." She leaned against him as he took up the reins and urged the horse forward. "Where are we going?"

Samuel winked. "You'll see."

He guided them toward the mountain. As they entered the trees, Lydia's gasp of delight made him grin. She clutched his arm. "Look, Sam." Awe tinged her voice. "The forest is beautiful covered with snow like this. I love how the branches are flocked white."

"It is lovely." He leaned closer, whispering in her ear. "But not as lovely as you."

Her cheeks, already red from the cold, flushed brighter.

Samuel chuckled. "Blushing becomes you."

She pushed his arm, laughing. "You're deliberately trying to embarrass me."

"Not embarrass, sweetheart. Compliment. There's a difference."

"I don't suppose there's any way for me to make you blush?"

He grinned. "Not a chance."

They settled into a comfortable silence. The sleigh barely made a sound as it sliced through the snow.

Lydia rested her head on his shoulder. "A sleigh ride through the forest. This was a wonderful idea."

"That's not all we're doing, sweetheart." He pointed ahead. "See?"

She leaned forward, squinting in the dim light. "Is that a cabin?"

"Not just any cabin. The cabin that's responsible for our marriage."

Lydia let out a small laugh. "We're returning to the scene of the crime?"

"So to speak."

Samuel smiled as they approached the warm, welcoming light pouring from the cabin's windows. He'd spent a good portion of the morning cleaning it out and making it cozy for their date. It had been seven years since their last date, and he wanted this one to be special.

He reined in the horse. "Stay here. I'll be right back."

After unhitching the horse and leading it to the small lean-to, he helped Lydia from the sleigh. "Close your eyes."

She arched a brow but complied. Samuel took her hand

and led her to the door. He pushed it open, then swept his wife into his arms. Lydia gave a startled gasp, her eyes flying open as her arms locked around his neck.

Samuel laughed, stepping through the door and closing it with a kick. "What do you think?"

Lydia took in the room. "Sam," she breathed. "When did you do all this?"

A fire blazed in the hearth. In the middle of the room stood a table, covered with a white tablecloth and a small candelabra. Two covered plates sat on either end. Winter greenery graced the hearth and shelves. It was downright beautiful.

"Cassie did a good job, didn't she?"

Lydia chuckled. "Cassie did this?"

"Well, she decorated. I cleaned everything, and she made it homey. She made the food too. Travis brought it up here." He glanced at his pocket watch. "Just about ten minutes ago, if everything went according to plan."

Lydia rested a hand against his chest, still snug in his arms. "This is very creative, Sam. I love it."

He grinned, gently setting her on her feet. "Wait until you see what Cassie brought for our supper."

She followed him to the table. Taking a deep breath, she sighed. "Whatever it is, it smells delicious."

Samuel took the warmer from her plate with a flourish. "Fried chicken with gravy, mashed potatoes, and canned string beans." He pulled out her chair. "After you..."

Lydia sat, and Samuel rounded the table to take his seat. They prayed a blessing over the food. After saying *amen*, Samuel lifted the glass of cider beside his plate. "Here's to new beginnings."

She clinked her glass against his. "To starting over."

They took a sip, then cut into their chicken. Lydia closed her eyes after taking a bite. "How have I lived here this long and never tried Cassie's fried chicken? I think I have a new favorite."

Flavor burst over Samuel's tongue—buttery breading, succulent chicken, and an array of spices he couldn't name. "Heavenly."

"I wish I could cook like this."

Something in Lydia's tone made Samuel sit straighter. He tilted his head, eying his wife. "Why do you say that?"

She ducked her head, taking a bite of potatoes instead of answering.

Samuel frowned. "Lydi?"

"Cooking has never been my strong point." Her cheeks bloomed with color. "That's all."

Not her strong point? He laughed, shaking his head. "You're a wonderful cook. I always enjoy your meals."

She glanced up. "Really?"

"Absolutely. In fact, I think you give Cassie a run for her money."

She chuckled, slicing her string beans into thirds. "I wouldn't go that far."

"I would."

Her blush deepened.

Samuel tapped her cheek. "And there's that lovely rose again."

She swatted his hand with a laugh. "You're such a flirt."

"As long as you don't object, it'll continue."

With another sip of her cider, Lydia changed the subject. "Tell me about your time in seminary. I remember the first few months were hard for you, but then..."

Samuel reached across the table to take her hand. "Then we lost touch."

She shook her head ruefully. "I broke contact, you mean."

"Considering what you were told, I can't blame you." He squeezed her hand. "What do you want to know?"

Lydia regarded him, her hazel eyes mesmerizing. "Was it

everything you hoped it'd be? You were so excited to learn theology and make friends with men of a similar calling."

"Over time, yes. I focused hard on my studies the first year, trying to get over the heartbreak of you being gone." At the flash of pain in her gaze, Samuel held up a hand. "I don't say that out of malice. It was simply my reality. In a way, it might have made me a better pastor."

"Oh?"

He chuckled. "Lydia, I was so in love with you, I was easily distracted in those initial months. When you disappeared from Aspen Grove, I had no choice but to throw myself into work to keep my mind and heart occupied." Shaking his head, he leaned back. "I got the highest marks all three years. It wasn't until my second year that I finally started to make friends. There were a few men I'd study with, and we'd talk theology and philosophy long into the night. After seminary, though, when we got our different assignments, we lost touch."

"Is that when you were assigned to John's church?"

He nodded. "I was happy to have him as a mentor. John had been a guest speaker at the seminary during my time there, and we connected easily. I found out later he requested I be assigned to his church once I graduated. That was the greatest gift he gave me. His mentorship over the next four years formed me into the pastor I am now. It gave me the courage to come out west, even though I'd always thought I'd end up in Aspen Grove again."

"Why did you come west?"

"Honestly?" Samuel took another bite of chicken, contemplating how to answer. "As much as I love Aspen Grove, it didn't feel like home without you there, and if I wasn't going to go back home, I wanted adventure. John talked often about how much pastors were needed in the American territories. When a request came through for a pastor here in Harmony Springs, I applied immediately. A few weeks later, they asked when I could come."

The smile that came over Lydia's face was soft. "You always did talk about seeing the territories someday. How wonderful that your dream came true."

Speaking of dreams... "What about you? Did you ever get to see the ocean? I remember how fascinated you were with the idea."

She shrugged with a shake of her head. "No. That was always a far-fetched dream. It would be wonderful, though."

An idea sprang to mind, one where he took his wife on a wedding trip. Samuel hid a grin. He'd have to look into logistics, but someday, he would take Lydia to see the ocean. If he could make that dream come true, he would.

She deserved it.

∾

*L*ydia ate the final bite of her chicken and potatoes. She released a small sigh of satisfaction and put a hand over her belly. "I don't think I could eat another bite."

Samuel wore a mischievous grin. "No? Then what am I gonna do with the cinnamon cake Cassie made for dessert?"

She sat a little taller. "Cinnamon cake?" Despite being full, her mouth watered. "I love anything cinnamon."

"So you do want some?" Samuel's eyes twinkled as he pulled two hefty slices of cake from a basket beside the table.

The sweet smell of cinnamon and brown sugar teased Lydia's nose. She dug in as soon as Samuel set the plate in front of her. Closing her eyes, she savored the treat.

"Mmm. This rivals chocolate cake," Samuel said.

Lydia opened her eyes. "High praise."

"This is highly delicious. I've never had cinnamon cake before."

Lydia took a sip of her cider. "It reminds me of cinnamon jumbles."

Samuel chuckled. "That might have been why I asked Cassie if she had anything like this. She said Travis loves this cake and hoped we did too."

Lydia finished her cake, then pushed back the plate. "This has been a wonderful date, Sam. You put a lot of thought into it. Thank you."

"Anything for you, sweetheart." He stood, holding out a hand. "Will you dance with me?"

She blinked. "Dance?"

Wiggling his fingers, Samuel grinned. "Yeah. Like we used to at those barn dances years ago."

She slid her hand into his. He pulled her up and into his arms. Slowly, they began to sway.

"Do you remember our very first dance?" he murmured.

Lydia pulled back enough to gaze into his eyes. "We were about Ruby's age."

"Yep." He tugged her closer. "That's when I knew I wanted to marry you."

Her mouth dropped open. Lydia stared up at him in disbelief. "We were six."

"When you know, you know." He spun her before pulling her close again. "I knew you were the one for me. Even then."

Her mind spun. How could he have known at such a young age? "You never told me that."

His expression turned sober. "I planned to, after I asked you to marry me the first time. But then, with everything that happened…" He shrugged. "The timing didn't feel right. And then we lost touch." With a chuckle, he tapped her nose. "Yet here we are. Married and happy." Another sober look. "Are you happy, Lydi?"

Slipping her arms around his neck, Lydia nodded. "Yes, Sam. You've made such an effort to be a good husband and father, and that makes me happy. I might have changed the circumstances that brought us here, if given a choice, but I think we'll have a good life together. Ruby is a wonderful daughter." Her cheeks heated. "And she'll be a good sister to any children we have."

Samuel winked. "Eventually."

Laughing, Lydia snuggled into his chest. "Exactly. For now, we can focus on the daughter we do have."

Samuel was quiet for a moment. When he spoke, his voice rumbled against her cheek. "Do you ever think it might be nice for Ruby to have a sibling around her age?"

Lydia's breath halted. "Do you mean you want to have children soon?"

"That's not what I meant." He tipped up her chin so they were face to face, his gaze serious. "Once we have more children, there will be a significant age gap between them and Ruby. But there are lots of kids who need a home. Maybe we could consider adoption at some point?"

This man. He was one of the most kind and caring people she'd ever met. How could she have doubted his heart for so many years?

Framing his face with her hands, Lydia rested her forehead against his. "That's very selfless, Sam. I think it's a good idea."

His breath puffed against her cheek. "I thought you'd be open to it, considering we adopted Ruby, but wanted to be sure." He ran a hand through her hair, pulling back enough to smile at her. "You're a wonderful mother, Lydia. Any children in our home will be blessed by you."

"I could say the same for their father."

His laugh was quiet. "I'm glad we're on the same page. Maybe we'll end up with ten kids, after all."

Lydia bit back a smile. "Maybe."

Samuel kept his hand on the back of her head, while his other came to rest against her back. He leaned down and pressed a soft kiss to her lips. She responded with a burst of passion that threatened to carry her away. Samuel's grunt of surprise vanished as he wrapped his arms around her tightly and deepened their kiss. A few blissful minutes later, he pulled back with a little groan. "My self-control has limits, sweetheart."

Lydia touched a finger to her lips. How easy it had been to give in to the feelings he evoked inside. That had gotten them in trouble seven years ago. Now that they were married, they could act on those feelings, but she wasn't ready. Not yet.

Inhaling a deep breath, she traced circles over his heart. It thumped heavily against her fingers. With a smile, she met his gaze. "Thank you for respecting me, Sam. I got lost in a fit of..." She blushed and ducked her head.

He chuckled low. "Yeah. Me too." Lifting her chin, he winked. "At least we know we still have that physical connection."

Oh, gracious. Her cheeks burned hotter. Her husband laughed and cupped one side of her face. "Have I ever told you how lovely you look with a pink face?"

She buried her face in her hands.

Samuel uncovered them. She glanced up, blinking at the abrupt change in his demeanor. His face had turned serious, his eyes locked on her. "Lydia, I know I tease a lot, but I want you to know something." He leaned closer, so close she could see the tiny flecks of gold in his blue-green eyes. "I love you, and I'm not going anywhere. As long as I draw breath, you will be loved—even if you never feel the same."

A lump grew in her throat while tears stung her eyes. Lydia rested her head against his chest, wrapping her arms around him. She wished she could say the words he wanted to hear, but she couldn't. Someday, though...someday, maybe she could. "Be patient with me, Sam."

He kissed the top of her head. "As long as it takes, sweetheart."

CHAPTER 20

"*D*o we have to go back to school, Mama?"

Lydia knelt in front of her disgruntled daughter. "Yes, sweetie. Christmas holidays are done. Aren't you excited to see your friends again?"

Ruby crossed her arms. Her bottom lip jutted out. "I only like Isaiah and Alice."

"Only?"

"I guess Marilla and Betsey are nice. Everyone else says I'm too little to play with them." Ruby huffed. "Why can't I play big-kid games?"

Lydia stifled a smile. "You need to do a little more growing, sweetie. Then you'll be able to play all the games." She tapped Ruby's nose. "But school is about learning, isn't it?"

"I guess." Ruby pouted. "I want to stay home with Papa."

"Papa's at work."

"Then I want to stay with Grandma and Grandpa."

"You'll see them at supper this evening."

Ruby stomped her foot. "I don't want to go to school!"

Lydia stood. She put a hand on Ruby's shoulder and guided

her to the door. "Sometimes the hardest part is getting out the door. Maybe you'll feel differently once we get there."

Grumbling, Ruby moped all the way to the schoolhouse. She slouched in a seat as Lydia arranged wood in the stove to heat the room. Even when warmth permeated every corner of the building, the child remained sullen. She only brightened once Alice came into the building and sat beside her. Lydia breathed a sigh of relief. Her daughter had been moody the past few days, an effect of the grief that still lingered over Pearl's death. Even with Grace and Paul giving her lots of attention over the last week, Ruby became more subdued. Having new grandparents likely reminded the girl of her granny.

Thankful to see Ruby perk up, Lydia began class. "Welcome back, everyone. Today, our first assignment is to write about your favorite memory from this Christmas season."

Excited chatter broke out in the room. Students took out their writing slates and got to work. For the next half hour, everyone remained engaged in their task. Lydia walked up and down the aisles to observe their writing.

"Wonderful work, class. I see you all had a lovely Christmas. Now, please…"

The door swung open. Everyone turned to see the visitor. Mr. Farrow walked into the room, hat in his hands. "Hello, children." His gaze swung to Lydia. "Mrs. Allen. Might I have a word?"

Tension clawed its way up her spine, but Lydia held her head high. "Of course. Class, please continue working on your writing. I'll just be a moment."

She strode to the back of the room, where the open door sent freezing air into the building. "Mr. Farrow, would you please close that?"

"Hmm? Oh, I'm sorry, ma'am."

He quickly shut the door, cutting off the frigid wind.

Lydia eyed him. "How can I help you, sir?"

"I came to tell you the school board would like to have your review tomorrow, immediately after classes end for the day."

Lydia blinked. "Tomorrow? I thought the review wasn't for a couple more weeks."

"The members voted to move it up."

Dread slithered through her. "Is there a reason for it being moved?"

He wouldn't meet her gaze. "Mrs. Allen, all I can say is that we're having it tomorrow. Please make arrangements to be here for an hour after school."

"Sir, my in-laws are leaving tomorrow. Pastor Allen and I are supposed to see them off."

Turning his hat in his hands, Mr. Farrow shook his head. "We really must insist..."

"No."

He met her gaze. "No?"

"Mr. Farrow, with all due respect, the board cannot expect me to be available on a moment's notice. I have a family, and with that comes certain responsibilities. We don't know when my in-laws will be back. I am not going to lose time with them because the school board suddenly decided to move up my review—*without* consulting me." She squared her shoulders. "You'll have to find another time for the review."

He stared at her. "Mrs. Allen, your contract states you must have three reviews a year. You cannot skip one because it's inconvenient."

"I'm not skipping anything, sir. I'm asking you to schedule it another time." Taking a step back, she waved a hand at her students. "Now, if you'll excuse me, I need to get back to the job you hired me to do." She opened the door. "Good day."

Still gaping, Mr. Farrow took his leave. Lydia shut the door firmly behind him. She rested her back against it and squeezed her hands together. Uneasiness clutched her stomach. Mr. Farrow was a decent man, but others on the board—like Mrs.

Holt—did not like being crossed. The woman already held a grudge against Lydia. This wouldn't help.

She'd made the right decision, but her gut said it might come at a cost.

Whatever happens, Lord, help me to accept it with grace and dignity.

With a deep breath, Lydia went back to the front of the room.

～

*H*er nerves didn't settle even after school let out. The tension inside only increased, until Lydia thought she might boil over. She needed to talk to Samuel.

Ruby seemed oblivious to Lydia's turmoil. She skipped along the path as they made their way home, talking the whole time about how much she enjoyed school. A wry smile tugged at Lydia's lips. At least her daughter had lost the surly attitude from this morning.

Reaching up, Lydia clasped the locket around her neck. Samuel's gift had quickly become a favorite part of her wardrobe. It rested over her heart and made her think of the man who insisted he'd win her love. Sooner or later.

Her smile turned genuine. Things with the school board might go south, but she had Samuel to lean on. She wouldn't go through this alone. The thought gave her a measure of comfort.

"Mama, it's cold."

Lydia took Ruby's hand. "We're almost home. Would you like some hot chocolate to warm you up?"

Eyes lighting with excitement, Ruby nodded. "Will Papa be home too?"

"Maybe."

Samuel's schedule varied, dependent on the needs of his parishioners. He'd left early this morning to visit a rancher who fell ill. Lydia prayed the man made a full recovery, and she prayed that Samuel be protected from the illness. After what happened to Charlotte and Frank, any threat of sickness made her nervous.

When they arrived home, Lydia built a fire to warm up the chilly room. Ruby wrapped herself in a blanket and huddled by the fire while Lydia gathered ingredients for hot chocolate. Just as the milk heated up enough to add the chocolate, Samuel came through the door.

"Papa!"

Ruby left her blanket in a heap and ran to her father.

Samuel caught her in his arms, chuckling. "Hello, Ruby. Did you have a good day?"

"Uh-huh. School was fun."

Lydia raised a brow. "Was it?"

"Yeah, Mama. I liked it after getting there, like you said."

Samuel turned a curious gaze on Lydia.

She shrugged and stirred the chocolate. "Ruby had a hard time getting out the door this morning."

"Ah." Samuel chucked their daughter gently under the chin. "It can be difficult getting back into a routine, huh?"

Ruby nodded emphatically.

Samuel smiled, setting her down. "I'm glad it turned out well." He draped the blanket back over Ruby's shoulders. "Why don't you sit, and I'll come read you a story in a minute?"

"Yay!"

Samuel ambled toward Lydia. He brushed a kiss on her cheek. "Did you have a good day?"

"Overall, yes. The children liked being back at school, and they did well in their subjects." She bit her lip.

Samuel's gaze drifted down. His brow furrowed and his eyes lifted again. "But?"

"But Mr. Farrow interrupted my lessons to inform me my review was moved to tomorrow."

"What? Can they do that?"

She sighed. "So it seems. I told him no."

"Did you?" A slow smile spread over her husband's face. "That took gumption."

"I suppose. We had plans already with your family, and I may have resented the fact that they expected me to be available on a moment's notice. I'm just nervous that they'll use this against me."

Samuel slipped his hands around her waist.

Lydia let him pull her close, resting her hands on his chest. "What if they fire me?"

He hummed thoughtfully. "How would that make you feel?"

"I'm...not sure." Lydia closed her eyes. "I love those children. It's a joy watching their faces light up when they learn something new. This job felt like a God-send when I first came to town."

Samuel studied her, letting her process her thoughts out loud.

"When I took the job, I had no expectations of remarrying or having a new family. I thought this would be my life. Now, with you and Ruby, it's still a good situation. She and I are in school at the same time, and you're home not long after us. But..." She swallowed hard, a blush heating her cheeks. "If you and I have more children, I wouldn't want to work. I'd want to be home to raise them."

Samuel's dimples deepened with his smile. "Yeah? So if the worst did happen and you were fired, you'd be okay with it?"

"I'm not sure if 'okay' is the right word. It'd be an injustice." She tapped his chest. "But it wouldn't be the worst thing, since I have my new family, with the prospect of it growing."

"Eventually," he said with a wink.

Lydia laughed. "Yes. Eventually."

Sobering, Samuel rubbed his thumbs over her back. "If

they do let you go, sweetheart, we'll fight it. They have no grounds."

Lydia chewed on her lip. "Actually, they might."

"What do you mean? You've done nothing wrong."

"No, but I remember something about female teachers being single or widowed. At the time, I thought nothing of it. Now, that could be a problem. I'm married." She frowned. "Come to think of it, I'm surprised they didn't mention that when they insisted I get married if I wanted to keep my job." They wouldn't have tricked her, would they? Unease tickled her insides.

"I thought you were hired without a teaching license because they couldn't find anyone else," Samuel said.

"They did." Lydia let out a breath, shoving away the unpleasant thoughts. "That could be the thing that saves my job. They may have no other choice."

Samuel's frown creased his brow.

Lydia reached up, smoothing his skin. "Whatever happens, I'll be able to accept it. I want to keep teaching, at least for now, but if it's taken away, it's not the end of the world." She smiled. "My husband is capable of taking care of the family."

He chuckled. "I can, but are you sure you'll be fine with either outcome?"

"I'm not sure, but based on your last sermon, having a holy detachment from two options can be a good thing."

"Ah, so you were listening?" His eyes twinkled as he tapped her nose.

Swatting his chest, Lydia giggled. "Of course, I was."

"I haven't heard that giggle in a while."

She rolled her eyes. "Don't you have a book to read?"

"Indeed, I do." He peered over her shoulder. "Is that hot chocolate?"

"It is. I'll bring some over for you and Ruby in a minute."

He kissed her cheek again. "Thanks, Lydi. You're the best."

He pulled back, but kept his gaze locked on hers. "The school board would be fools to let you go."

She rested a palm on his cheek. "I appreciate your support."

"You'll always have it."

$\sim$

*T*he lump in Samuel's throat made swallowing difficult. He hugged his parents again, tears welling in his eyes. "We're going to miss you."

Pa squeezed him back. "We'll come visit soon. Maybe in the spring."

"I'd like that."

"Me too." Ruby piped in, locking her arms around each grandparent's leg.

Ma crouched down in front of his daughter. "It's been a pleasure getting to know you, Ruby. I'm so glad you're part of our family now."

"I'm glad too. I miss Granny, but now I have two grandmas. That makes me feel a little better."

Samuel exchanged glances with Lydia. Her gentle smile soothed the sense of loss threatening to overtake him. He'd never found it easy to say goodbye, and after he'd been reconciled with his parents, their visit had become the highlight of the new year.

Ma and Pa embraced Ruby, then did the same with Lydia. "You take care of our boy, young lady," Ma said, patting Lydia's cheek.

"I will, Grace." Lydia shot him a cheeky grin. "As long as he behaves himself."

Pa laughed. "That's a tall order."

"Hey!" Samuel plunked his hands on his hips. "I always behave."

Lydia's brow quirked along with her lips.

Samuel rolled his eyes. "Fine—almost always."

The train whistle blew. Passengers disembarked, milling around those waiting to board.

Pa clapped his shoulder and looked directly into his eyes. "Son, I'm proud of the man you've become. I love you."

The words threaded through him. It was rare his father spoke such sentiment, and for a moment, Samuel couldn't form words of his own. When he did, he threw his arms around Pa. "I love you too."

Ma watched with watery eyes. She embraced Samuel as soon as Pa let go. "I also love you, son. You're doing good work here." She lowered her voice to a whisper. "And I'm sure that your wife will be fully in love with you soon enough. How could she resist?"

Heat crawled up Samuel's ears. He shot a glance at Lydia, thankful to see her occupied with Pa and Ruby. "Thanks, Ma. I hope so." He kissed her cheek. "I love you. You're my favorite ma."

She laughed, shaking her head. "Your only ma, you mean."

Far too soon for Samuel's liking, his parents said their final goodbye and headed for the platform. A couple tears escaped his eyes, falling down his cheeks. He waved until they were out of sight, swallowed up by metal.

Lydia slid her arm through his. "Saying goodbye is hard. I enjoyed their visit."

"As did I."

Ruby sighed. "Maybe they can move here. Then we can have Grandma Dorothy *and* Grandma Grace with us. And Grandpa Paul."

"That would be great." Samuel took Ruby's hand as they began their walk back home. "I'll mention it in my next letter to them."

Ruby stopped and tugged at his hand. "Papa, Alice is waving at us."

"Your friend from school?"

He searched the street until he spotted Alice. The little girl hurried over with her mother in tow. "Hi, Pastor Allen, Mrs. Allen." Alice bounced on her toes, excitement in her brown eyes. "Mama said I could have Ruby over for supper if it's okay with you."

Samuel leaned close to Lydia, brows raised in question. She smiled with a nod. "Of course. As long as you're home by seven."

Alice's mother—whose name escaped Samuel—promised to bring Ruby home in time, and the two girls squealed with delight before running off together down the lane. He chuckled, pulling Lydia a little closer. "I guess it's just us this evening."

"That doesn't sound so bad."

Lydia's smile sent his heart racing. He leaned down, nuzzling her cheek. "How about a supper date at the café? I heard Cassie is experimenting with larger cinnamon jumbles. She might need a taste tester."

Eyes lighting up, Lydia grinned. "What are we waiting for? Let's go."

As they walked together, Samuel reflected on the past few weeks. He slipped his arm around Lydia's shoulders and lowered his voice. "Thank you for leading by example."

She turned her hazel eyes on him, confusion creasing her brow. "Me?"

"If it weren't for you, I'm not sure I could have forgiven my parents that fast."

Lydia chuckled under her breath. She leaned into him, their steps slowing. "It took me years to forgive, Sam. I'm glad you can do so more easily than me."

A shrill voice pierced the air. "Mrs. Allen. A word, if you please."

Samuel groaned. "Mrs. Holt? Speaking of forgiving..." he whispered.

Elbowing his ribs, Lydia turned. "Good afternoon, Mrs. Holt. How are you today?"

The woman bustled toward them, out of breath, brown hair slipping from her bun. "I would like to discuss your review. Since you found the time we assigned inconvenient, we scrambled to select another that worked for the board."

"With all due respect, ma'am, the board moved up the original time without consulting me. It seems prudent to ask the person being reviewed if the time selected works for her."

Mrs. Holt bristled. She crossed her arms. "Mrs. Allen, we expect our teacher to be readily available, unless circumstances are extreme. Yours were not."

Samuel's eyes narrowed. "Are you calling family obligations unimportant, Mrs. Holt?"

"Of course not."

"What was so pressing that you had to inconvenience my wife and move her review up two weeks? It must have been a grave reason for such a sudden change."

Mrs. Holt cleared her throat. "Pastor, if you don't mind, this conversation is between me and Mrs. Allen. It doesn't concern you..."

"I assure you, it does." Samuel stepped forward, his voice lowering to a growl. "Lydia is my wife. Anything that concerns her concerns me, and vice-versa."

Eyes wide, Mrs. Holt hopped back. "I'm not at liberty to say. She'll find out at the review in a week."

"One week?" Lydia leaned into Samuel. "After school?"

"Yes. Will that be convenient?"

Samuel clenched his hands. The way Mrs. Holt stressed the last word set him on edge. Before he could say anything, Lydia stopped him with a gentle hand to his chest. She gave him a smile, then spoke to Mrs. Holt. "That is fine."

"Then we'll see you next Thursday at three o'clock sharp. Good day." With a brusque nod, Mrs. Holt flounced down the street.

Lydia turned her back on the woman and faced Samuel. Cupping his cheeks, she rested her forehead against his. "Thank you for defending me."

He slid his arms around her. "Always. Do you want me to be at the review?"

Her breath caught, her hazel eyes going misty. "I'd like that."

"Then I'll be there." He kissed her forehead. "You can count on me."

CHAPTER 21

*N*erves fluttered in Lydia's stomach when she dismissed her students the following week. The upcoming review had been on her mind all day. She prayed the children hadn't sensed anything amiss. Whatever happened, she could accept it—she just didn't like the time of waiting.

I know You're in control, Lord, and that You have a plan. Help me be at peace.

Someone coughed, drawing her attention. Her gaze swept the classroom. Everyone had left—everyone except Ruby and Alice. The girls huddled on a bench near the front of the room. The cough sounded again, wracking Alice's little body.

The child seemed fine when she first arrived that morning, but throughout the day, she'd had fits of coughing. Winter often brought colds and sniffles, yet the way Alice shivered now concerned Lydia.

"Are you all right, sweetie?"

The little girl shook her head, leaning against the bench. "My throat hurts."

"I have some peppermints in my desk. It might help the ache. Would you like one?"

Alice nodded.

Lydia led her to the desk. She pulled a candy from her top drawer and unwound the wrapper. Alice accepted it with a small smile, putting the round peppermint into her mouth.

Lydia knelt. Alice's face had flushed, and her small body still trembled. Lydia pressed her hand against the girl's forehead.

Hot.

Worry shot through Lydia. She stood, taking Alice's hand. "Let's see if your father arrived yet." The man had been picking her up all week. Lydia frowned. Why hadn't she noticed how unusual that was? She'd never seen him before Monday.

Come to think of it, he'd been awfully haggard this morning...

Ruby slid off her bench. "Mama, what's wrong with Alice?"

"She's not feeling well."

The door opened, sending a gush of freezing wind inside. Alice yelped and hid her face in Lydia's skirt. "It's too cold."

Mrs. Holt bustled in, shutting the door with a bang behind her. She nodded at Lydia even as her gaze fell on Ruby and Alice. "Will these children be leaving soon?"

A retort burned the edge of Lydia's tongue. She bit it back, striving for a calm she didn't feel. "Alice's father should pick her up shortly. Ruby will remain here with me."

Disapproval shone in the other woman's eyes. Before she could speak, the door opened again. Other members of the board flocked inside. Samuel came behind them. His gaze found Lydia's at once. Relief pulsed through her. She moved forward to greet him, but a moan at her side stopped her, followed by a worried little voice.

"Mama, Alice is crying." Ruby tugged her arm, pointing at Alice with a worried expression.

Lydia knelt again. Tears streamed down Alice's cheeks in silent rivulets. Though the girl made no other sound, the misery on her face pulled at Lydia's heart. She hugged Alice close. "We're going to get you home, sweetie."

Alice's hot skin burned through the layers of Lydia's warm winter dress. How had she missed the signs of her student coming down with fever?

Fear slithered through her heart. Fever. Chills. A cough and sore throat. All symptoms Charlotte once had before her death.

"Sam, did you see either of Alice's parents in the schoolyard?"

He shook his head. "I didn't see them on my way here either."

Her gaze swung to the board members. "Did anyone see Mr. or Mrs. Curtis?"

The chorus of *no*'s made her stomach drop.

Mr. Farrow clasped his hands behind him. "I'm sure they're simply delayed. It happens, doesn't it?"

"I suppose." Lydia blew out a breath. Perhaps she panicked because of her experience with a sick child. "But Alice needs care. What if a doctor must be fetched?"

"The closest doctor is ten miles away," Mrs. Holt said. Her eyes, usually hard, softened slightly. "It's natural to worry, Mrs. Allen, yet children recover all the time. With a little rest, she'll be fine."

Tears welled in Lydia's eyes. *You don't know that.*

Samuel bent beside her. He pressed one hand to her back, the other to Alice's. A solution formed in her mind. "Sam, will you take Alice home?"

His gaze searched hers. "Are you sure? I promised to be here for your review."

"I know." She rested her hand on his cheek. "But it would mean more to me if you made sure Alice was home with her family and getting whatever care she needs."

He studied her for a few moments, then murmured, "Charlotte."

Throat tightening, she nodded.

"All right. I'll take her home. Would you like me to take Ruby as well?"

Lydia glanced at the board surrounding them. She lowered her voice. "That would probably be best."

He kissed her cheek. "I'll be praying, Lydi."

"Thank you."

Samuel gathered Alice in his arms. "Come, little one. Let's get you home."

The child burrowed against him. Though she shivered still, sweat beaded on her brow. He leaned close to Lydia and murmured, "Several of our parishioners have similar symptoms. This may get worse before it gets better. I'll ask Travis to wire the doctor."

She clutched his arm. "You'll have to visit the sick, won't you?"

He nodded, a somber expression on his face. "I'll be careful."

Lydia swallowed hard. She crossed her arms over her body. No words formed, but the fear of Samuel getting sick pressed hard against her heart.

Alice lay cradled safely in his arms. Just holding the girl could mean he'd be infected. But if given the chance to avoid illness or help someone in need, she knew he'd choose the latter every time. It was who he was.

"Mrs. Allen, are you ready to get started?" Mr. Farrow's question pulled her from her musings.

Samuel gave her a gentle smile before leaving the school with Ruby in tow. With him gone, her nerves returned in full force, competing with worry for Alice and her family.

Once they were all seated, Mr. Farrow cleared his throat. "We won't keep you in suspense, Mrs. Allen. The purpose of this meeting is more than a review." He pulled a piece of paper from his briefcase. "As you can see in your contract, married women are not supposed to be teachers. We allowed an exception for you after you married the pastor."

Lydia blinked. "Mr. Farrow, if you recall, the board required that I marry Samuel in order to keep my job. You didn't give me a choice."

"Yes...well..."

Mrs. Holt interrupted. "That was a matter of propriety. Your indiscretion was known to all. It wouldn't have been proper to allow you to teach without getting married."

Gritting her teeth, Lydia drew in a sharp breath. "There was no indiscretion."

"You were found in each other's arms after spending the night together." Mrs. Holt shook her head, a faint smirk on her lips. "Now, back to the matter at hand."

The woman's condescension raised Lydia's hackles. "How dare you assume the worst? I believe you would have done the same thing to survive. And we had a *child* with us."

"That's no matter..."

"Ladies," Mr. Farrow broke in, glancing between them. "There's no need to argue. We're here today for a purpose, and that is not it." He focused on Lydia. "Mrs. Allen, since you are now married, and presumably will be having children, the board deemed it necessary to search for your replacement."

"What?" Blood whooshed through her ears. "How long have you been searching?"

Mr. Farrow didn't meet her gaze. "Since your wedding."

She stood, fists clenching. "And you didn't see fit to tell me? You said I had to get married to keep my job, then turned around and started looking for a replacement?"

"Erm...yes. It's in the contract."

Heat simmered inside. "It might be in the contract, but you willfully deceived me. That is not just."

"Nevertheless, it is our decision. The new teacher will be

here in the summer. He couldn't make it any sooner, so you may stay on for the rest of the school year."

"How generous," she muttered, plopping back in her seat. Indignation boiled inside. "Why move this review up?"

"We thought it best to give you the news as soon as possible."

Lydia glared at Mrs. Holt, then Mr. Farrow. "You both acted as if my refusal to meet last week was a glaring inconvenience. For this?"

"Mrs. Allen, we expect our teachers to be available..."

"Save your excuses." She stood once more. "If that's all, I'm going to check on Alice."

"Why, I never!" Mrs. Holt waved a hand, her face going purple. "We're not done here."

"Oh? What else have you to say?"

When no one answered, she huffed. "I thought not. Good day."

Grabbing her coat, Lydia marched outside. The biting cold wind cooled her heated face. She yanked on her gloves. "Hiring someone without telling me. The audacity!"

Her steps slowed as reality crashed in. She would not teach again once the school year ended. These were her last months with her precious students.

Lydia closed her eyes, fighting tears. To be so brusquely dismissed hurt, despite knowing it had been a possibility...

"Lydia?"

Her eyes snapped open. Cassie hurried toward her. Something in her friend's expression sent Lydia's heart into her stomach. "What's wrong?"

"It's the Curtis family. They're all sick."

Fear curled inside. "Is Samuel with them?"

"Yes. He asked me to watch Ruby while he went into the house. I think he wanted to keep her from the illness. He wanted me to find you."

If he asked that, knowing she had her review, things must be dire. "I was headed there anyway. Thanks, Cassie."

"If you need us to keep Ruby overnight, just let me know. We're happy to have her stay."

"I appreciate that."

They parted ways at the main street, and Lydia hurried toward the Curtis home, afraid of what she'd find when she got there.

~

Samuel knelt beside a sofa, pressing a damp cloth to Alice's forehead. The little girl whimpered. "Cold."

"I'm sorry, but it will help with your fever."

Tears fell down her cheeks. "Everything hurts."

Semi-conscious groans from the other room spoke of the pain Alice's parents experienced even in their sleep. When he arrived, it had been to find them slumped over the table, untouched bowls of oatmeal before them. He'd gotten the Curtises into bed after having them drink a few mouthfuls of water—all they could stomach. They'd fallen into a fitful sleep moments later.

When a knock sounded at the door, he stifled his own groan. Cassie must have found Lydia. He'd questioned the wisdom of asking for his wife as soon as the words left his mouth. The last thing he wanted was her to suffer this same illness.

"Sam?"

Lydia opened the door herself. He shot to his feet, holding out his hands. "Lydia, stay there. Don't come in."

She shut the door behind her. Removing her coat, she leveled him with a piercing stare. "Didn't you ask me to come?"

"I thought the better of it. Whatever they're sick with, it's bad. Alice said her father wasn't sick this morning, which means this illness came on sudden and intense."

"Sam..."

Another knock came. Lydia opened the door. Travis stood on the other side, hat in hand, face somber. His gaze landed on Samuel. "Sorry for the interruption. Cassie said I could find you here."

Getting to his feet, Samuel pressed his hand to Alice's forehead. "Try to rest, okay?"

Alice cried, reaching for him. Before Samuel could react, Lydia slipped around him and took his spot beside the girl. "I'm here, Alice."

"Mrs. Allen?" Alice lifted her arms, and Lydia gently lifted the girl onto her lap.

Torn between a love of her tender care and concern for her safety, Samuel swallowed and turned to Travis. "What's going on?"

Travis motioned him onto the porch. When they were both outside, the sheriff shook his head. "Things are bad, Samuel. Four people were found dead this morning, folks who recently showed signs of illness. More people are falling sick. We need a doctor." He clamped a hand on Samuel's shoulder. "I came to see if you'd fetch him from Elkhorn. I'd go, but there are reports of severely ill ranchers who might need help."

"Of course, I'll go. Let me tell Lydia, and I'll be on my way."

He slipped back into the house to find his wife laying Alice back on the sofa and covering her with a blanket. She put a finger to her lips. "Alice fell asleep as soon as you went outside."

"Lydia." Samuel grasped her hands and held them against his chest. "Travis said this illness is spreading. People are dying. I'm going for a doctor."

Fear flashed in her eyes. "Dying?"

"We're going to get them help."

Her throat worked. "When you get back, you're going to visit the sick, aren't you?"

"I'm a pastor. It's part of my ministry."

Lydia lifted her chin. Her hazel eyes sparked with determination. "Then I'm helping too."

"No. It's too dangerous. I can't lose you again."

"I'm a pastor's wife. Your ministry is my ministry." She placed a hand on Alice's head. "Besides, someone needs to care for the Curtis family. I can't just leave them like this."

"Lydia…"

"Go, Sam. The sooner you leave, the sooner the doctor can help people." She rose on tiptoe, pressing her lips against his. "Stay safe."

He returned the kiss, his arms wrapping around her in a tight embrace. "You, too, sweetheart." Letting her go, he fetched his coat. "When I get back, I want to hear about your review."

Her eyes dimmed. "You will."

Something in her tone stopped him. "Was it bad?"

Lydia blew out a breath, a faint smile on her lips. "That's still to be determined." She nudged him toward the door. "Go. We'll talk later."

He embraced her once more, then headed out into the cold.

CHAPTER 22

A child's cry woke Lydia from sleep. She jerked up, disoriented. *Where am I?*

Hard wood pressed against her stomach. Blinking sleep from her eyes, she frowned at the table. Why had she fallen asleep in the kitchen? And why was it so dark?

The cry sounded again, and in a rush, it all came back. Alice. Mr. and Mrs. Curtis. The sickness they carried.

Lydia stood, smoothing down her wrinkled dress. The room felt far too cold. She glanced at the embers dying in the hearth. The fire needed to be rebuilt. But first, she needed to check on the family.

Alice slept fitfully in her room. Breathing a prayer of thanks, Lydia slipped into the main bedroom. "Is anyone awake?" she whispered.

Sobs were her only answer. She tiptoed closer to the bed. Mr. Curtis sat up suddenly, flailing. "Doctor. We need a doctor. Please. Jane is so cold."

"The doctor is coming, Mr. Curtis."

He choked on his words. "Something's wrong. Jane's been sick all week. She ain't gettin' any better."

All week? Lydia bit her lip, remembering comments from Alice during school that her mother wasn't well. "Let me get a fire going, then I'll get you some water."

"Don't want no water. Want the doc."

Lydia built the fire as quickly as she could, then reapproached the bed. "Are you still feverish, sir?"

"Don't know," he muttered. His eyes rolled back as he slumped back on the bed.

Lydia put her hand on his brow. His skin was hot. She moved to Mrs. Curtis to check her temperature.

Cold. Lydia frowned. Far too cold. She sat on the edge of the bed, picking up one of the woman's hands to rub. Maybe that would help warm her. Mrs. Curtis's hand was stiff in hers. Stiff —and lifeless.

Lydia dropped her hand with a gasp. Leaning down, she felt for any puff of breath against her ear.

Nothing.

"No, no, no." Lydia pressed two fingers against Mrs. Curtis's neck, searching for a pulse. Nothing. She tried again over her chest.

No sign of life.

Bolting to her feet, Lydia blinked back tears. Mr. Curtis fell back to an unconscious sleep as his wife lay dead beside him.

Moans from the parlor tore through her. Alice. How would Lydia tell her that her mother was gone? Her stomach tightening, Lydia went to the child.

Alice sat up in bed when she entered the room. Rubbing her eyes, the little girl appeared disoriented. Lydia strove for calm as she sat beside Alice. "How are you feeling?"

"Bad. My throat is tight."

Lydia reached for the cup on Alice's bedside stand. "Drink this."

Alice took a few sips, then sank back into her pillows. "Why does everything hurt?"

"You are very sick. It's going to hurt for a little while."

"When will I get better?"

You'll make me better, right, Mama?

For a moment, Alice's face turned into Charlotte's. A lump grew in Lydia's throat while tears stung her eyes. She blinked hard. Alice came into focus once more. Her blond curls hung limp around her face, brown eyes wide with fear.

Lydia took Alice's hand. "I don't know, sweetie, but Pastor Allen went to get the doctor. Hopefully, they'll be back soon."

"I want Mama."

Pain pierced Lydia's heart. The tears she'd been fighting fell from her eyes. "Your mama can't come, Alice."

"Why not?"

A knock at the door saved her from answering. Heart breaking for Alice and the grief to come, Lydia stood. "I'll be right back, okay?"

Alice turned on her side with a nod, eyes drooping.

Lydia hurried to the front door. She opened it, the black of night broken by a lantern in a strange man's hand. Samuel stood behind him, weary and wind-blown. "Lydia, this is Dr. Lewis. We got here as soon as we could."

Relief swept through her, followed quickly by sadness. "Alice and Mr. Curtis are still sick. Mrs. Curtis..." Her stomach tightened. "She didn't survive the night."

Shock registered on both men's faces. Dr. Lewis's brow creased. "Show me the patients."

Lydia led him to the main bedroom. The doctor went in. After setting down his bag, he checked Mrs. Curtis first. Lydia couldn't make herself enter the room. Too many memories flooded in, and tears poured down her cheeks.

Samuel took her in his arms. Lydia buried her face in his chest and cried.

"Mrs. Allen?"

The weak call broke through her haze. Lydia pulled back, wiping her cheeks. "Alice needs me."

Samuel nodded. "I'll help Dr. Lewis."

"Thanks for getting him. I hope he can help those who are ill."

He studied her face. "This must be bringing back hard memories."

"It is. I can't...what if Alice dies, Samuel? What if my other students get this illness?" Fear clutched her. "What if Ruby gets sick?"

Samuel cupped her cheeks, his steady gaze bringing her a measure of comfort. "We're directed not to worry about tomorrow, love. Sufficient for each day is the trouble of its own."

She sniffed and wiped her eyes. Samuel pulled a handkerchief from his pocket. He gently wiped away her tears. Lydia took his hand as he lowered it. "I can't help worrying, Sam. Not after what happened to Frank and Charlotte."

He traced her jawline with his thumb. "I know it's hard, but this is not in our hands."

Tears threatened again, but Alice called once more.

Samuel nodded toward the girl's room. "She needs you." He hugged her close. "Do what you can. Leave the rest to God. We may not understand why He let this happen, but He can bring good from it. Somehow, some way."

"Somehow," Lydia repeated softly. Feeling a little uplifted, she turned and went to Alice.

~

Two weeks after Dr. Lewis confirmed influenza struck the Curtis family, Samuel felt like collapsing. He'd worked with the doctor from dawn to dusk daily, trying to help stem the spread of influenza. The illness spread rapidly, affecting nearly a third of Harmony Springs residents in town. The ranchers and their families fared better.

Samuel did what he could to help. Many asked for his prayers and comfort, especially as the death count rose. More recovered than not, but there were far too many families who grieved the loss of a loved one.

Families such as the Curtises. Mr. Curtis and Alice both recovered, but shock and grief swallowed them after Mrs. Curtis's death. Mr. Curtis took the loss particularly hard. He remained bed-bound, at the mercy of a crippling sadness. Nothing could persuade him to get up, not even to care for his daughter. Once Alice was past the point of contagion, Lydia asked to take her for a while, receiving only a grunt in return. She took it as permission. Alice had been with them for a week, quiet and sad, but she shared a room with Ruby, and it seemed that having a friend who'd experienced a similar loss helped her process the loss of her mother.

Thank God for his wife. Lydia worked with Cassie to make gallons of soup and loaves of bread, bringing nourishment to the sick. Samuel delivered the food and prayed with the families.

Dr. Lewis recommended that people stay in their homes as much as possible, hoping to contain the spread of illness. He also bade people to wash their hands regularly with soap, a practice some doctors thought killed off whatever caused sickness.

It appeared to be working. Less people were getting sick, and those who did recovered several days later. Still, there was much work to be done. Wherever Dr. Lewis was, Samuel attended as both assistant and spiritual comforter. They had just finished a house call at the Greyson residence, where mother and son had finally begun to recover.

"That was a close one." Dr. Lewis sighed, his breath puffing white in the cold air.

Samuel buttoned up his coat. "Thank God they pulled through. Mr. Greyson looked greatly relieved."

"As well he should." The doctor pulled on his gloves. "Pastor, there's something I've been meaning to mention."

Samuel motioned for him to continue. Dr. Lewis spoke in low tones. "This town needs a doctor of its own. I'm glad I could be here for a time, but this came over wire today."

He handed Samuel a piece of paper. Opening it, Samuel scanned the short message. His gaze shot back up. "The illness has reached your town."

"Unfortunately. I'll be needed there." He took the paper back and tucked it in his pocket. "I wish I could be in two places at once, but that's not possible. As much as I hate to leave the residents of Harmony Springs, I need to go home. Do you think you can handle things without me?"

Samuel blew out a breath. "Possibly." Lydia wouldn't be thrilled that he continued to put himself in danger, but so far, he'd remained healthy. He prayed that continued.

"Put an advertisement in papers out east. It's how I found the job in Elkhorn. Many young men would be grateful for a chance to start a practice of their own here in the west."

"That's not a bad idea. As far as I know, we've only advertised for a doctor in the territories."

"Send the message out soon. You want a permanent physician here."

Samuel nodded. A hospital would be nice, too, but that would take money and resources they didn't have.

He paused, a conversation coming to mind. "One of my friends has a sister who is just finishing medical school. Perhaps we could offer her a job."

Dr. Lewis whistled low. "A woman? You might face some opposition to that. Many folks don't trust lady doctors as well as men."

"That's ridiculous."

"I agree, but it's an unfortunate reality."

Samuel grunted. Despite Dr. Lewis's hesitation, he'd broach the subject with Ella, see if her sister would be open to the possibility of relocating to Harmony Springs. They couldn't afford to be choosy about their physician. If it came down to life or death, the townspeople would choose a woman doctor over none at all.

"Are there any more stops today, Doctor?"

"One more. The Holt residence."

Samuel's stomach dropped. "The Holts?"

"I got word that two of them fell ill. Mrs. Holt and her daughter Francine."

His feet stuck to the ground. Samuel pressed his lips together, fighting the anger that surfaced. When Lydia first told him she was being ousted from her job, he'd had some very uncharitable thoughts, leading to a plea for God to forgive him and to help him overcome his anger. She'd been treated unjustly, and he didn't like it. Lydia had managed to calm him. *"It'll be all right. Now I can simply be a pastor's wife and help you in the community."*

He liked the sound of that. Still, it bothered him that the school board treated her unfairly. Most of his frustration had been directed at Mrs. Holt.

Now she needed his help.

Samuel glanced up toward heaven. *Help me, Lord.*

When they reached the Holt home, Samuel stared at the exterior. Made of brick instead of clapboard, it rose two stories above the street and had a large wraparound porch like the ones he'd seen on ranchers' homes. It must have been custom built.

They climbed the porch steps and knocked. Abigail let them in. The young woman's face was haggard. Some of Samuel's frustration melted away. "How is your family?"

Tears welled in her eyes. She shook her head. "Not good.

Francie isn't well, but it's Mama we're worried about. She's bad off."

"Can you take us to her?" Dr. Lewis asked.

Abigail nodded and led them up a flight of stairs. Pointing to a door on the right, she said, "Mama's in there. Francie is in the room next door."

They entered the room to find Mr. Holt sitting beside his wife, his hand clasping hers. Relief flashed over his face when he saw them. "Thanks for coming. Please, do what you can."

Samuel knelt beside the bed, bowing his head in prayer while Dr. Lewis examined Mrs. Holt.

"Mr. Holt, your wife appears to be dehydrated. It's very important to get her to drink water whenever possible."

The man wrung his hands. "I'll do my best."

"I have more instructions for you, but perhaps we can discuss them while I examine your daughter?"

Mr. Holt nodded. "Of course. This way." He paused with a glance at Samuel. "Can you stay with my wife until I'm back?"

A little stunned at the request, Samuel stuttered. "Y-yes."

"Thanks, Pastor."

Samuel took the chair beside the bed. He wasn't sure what to do, so he bowed his head in prayer once more.

"Pastor?" Abigail stood in the doorway.

He straightened. "Yes?"

She came forward, a cup in her hands. "Here's some water for Mama. If she wakes up."

"Thanks, Miss Holt." He accepted the cup. "How are you faring?"

Abigail sat on the bed, gaze on her mother. "It came on so sudden yesterday, for them both. We didn't call for the doctor because we knew he was busy. Papa thought maybe they would be better today." She sniffed, swiping her nose with her sleeve as tears slipped down her cheeks. "But they got worse. I'm scared for Mama."

Despite his grievances with the Holt family, Samuel hated seeing people suffer. He offered her his handkerchief. "I won't tell you everything will be all right, because we don't know the future. But I can tell you, you're not alone in this."

She wiped her eyes with the square of cloth and gave him a wobbly smile. "Thanks, Pastor Allen. I'm going to see what the doctor says about Francie."

Samuel turned back to Mrs. Holt, then nearly fell from his seat. Her eyes were open, staring at him.

Recovering from his shock, Samuel took the water cup in hand. "Here. Drink this."

She opened her mouth, and little by little, Samuel dribbled water in. When she'd drunk half the water, she shook her head. "No more."

"Mrs. Holt—"

"I need to tell you something."

He slowly lowered the cup. "Can you drink just a little more?"

"After," she rasped. "Need to apologize."

"Apologize?"

She nodded, eyes closing. "I've been awful to your wife, Pastor. There's no excuse for my behavior. I was angry that you showed interest in her over one of my girls. It was petty of me to seek revenge for a perceived wrong." She sighed, opening her eyes once more. "Please forgive me."

Mouth falling open, Samuel sat back in his chair.

Mrs. Holt wheezed. He reached for the water again, but she waved it away. "If I recover, I'll beg Mrs. Allen's forgiveness myself. But...if I don't...please tell her for me."

She thinks she's going to die.

All of Samuel's frustration and anger melted away. He put a hand on her shoulder. "I forgive you. And I'm certain Lydia will too."

Mrs. Holt's body relaxed. "Thank you." Her eyes slipped shut.

"Not yet, Mrs. Holt. You need more water."

She cracked one eye open. "I'm tired."

"The doctor wants you to be hydrated. You need to drink."

"Fine."

She let Samuel give her half of the remaining water before pushing the cup away. Her motions were weak, but he didn't force her to take more. Mrs. Holt's eyes closed again. Her body shivered much as Alice's had two weeks before.

Samuel stoked the fire. When he resumed his seat beside her, he breathed a prayer of thanks for her apology. Lydia would appreciate it, even if it came too late to save her job.

Now he could only pray that Mrs. Holt recovered.

CHAPTER 23

*L*ydia kept watch at the window. Samuel should have been home by now. It had been a week since Dr. Lewis left Harmony Springs to care for the people of Elkhorn. By some miracle, neither the doctor nor Samuel had contracted influenza, but Lydia feared daily for her husband's safety. He continued to minister to the people in town. Most had recovered, but a few still had the dreaded illness.

Little feet pattered into the kitchen. Lydia turned, smiling at Ruby and Alice. "Are you girls ready for supper?"

Ruby glanced around the room, her brow furrowing. "Where's Papa?"

"He's still out."

"When will he be home?"

"Hopefully soon."

The door opened. Cold air rushed in as Samuel stepped over the threshold. Lydia gripped a chair, relief weakening her knees. He gave them a tired smile. "How are my girls today?"

"Good, Papa. Alice and I learned how to make winter wreaths."

Samuel chuckled. He shrugged out of his coat. "Mama is still teaching you even with school shut down?"

"Yeah." Ruby made a face. "Most of it is boring, but we liked the wreaths."

Lydia shook her head with a little laugh. "Boring it might be, but education is important."

"I like it," Alice said softly.

Lydia had noticed over the past weeks that Alice aimed to please. It was almost as though she worried a differing opinion would get her in trouble. She'd done the same in school, though Lydia had assumed it was a love of learning. Now, she wondered what Alice's home life was like.

"I'm glad to hear that. Why don't you two wash up so we can have supper?"

Samuel rubbed a hand over his face. Lydia went to him. His face was lined and weary, his eyes dull. Worry pricked her heart once more.

He sighed, deep and long. "There's good news and bad news, Lydi. The good is that there have been no new cases of influenza yesterday or today. I'm praying we're past the worst of it."

"That's encouraging." She took his hand. "Did we lose anyone else?"

His eyes drooped at the edges, sadness clear in the blue-green depths. "In a manner of speaking, yes."

What did that mean? She started to ask, but Samuel swayed on his feet.

Lydia led him to the sofa. "Sit, Sam. You look exhausted."

"I've never been this tired before." He sank onto the cushions and leaned his head back.

"Do you feel sick?"

He smiled without opening his eyes. "No, sweetheart. Just tired."

She studied his pale face. Fear threatened, but she shoved it down. Maybe it was simply exhaustion. He'd been ministering to the town nonstop since influenza broke out.

The girls came back from washing, their hands still damp.

Lydia put a hand on Samuel's shoulder. "I'm going to feed the girls. Do you want supper now?"

He shook his head. "Not just yet."

"All right. I'll be back shortly."

A soft snore was her only reply. Exhausted, indeed.

Lydia served supper. Afterward, she and the girls played with dolls in their room for a while, then she put them to bed. When she came downstairs, Samuel sat at the table eating a bowl of soup.

She made two cups of tea, then joined him. "What did you mean earlier? About losing someone in a manner of speaking?"

Samuel took a sip of tea. He stared into the cup as it lowered. "It's not good." His jaw clenched. "How can a father abandon his child?"

She blinked. His subtle display of anger meant he was truly upset. "What do you mean?"

He set the cup down with a clink. "I checked on Mr. Curtis today. He was my last stop before coming home. I expected to find him still in bed."

"He wasn't?"

"No. When I came in, he was stuffing clothes into a bag. It took me a minute to process what I was seeing. When I asked what he was about, he said he was leaving Harmony Springs. Alone."

Lydia's thoughts swirled. Her mind latched on one word. "Alone? What about Alice?"

"That's what I asked." Samuel's throat constricted, a vein throbbing in his neck. "He said he couldn't care for her without Mrs. Curtis, that he was going to drop her off at an orphanage before going farther west."

"What?" Lydia bolted to her feet. "No!"

Samuel took her hand. "I made a rash statement, Lydi. He was insistent on the orphanage, saying he didn't want to be a father anymore, and I...I told him we'd keep her."

Lydia dropped back into her chair. She stared at her husband, mouth gaping open. He must have taken her silence for disapproval because his words tumbled out fast and earnest.

"I know I should have talked to you first. It was rash, impulsive, but all I could think about was Charlotte and how you thought I'd abandoned you both, and I couldn't bear the thought of that happening to another child, especially one as sweet as Alice, not after everything she's been through. We did talk about maybe adopting, after all, and she deserves to have a happy home, and who knows how long she'd wait for that at an orphanage, or even if she'd get a happy home... Why are you crying?"

How hadn't she seen it sooner? Samuel had promised to love her, to cherish her, and to wait as long as it took for her to love him back. This man—this good, caring man—wanted to take in another child because he didn't want Alice to be alone. He'd taken on care of the town because it was his ministry. He was everything she'd known before and more. There was a maturity about him that hadn't been there at eighteen, but he was still her Samuel.

She'd fallen in love with him again. Hearing that he'd take in another man's daughter that easily sealed the realization.

"Lydia?" Samuel took her other hand, concern on his face. "I'm sorry if I made the wrong decision. But I think we could be good parents to..."

She cut him off with a kiss.

When she pulled back, he chuckled softly. "Does that mean you approve?"

"Yes. I love that your heart is so big."

Despite the exhaustion in his eyes, they twinkled. "Yeah?

That's a step in the right direction." He winked. "One of these days, you'll be telling me that you love me."

His tone was teasing, lighthearted, but hope hid under the surface. She knew he wanted to hear those words, and she could finally say them. Lydia squeezed his hands. "And if that day is today?"

Confusion blanketed his face. He tilted his head, squinting at her. "What are you saying?"

"I'm saying I love you, Sam, and I'm blessed to be growing our little family with you. Alice will be a wonderful addition. I think Ruby will like having a sister."

"Lydi," Samuel breathed. He dropped her hands, reaching up to cup her cheeks. "Truly? You love me?"

She laughed. "I don't know when exactly I fell, but yes, I'm in love with you. It was inevitable, I think, especially once I discovered you'd never abandoned me or Charlotte. My biggest regret is that we lived apart for so many years, with me angry at you over something out of your control."

He huffed, some of the joy fading from his eyes. "Considering how I feel about Mr. Curtis right now, I can't say I blame you."

"I don't understand how he could do this, but his loss is our gain. Did he leave?"

"Yeah. He bolted out the front door for the train station as soon as I said we'd take Alice. Never once looked back."

Lydia frowned. "I wonder if he wanted to be a father when he married Mrs. Curtis. It was obvious he loved his wife, but he never asked about Alice when I was caring for them. That struck me as odd." She gasped. "Oh! Sam, how are we going to tell her?"

Samuel shook his head. "I don't know. We could say she's gaining two parents and a sister, all of whom will love her, but that's not going to ease the pain. It's going to take time. Being abandoned so young..." Tears shone in his eyes.

"And she's grieving her mother."

He rested one hand on her shoulder. "We'll figure it out. We're in this together, and we'll find a way to break the news."

"All right." She pushed his bowl toward him. "Finish eating. You need the nourishment."

"Food can wait. I want to make sure I wasn't dreaming a moment ago."

When she raised her brow, he grinned. "You know—about us and love."

"Do you want me to say it again?"

Samuel looped his arms around her waist. "If it's not too much trouble."

Laughing, she leaned closer. "I love you, Samuel Allen. 'Til my dying day."

He responded with a kiss that curled her toes.

❧

*L*ydia hummed as she cleaned her classroom. School was back in session, and her students had just departed. Alice and Ruby played in the schoolyard, enjoying the mild winter day. Lydia ran her dust cloth over a windowsill. She paused, gazing out at the mountains. They rose tall and majestic, white-capped against the cloudless blue sky.

Beautiful.

She smiled. Resting her head against the glass, she thanked God for the peace that had settled over her family. She'd finally convinced Samuel to take a few days off, to allow himself some rest after a grueling several weeks. They planned to have a dinner date this evening. Cassie offered to watch the girls while Samuel and Lydia enjoyed their time together. The only thing left to do was tell Alice about her father—something they hadn't quite figured out yet.

Footsteps sounded outside, coming closer until they moved into the classroom.

Lydia turned with a smile. "Are you girls ready to go—oh."

Mrs. Holt stood nearby, twisting a handkerchief in her hands. "I hope I'm not interrupting."

"Not at all." Lydia clenched the dust cloth behind her back. "Do you feel fully recovered?"

"Yes, thank you. Your husband was very helpful."

"I'm glad."

Silence pulsed heavily between them. What more could Mrs. Holt have to say?

Lydia walked to her desk, putting the dust cloth back in its drawer. She put one hand on her stomach and faced the other woman. "Can I help you with something?"

"I've come to ask your forgiveness."

She'd have been less surprised if Mrs. Holt turned a cartwheel and stood on her head. Lydia gaped, her hand falling to her side. "What?"

"Mrs. Allen, I've been petty and rude to you, even before Pastor Allen came to town. During my illness, I was convicted of my actions. I did not behave the way a Christian should. There are no excuses. Please forgive me and allow me to make things right."

"I...how?"

Mrs. Holt took a step toward her, hands reaching out. "I'll talk to the school board, ask them to let you keep your job."

That, at least, had an easy answer. Lydia shook her head. "Thank you for the offer, but over the last few weeks, I've prayed about what to do next. While I love teaching, my place is beside Samuel, helping him with his ministry and raising our family. That's where I want to be."

Mrs. Holt's face fell. "Are you sure?"

Lydia moved around the desk, coming to a stop in front of

her. "I'm sure. I appreciate your offer, though." She placed a hand on Mrs. Holt's shoulder. "And I forgive you."

Tears filled the woman's eyes. "Thank you, Mrs. Allen." She released a breathy laugh. "I told all this to your husband but asked him not to say anything unless...well, unless I died from my illness. I promise to be civil from now on."

Smiling, Lydia stepped back. "Good to know."

They said their goodbyes, Mrs. Holt looking less pinched than Lydia had ever seen her, and parted ways. Lydia closed up the building, then smiled at her girls. "Are you ready to go home?"

Ruby skipped toward her. "Mama, Alice wants to ask you something."

"All right." Lydia held out a hand to each girl. As they started walking, she asked, "What's on your mind, Alice?"

Alice's grip on her hand tightened. "Do I have to go back home?" Her voice sounded tight, strained.

Breath whooshed out of Lydia's lungs. She strove for calm. "Why do you ask?"

"I don't want to go back. I want to stay with you and Pastor Allen and Ruby. You're nice." Alice flung her arms around Lydia. "Please let me stay."

Lydia knelt. "What's wrong, Alice?"

Alice sniffed. "Papa doesn't want me." Her lips wobbled as she spoke. "I heard him tell Mama I'm a burden."

Heat rushed through Lydia's body. She pulled Alice into a tight hug, angry for her. No child should hear or believe such things. If Mr. Curtis were here, he'd have a mama bear to contend with.

Pushing down the anger, Lydia framed Alice's face. This wasn't how she thought telling Alice would come about, but maybe it wouldn't be as devastating as she thought. "Sweetie, your papa left town. He's not coming back."

Alice stared at her. "He's not here?"

"No."

"And he didn't take me with him?" Hurt flashed over Alice's face.

Lydia bit her lip. Or maybe her first instincts were correct. "No, Alice. I'm sorry."

Fear joined the hurt. Alice trembled and grabbed Lydia's shoulders. "Do I have to go to an orphanage?"

Ruby paled. "No! You can stay with us." She grabbed Lydia's arm. "Right, Mama?"

"Pastor Allen and I already talked about this," Lydia said, giving Alice a reassuring smile. "If you want, you can live with us and be our daughter. Would you like that?"

Alice huffed a half laugh. She clasped her hands together. "Do you mean it?"

"Absolutely. We'd love for you to be part of our family."

Worry flitted over Alice's face. "I wouldn't be a burden?"

Wishing Mr. Curtis were here to get a piece of her mind, Lydia shook her head. "Never."

"Are you sure Pastor Allen won't think so?"

The tremor in Alice's voice broke Lydia's heart. "Sweetie, it was his idea to take you in. He didn't want you going to an orphanage."

Hope lit Alice's eyes.

Lydia stood, holding her hand out again. "Why don't we go ask him what he thinks about this?"

"Papa will be happy," Ruby stated. "He likes kids. He wants a whole passel of 'em." She paused. "What's a passel, Mama?"

Holding back a smile, Lydia said, "It means a lot."

"Does that mean me and Alice will get more sisters?"

"God willing. And probably some brothers too."

Ruby wrinkled her nose. "But I like sisters."

"You like Isaiah. Wouldn't it be fun to have a brother like him?"

Alice's gaze turned wistful. "I always wanted brothers and sisters, but Papa said one was enough."

Ruby tugged on Lydia's hand. "Can we have a sibling tomorrow?"

"That's not how it works, Ruby. It will probably be a year or so before a baby comes along." Even as she said it, Lydia was surprised at how much she wanted another child.

So much for *eventually*.

"I'll pray for a brother or sister before bed tonight," Ruby said.

Alice nodded. "Me too. Maybe we can have both."

Lydia laughed. "Slow down, girls. Let's start with one at a time, shall we?"

"We'll ask Papa what he thinks about that too. C'mon, Alice, I'll race you home." Ruby shot off down the lane, Alice close on her heels.

Since their house was in sight, Lydia picked up her pace as well. She missed Samuel. It would be good to talk with him, to discuss their respective days. How had his day off gone?

When she reached the threshold, Ruby hurried to her. "Papa's sleeping."

Lydia frowned, glancing at the clock. "Sleeping? At this hour?"

Trepidation swept over her. She raced for the stairs, not stopping until she reached their bedroom.

Samuel lay motionless under the quilt. His face was pale in the afternoon light. Sweat beaded his brow. Lydia gasped, sitting beside him and placing her hand on his forehead. Heat burned her palm.

"No," she whispered, her other hand flying over her mouth. "No!"

Sick dread slithered through her gut.

Influenza.

CHAPTER 24

*E*verything hurt.

Samuel groaned. His limbs felt heavy, his head ached, and his throat burned. Something cold pressed against his brow. He flinched, then groaned again as his head exploded in pain.

"Shh. Rest, love."

Lydia's soft voice calmed him. He tried to open his eyes, but they wouldn't move. The calm vanished, replaced by panic.

"Samuel, I'm right here. Please be still."

His wife's hands moved over his shoulders. Though it hurt, he craved her touch.

"Can you drink something?"

He couldn't even open his eyes. How was he to drink?

A cup was pressed to his lips. Samuel parted them enough to let some of the water in. He swallowed, his throat screaming as the cool liquid went down. After a few more sips, he turned his head away.

Why couldn't he open his eyes?

"You've been sleeping for days." Worry tinged Lydia's voice. He wanted to reach out to her, to comfort her, but he couldn't.

She went on. "You need to fight, Sam. I've lost you once. I can't lose you again." Her voice broke. "Not when there's so much for you to live for. Your ministry. Our love. Our girls. Our future children."

Something wet fell on his cheeks. Was she crying?

"Come back to me, Sam. Please. I love you."

Words he'd longed to hear again for years. When she said them the other day, he'd been out of his mind with joy. They'd stayed up late that night, talking about their hopes for the future and for their family. Everything had fallen into place. As he held Lydia close as she slept, he thanked God for bringing them together again.

It wouldn't all be taken away now, would it?

A cold, damp rag brushed across his fevered skin. Samuel shivered, wishing he could push it away. As it passed over his eyes, they cracked open. He blinked in the dim light.

Lydia gasped. "Sam?" She gripped his hand. "Open your eyes more, love."

His eyelids drooped. They were too heavy. He could just make out Lydia's features. So beautiful, his wife. So passionate and loving. She felt deeply, for good or ill. He could only imagine how she felt now.

He struggled to fully wake. Blast this fevered delirium. He couldn't get his body to cooperate. Giving Lydia's hand a weak squeeze, he sank back into the bed and let himself rest.

$\sim$

"*L*ydia, you need to eat."

She shook her head, holding Samuel's hand tighter. "I'm not leaving him."

Ella crossed her arms. A motherly look shone from her green eyes. "Do you remember when Cody was in the hospital, and you made sure I ate? I'm returning the favor."

"I'm not hungry," Lydia mumbled. "And you shouldn't be here. You might get sick."

"I already was."

Lydia snapped her gaze up. "What? I don't remember Samuel being called to your house."

"It was mild. I didn't feel well for about three days, then recovered. There was no danger. Isaiah and Addie also had mild cases. We were fortunate." Her eyes softened as she studied Samuel. "How's he doing?"

"He's been in and out of consciousness for four days. I try to have him drink when he's awake, but it never lasts long." Her chest tightened. "Frank wasn't this bad, and I lost him. What if I lose Samuel, too, Ella? I couldn't bear it."

"You'd do what you had to in order to go on. But the whole town is praying it won't come to that."

Lydia pressed her husband's hand to her heart. She watched him for any sign of wakefulness. At least he slept peacefully now. His sleep over the last few days had been fitful and restless.

"How are the girls?" she asked, her gaze remaining on Samuel.

"They're worried about him, but I think having Isaiah and Jonah to play with helps distract them."

Something in Ella's tone made Lydia look up. "What aren't you telling me?"

Ella sighed. "Come eat, Lydia. We'll talk downstairs."

"But..."

A knock sounded at the bedroom door. Travis stood just outside, hat in hand. "Howdy, ladies. Sorry for letting myself in, but I thought Lydia might need a break."

"She does. Thank you, Travis." Ella smiled at him, then looped an arm through Lydia's, pulling her to her feet. "She also needs some rest."

"No," Lydia protested. "I'll eat, but I want to be back at his side after."

Travis put his hand on her shoulder. His hazel eyes, much like hers, were serious. "Lydia, we don't need you getting sick too. You need food and rest to keep up your strength. Take some time to care for your needs. Samuel isn't going anywhere."

Her throat pinched. She took in her sleeping husband, heart hurting. "Do you promise to call me if anything changes?"

"Yes, ma'am."

"Thank you."

Ella led her to the kitchen. "Sit. Cassie sent over some hearty stew. I'll ladle it up, then we can talk."

A numb ache spread through Lydia's body. She slumped in her chair, resting her chin in her hands. "I appreciate you being here, Ella. And I'm glad you're the one watching my girls."

"They're sweet children." Ella set a steaming bowl in front of Lydia, along with a hunk of bread and a cup of tea. Lydia breathed a prayer of thanks for the food, then spooned some broth into her mouth.

The savory, meaty stew woke her hunger. Lydia ate several bites in quick succession, filling her empty belly. How long had it been since she ate something? Travis was right—she risked illness herself if this kept up.

Once she'd eaten a third of her stew, she slowed. "Now, what didn't you tell me upstairs?"

Concern flashed over Ella's face. She released a soft sigh. "The girls are scared, Lydia. Alice asks about Samuel every hour, and I can tell she worries for him. But Ruby...she's terrified. She said everyone she loves leaves her and thinks Samuel is next."

Lydia's appetite vanished. She forced herself to keep eating, but her heart ached for her girls, especially Ruby. Of course, this would be a frightening time for her.

The worst part was that Lydia couldn't reassure her daughter otherwise. Samuel's life hung in the balance. But perhaps seeing Ruby would help.

When she finished the stew, Lydia stood. "Do you think Travis would stay for a while with Samuel? I hate to leave him, but I'd like to see the girls, even if for an hour."

Ella smiled. "Cody took all the children to the café, so Ruby and Alice are nearby."

"Bless you both."

Lydia rushed up the stairs to ask Travis about staying.

He nodded. "Take all the time you need. Cass will make sure you have supper this evening too."

She thanked him again before hurrying downstairs, where Ella waited with her coat. They set off at once, and Ella let the horses trot faster than normal as they headed to the café.

Just as Ella pulled the wagon to a stop, a familiar voice reached her ears. "Lydia!"

Eyes wide, Lydia shaded her eyes from the bright sunshine. Dorothy strode down the street, beaming and waving an arm.

Lydia jumped down from the wagon and rushed to her. "Mother! You're back." She collapsed into Dorothy's arms. To her horror, sudden sobs shook her body.

"Oh, my dear girl, whatever is wrong?"

"S-Samuel is sick. Influenza."

Dorothy's body stilled. Her grip on Lydia tightened. She didn't have to speak. She'd gone through the horror of losing Charlotte and Frank as well, had experienced the sickness herself. If anyone understood what Lydia was going through, it was Dorothy.

Once she got her tears under control, Lydia pulled back slightly. She searched Dorothy's warm brown eyes. "I'm glad you're home."

Only then did she notice Dorothy wasn't alone. Her eyes widened. "John."

Samuel's mentor walked a few steps closer, coming to a stop beside Dorothy, holding two valises. Wrinkles creased his brown jacket, and his face appeared more lined than usual, but he gave her a warm nod. "Hello, Lydia. You said Samuel is ill?"

She nodded. "We had an outbreak of influenza. Samuel has been working himself to the point of exhaustion caring for the sick. We thought the worst was behind us. Everyone was getting better, and there were no new cases. Then Samuel..." She struggled to keep more tears at bay.

John dropped one of the valises to put a hand on her shoulder, his expression soft. "That sounds like Samuel. Always caring for others. Can I see him?"

Sagging with relief, Lydia nodded. "He's at home. Travis is watching over him."

"Then I'll go straightaway."

John and Dorothy exchanged a look before he left, one that had Lydia staring at her mother-in-law. "Mother..."

Dorothy shook her head. "Later, dear girl. Where were you headed?"

"To the café to see Ruby and Alice."

"Alice? Your student?"

There was so much Dorothy didn't know. Lydia took her arm. "Let's go inside, and I'll explain everything."

As soon as they entered the café, Ruby barreled into Lydia, clinging to her. "Mama!"

Lydia hugged her back, inhaling her daughter's sweet scent. "Hello, Ruby."

Ruby cried onto her shoulder. "Is Papa still sick?"

"I'm afraid so, honey. But he's being taken care of."

"He's going to leave us, too, isn't he?" Ruby asked, her eyes wild.

Lydia swallowed. "I hope not. We need to keep praying he gets better."

"My first mama and papa got sick and left. Granny got sick

and left. Now Papa is sick." Ruby sobbed, burying her face in Lydia's neck. Her words came out muffled. "Everyone leaves."

Dorothy knelt beside them. "Your papa is young and strong, Ruby. If anyone can pull through, he can."

Lydia bit her lip. Frank had been young and strong, but the same illness took him.

Ruby pulled back, blinking rapidly. Her mouth dropped open. "Grandma?" She flung herself into Dorothy's waiting arms.

Lydia stood, searching the room with her gaze. Alice stood with Ella and Cody. Lydia opened her arms, and the little girl flew to her. For several moments, they embraced without speaking.

Finally, Ella tapped her shoulder. "Why don't you all have a seat? Cassie will bring you cookies and hot cocoa."

It took some coaxing to get Ruby to a chair, but soon they were all seated with their treats.

Dorothy took a sip of cocoa before turning her gaze to Lydia. "Now, why don't you tell me what's happened since I left?"

Words flooded out of Lydia. She told Dorothy about settling into married life, the Allens' visit, the revelation that Samuel never knew about Charlotte, and Alice's story.

When she finished, Dorothy sat back with wide eyes. "Oh, my. You've had a rather intense three months."

"Yes."

Her mother-in-law's gaze softened, a small smile pulling at her lips. "And you've fallen in love with Samuel, haven't you?"

"I have." Tears burned Lydia's eyes yet again. Was there no end to the water her body produced? "I finally told him—the night before he got sick."

Dorothy squeezed her hand. "Oh, my dear."

Lydia glanced at her girls. They were talking with Ella as they ate their cookies. Lowering her voice, Lydia leaned closer to Dorothy. "I can't lose him again. My heart might never recover."

"He's strong, Lydia. I think he'll make it."

"Mother, you of all people know it can take anyone. Frank should have pulled through."

With a sad smile, Dorothy shook her head. "Frank had scarlet fever when he was three. It weakened his heart. There were several times after that he got sick and had to fight harder than most to overcome the illness." She heaved a sigh. "Unfortunately, his body wasn't strong enough to fight the influenza when it came."

Stunned, Lydia sat back. "I didn't know."

"We didn't talk about it much. I think Frank hoped to put the past behind him." Dorothy picked up her cup again. "All that to say, Samuel should pull through." She smiled, her gaze on the girls. "Besides, he has so much to live for."

A thread of hope wound its way through Lydia's heart. "I pray you're right." She leaned forward, desperate for a distraction. "Tell me about that look you and John shared."

Dorothy's eyes sparkled. "I have some news..."

~

*I*t was so hot.

Samuel cracked his eyes open. He thrashed, his legs churning to kick the heavy weight off his body

"Easy, Samuel. No need to mutilate the poor blanket."

He must be dreaming. Turning his head to the side, Samuel blinked several times. His mentor did not disappear from sight. "John?" he croaked.

"Hey, son."

"Wh-what are you doing here?" He blinked again, hard. "Am I asleep?"

John chuckled. "No, you're quite awake. Dorothy and I just

got back to town. We met Lydia near the café. She seemed pretty torn up."

Lydia.

Samuel pushed himself upright, but a wave of nausea made him groan. "Oh..."

"Take it easy." John lowered him back onto the bed. "I'm guessing you've been sick a while. Still are, if that flush on your face is any indication. Here, drink this."

John pressed a cup into his hands. Samuel lifted it and took a sip. The cool water felt good against his parched throat. He gulped down more, suddenly realizing how thirsty he was. And hungry.

In confirmation, his stomach rumbled.

John grinned. "That's a good sign. Let me go rustle up some food."

Samuel rested against the headboard. His head ached, but it felt good to be sitting rather than lying down. Flashes of memory during his illness flitted through his mind. Lydia had cared for him ceaselessly. Was she safe from influenza? Or would she come down with it as well?

Please, Lord, keep her safe.

His mind turned over the words she'd spoken the night before he fell sick. She loved him. Just the memory sent warmth rushing through his body. The great desire of his heart had been fulfilled. He had a wife who loved him, two beautiful daughters, and a future full of hope. Despite his current weakness, he'd never been so happy.

Thank You, Lord.

John returned with a bowl of soup. "Do you want me to feed you, or can you handle it?"

"I think I can manage, thanks."

Samuel settled the bowl in his lap. The first sip nearly made him groan. "It's delicious."

"I reckon so." John crossed his arms, leaning back in his chair. "You've likely not had a meal in some time."

Taking another bite, Samuel frowned. "How long was I sick?"

"I don't know, but Lydia looked exhausted. My guess is at least a week."

His heart ached at the thought of Lydia caring for him, worrying for him—especially after what happened with Charlotte and Frank. A sudden longing to see her, to hold her, took hold.

"You're not getting out of that bed."

Samuel blinked. "How did you know what I was thinking?"

Chuckling, John shrugged. "It's in your eyes. You were about ready to charge after your wife, but you wouldn't have gotten far. You're still sick, remember?"

His pounding head and aching body confirmed that.

"Don't worry, Samuel. Lydia is with Dorothy, and that means she'll be getting the care she needs. I'm sure they'll be back before too long. A woman in love wants to be with her husband when he's sick."

Samuel froze, the spoon halfway to his mouth. "How'd you know she's in love with me?"

"Other than my uncanny perception skills?" John grinned. "You just confirmed it."

Shaking his head, Samuel laughed softly. "You're right. As usual."

"I'm happy for you, son. Dorothy and I prayed you two would overcome the past."

"It's quite a story, and you'll hear it soon." Samuel cocked his head. "But first, I have some questions."

"Go ahead."

"As glad as I am to see you, what are you doing here? I thought you'd be back in Chicago by now."

A wide grin spread over John's face. "Dorothy and I are getting married, and we want you to perform the ceremony."

CHAPTER 25

*L*ydia wasn't sure she'd ever fully understand the workings of the heart. Dorothy hadn't shown interest in another man since her husband died ten years ago. Now, a matter of months after meeting John, they were getting married.

Dorothy took her arm as they walked back to the house. "Are you sure you're okay with this?"

"I'm surprised but happy. You deserve it, Mother. John is a good man."

"He is, isn't he?"

Dorothy glowed. She let out a girlish chuckle. "Finding love again at my age. I never thought it possible."

Lydia smiled. She hugged Dorothy's arm close. "I'm also glad you'll have someone to spend your days with. I was a little concerned with you living alone."

"I certainly won't be alone." Dorothy's grin softened. "With John retired, he can move to Harmony Springs without needing permission. He has said if Samuel needs help, he's happy to provide it as a secondary pastor."

The mention of her husband made Lydia's heart squeeze. She paused, bringing both of them to a stop.

Dorothy watched her silently for a moment. "Lydia, do you trust that God has a plan?"

The abrupt change in topic proved her mother-in-law knew where Lydia's mind had gone. "I...of course."

"Do you trust that His will is best?"

"Yes."

"Even if it means Samuel is taken from you?"

Lydia caught her breath. Her voice refused to work.

Dorothy leaned closer. "My dear girl, you can't let fear hold you captive. We can't change what's going to be. But we can choose to trust, no matter what may come."

Tears warred with a wry laugh. "You sound like Samuel."

"He's a wise man." Dorothy patted her hand. "And the odds are good that he'll pull through."

One by one, the muscles in Lydia's shoulders relaxed. She hadn't realized how much tension she held until it released. As they began walking again, Dorothy remained quiet, giving Lydia time to think.

She shuddered at the thought of life without Samuel. Now that they'd found each other again, she couldn't imagine letting him go.

But if she was asked to? Could she trust God through such a tragedy?

Looking up at the sky, Lydia crossed her arms over her stomach. *I don't want You to take him, Lord. Please...please let him stay with me, with our girls.*

A voice whispered through her soul. *And if he dies?*

Her throat felt thick, tears pricking her eyes. She inhaled a long breath and held it for a few seconds. Letting go, she allowed the tears to fall. *Thy will be done.*

Peace enveloped her. The fear didn't dissipate, but she knew whatever happened, she'd have the strength to bear it.

Come what may.

When they arrived home, she stood outside the door, not ready to go in. Not ready to face what she might find.

Dorothy took her arm. "Come, dear girl. We'll check on him together."

Giving Dorothy a shaky smile, Lydia stepped inside and moved toward the stairs. She clung to the banister and prayed for strength. When they reached her and Samuel's room, she breathed one more prayer and pushed the door open.

Her gaze landed on her husband. He sat in the bed, chuckling at something John said. Lydia's knees buckled. She sank to the floor, tears of relief pouring from her eyes.

Samuel straightened, panic in his gaze. "Lydi!" He pushed aside the covers and tried to rise.

John restrained him. "Sam, stay put. You're not strong enough to get up."

Dorothy helped Lydia to her feet. "Go to him, dear girl, or the man is liable to hurt himself."

Weeping, Lydia climbed onto the bed. She grasped Samuel's hands and held them to her heart. "You're awake."

He gently freed one of his hands, reaching up to wipe tears from her cheeks. "Sweetheart, why are you crying?"

"I was so scared, Sam. I thought we might lose you." She buried her face in his neck. The heat from his skin was warm but not hot. Thank God. "But you're still here."

His fingers combed through her hair. "Tears of relief?" he murmured.

She nodded. "Ruby and Alice will be happy you're on the mend too." With a gasp, she bolted upright. "The girls! They need to know you're all right."

John held up a hand. "Let's wait until morning, see where Samuel's at. He still has signs of sickness. We don't want the girls to be exposed unnecessarily."

Samuel slumped back against the pillows. "I am pretty

tired." His gaze never left Lydia's. "Maybe you should sleep in the girls' room tonight. I don't want you getting sick either."

She clung to his hand. "I'm not leaving you."

"Lydi..."

"No arguing, Sam. I've been caring for you for days. If I were infected, it would have happened by now." She snuggled beside him. "You're not getting rid of me."

Dorothy put a hand on John's shoulder. "I think that's our cue to leave. Why don't we go pick up the supper Cassie made for these two?"

"Excellent notion." John stood, smiling at Lydia and Samuel. "Once we get the food, we'll be downstairs if you need anything. Holler when you're ready to eat. Or if you'd rather sleep, we'll put the meal in the icebox."

"Thanks, John, Dorothy." Samuel's eyes slipped shut. "I'm glad you're back, and I look forward to officiating your wedding."

John clapped his shoulder. "There's no rush, Sam. Focus on getting better."

He and Dorothy slipped from the room, leaving Samuel and Lydia alone. She wrapped her arms around her husband and pulled him close. "Don't ever scare me like that again, Samuel Allen."

Nuzzling her cheek, Samuel whispered, "I'll do my best."

"Good."

He lay still for a moment, eyes still closed. "How do you feel about John and Dorothy?"

"I'm happy for them. When do they want to get married?"

"As soon as I'm well again."

Lydia sucked in a breath. "So soon?"

"Mm-hmm. Something about being old enough to know their hearts and not wanting to waste precious time."

His slightly slurred sentence had Lydia pulling the covers over both of them. "You're exhausted, Sam. Get some rest."

The words had hardly left her mouth before Samuel's soft snores echoed through the room. Lydia held him, content to watch as he slept. Gratitude overwhelmed her. Smiling, she closed her own eyes.

Thank You, Lord, for bringing Sam back to health.

~

The first thing Samuel noticed the next morning was the lack of aches in his body. He stretched, delighted to move without pain. His head felt clear and cool. He breathed a prayer of thanks before realizing something warm and soft pressed against his side.

Lydia.

He ran a knuckle over her cheek. Her smooth skin was warm but not hot. He wouldn't rest easy until a week passed without her getting sick, but if she hadn't gotten influenza yet, hopefully, she wouldn't at all.

Samuel wouldn't wish what he went through on anyone. He couldn't remember ever having been so sick. Thank God the epidemic seemed to be over.

Lydia's eyelashes fluttered. Samuel turned to his side and ran a hand along her waist in slow circles. She blinked slowly, hazel eyes heavy with sleep.

"Good morning, sweetheart," he whispered, leaning forward to press a soft kiss against her lips.

She hummed in response. He nuzzled her cheek until she giggled. "Sam! I'm awake."

He could listen to that giggle all day. With deliberate movements, he found the ticklish part of her neck and rubbed his nose against it.

Lydia squealed. She kicked off the blanket and tumbled over the side of the bed. Peeking over the edge, she giggled again. "You're feeling better, I see."

"Much better." He sat up, stretching once more, a grin spreading over his face. "It's nice to feel myself again." His stomach rumbled. With a sheepish smile, he put a hand over it. "Seems I'm hungry, though."

His wife jumped to her feet. She smoothed her rumpled dress before grabbing his hand. "Let's get you fed. You've only had water or broth for the last week." She eyed his night-clothes. "Though maybe you should wash up and change first."

They both took time to wash their faces, and Samuel happily shaved the beard that had grown in during his convalescence. He changed into brown pants and a dark-blue shirt while Lydia put on a navy dress.

As they walked into the hallway, the smell of pancakes, bacon, and coffee teased his nose. Samuel winced as his stomach protested its emptiness again. Mouth watering in anticipation, he took Lydia's hand and practically pulled her down the stairs.

Dorothy met them in the kitchen with two mugs of coffee. Her warm gaze swept over Samuel, a smile on her lips. "I'm so glad to see you up and about, young man." She handed him the coffee. "Drink up. John will have breakfast ready in a couple minutes. You must be hungry."

"Famished."

He got Lydia situated before taking the seat beside her. Sipping his drink, he nearly moaned. Coffee had never tasted so good.

It paled in comparison to the food John set in front of him. After one bite, Samuel wolfed down his meal, salty and sweet flavors bursting on his tongue.

John chuckled as he watched. "Slow down, son. The food's not going anywhere."

Samuel took another drink of coffee. "I've never felt this hungry before."

"Good reason to be," Dorothy said, cutting into her

pancakes. "Now, are you two planning on getting those girls today?"

Lydia raised her brows with a glance at Samuel. "Do you feel ready for that? Are you fully recovered?"

"Yes," he replied. "I feel good, and it will be good for the girls to be home again. Alice has had so much change lately, and I imagine Ruby has been worried."

"Very much so. She was terrified we'd lose you. Both girls will be happy to see that you're better."

"Then it's settled," Samuel said. "After breakfast, I'll hitch up a buggy and we'll get our girls."

Thirty minutes later, they were on their way to the Brooks' farm. Samuel's stomach was pleasantly full, and he drew in deep breaths of the cold air. Spring would be upon them soon. He looked forward to the warmer temperatures and budding trees. For now, though, winter still held on to Harmony Springs.

When they pulled into the Brooks' yard, Samuel smiled at the familiar log house. The large porch gave a welcoming feel, and the pastureland that stretched as far as he eye could see made him feel peaceful. Ella came out the front door onto the porch, Rosie on her hip. Her eyes lit up when she saw Samuel. "Ruby, Alice, come see who's here," she called.

The girls came skittering out of the house, followed closely by the three older Brooks children. Samuel's gaze went right to Ruby and Alice. He jumped down and held out his arms.

Ruby shrieked. She flew down the porch steps and threw herself against him. "Papa, you're better!"

"That I am, sweet girl. I missed you."

"I missed you too. We prayed every night that you would get well."

He eased back, smiling at his daughter. "Thank you for the prayers."

Alice still stood on the porch. Her hands clasped in front of her, and she bounced on her toes, but she didn't move.

Samuel held out a hand to her. Hesitating just a moment, Alice walked toward him, her steps slow. Ruby stood with Lydia while Samuel gave Alice a hug. "Are you all right, Alice?"

She nodded, eyes on the ground. He ducked down, peering up at her. "What's wrong?"

A little sniffle emerged from the girl. She wiped her eyes and took a shaky breath. "I'm glad you're better, but…"

Another tear trailed down her cheek. Samuel caught it with his thumb. "But what, sweetie?"

The girl's brown eyes shone with more tears. "Why didn't God let my mama get better? Why did she die?"

His heart dropped. The child's grief was palpable. Samuel put his hands on her shoulders, maintaining eye contact. "I don't know, Alice. We'll probably never know why God took your mama to heaven when He did. You know what I do know, though?"

"What?" she asked, her voice small.

"I know that you'll always be loved and cherished in our home. Mrs. Allen and I will treat you as our daughter, because you are. You'll be safe with us, and hopefully, happy."

She bit her lip, her gaze falling once more. "Are you sure? You didn't change your mind about wanting me? I don't want to be a burden."

His grip tightened slightly. "Alice, look at me." He waited until her gaze met his. "You are not a burden. You never will be. You are a precious gift from God. If your pa couldn't see that, it was his loss. I'm happy to have you with us."

With a little sob, Alice threw herself into his arms. Samuel held her and let her cry. Lydia knelt beside them, Ruby at her side, and the four of them formed a small family circle, providing comfort where they could.

Ruby laid her head on Samuel's shoulder once Alice's tears abated. "Papa, can we go home now?"

"Yeah. Let's get your things from Mrs. Brooks."

They climbed the porch steps to where Ella waited with a smile, her children surrounding her. Jonah and Addie hugged Samuel when he reached the top, one on each leg. Isaiah gave Lydia a hug before shaking Samuel's hand.

Ella gave her children a warm smile, then shifted Rosie in her arms while facing Samuel. "It's good to see you up and about, Samuel," she said.

"Thanks, ma'am. I appreciate you and Cody caring for the girls over the last week."

"It was no trouble. They played well with my children." Ella put a hand on Isaiah's shoulder. "I think this one will miss them the most."

Isaiah crossed his arms, a pout on his lips. "Do they have to go? Can't they stay a little longer?"

Lydia crouched in front of her student. "Tell you what. Why don't we set up a day for you to come over and play with the girls after school? Would you like that?"

He perked up at once. "Yeah! How's tomorrow?"

Lydia laughed. She ruffled his hair and straightened. "I'll set it up with your mama."

"Thanks, Mrs. Allen!" He bounced on his toes. "We'll go get Ruby's and Alice's things."

The two girls hadn't left Samuel's side. Isaiah took his brother's hand and darted into the house.

Samuel rested his hands on the girls' shoulders. "Do you want to go help them get your things together?"

Ruby's gaze darted between him and the house. "You'll stay right here?"

"I promise."

"All right." She took Alice's hand. "C'mon. Let's pack so we can go home."

Ella bounced a fussy Rosie. "Can I offer you anything to drink while you're here?"

"Thank you, but no," Lydia said. "We're going to take time to readjust to having everyone home." She chuckled. "And there's a wedding to plan."

"I overheard that at the café." Ella grinned. "How lovely for Dorothy and John."

"You're invited, of course," Samuel said. "They don't want a big to-do, but I know Dorothy loves your family and would want you there."

"That's sweet of her." Ella switched Rosie to her other hip. "We'd be happy to come."

The children returned moments later. Isaiah handed one sack to Ruby and another to Alice. "Remember, we'll get to play again soon."

Ruby hugged her friend. "Thanks, Isaiah."

The little boy's cheeks turned red. He mumbled something about seeing to Addie and darted back into the house.

With a laugh, Samuel slid an arm around Lydia. "That brings back memories," he whispered.

His wife grinned.

He turned to Ella. "We might have to watch those two in about ten years."

She laughed. "Maybe so."

They said their goodbyes, and Samuel led his family to the buggy, lifting each one in by turn. When he climbed in beside them, he took up the reins with a grin.

"Let's go home."

CHAPTER 26

Three days later, Samuel stood at the front of the church, John by his side. The older man fidgeted with his blue tie. "Are you sure I look all right?"

Chuckling, Samuel clapped John's back. "Yep. Dorothy won't be able to take her eyes off you."

John straightened his tie yet again. His gaze darted from the church doors to Samuel. "Thanks for helping us get this wedding together. I know it was short notice."

"Happy to be of service. After all you've done for me over the years, this is the least I could do." He glanced at his pocket watch. "The ladies will be here in about five minutes. You ready?"

John's grin answered him.

The door opened, revealing the Brooks and Doyle families. Samuel greeted them and escorted them to their seats in the front row.

Isaiah tugged on his jacket. "Pastor Allen, can Ruby and Alice play with me after the wedding?"

"Of course. We're all heading to the café afterward, and

there will be plenty of time to play." He leaned closer and winked. "I hear there's going to be cake too."

Isaiah's eyes lit up. He poked his brother. "Did ya hear that, Jonah? Cake!"

Ella laughed, shaking her head. "They'll be running circles around us after that."

Her husband nudged her. "At least that means they'll crash tonight and sleep well."

"Hopefully."

Samuel chuckled. Before he could respond, three taps sounded at the door, the signal that Dorothy had arrived. He resumed his place at the front. "All right, everyone. The bride is here." Turning to John, he clasped his hand. "Let's get you married."

Lydia opened the door. Samuel caught his breath at the sight of his wife. She wore the same rose dress she'd donned for their wedding. Just as stunning now as she'd been then, she took his breath away.

John elbowed him in the side. "Breathe, man. You're turning red."

Lydia grinned, her knowing gaze on him. Samuel straightened his shoulders and grinned back. Let her see how she affected him. It wasn't a secret.

She turned to usher Ruby and Alice into the room. The two girls wore their best dresses, both in pink, and they started down the aisle with winter greenery as small bouquets. Once they reached the front of the church, they stood on either side of John and Samuel.

Dorothy came through the door. Her blue dress, matching John's tie, swished as she walked. She slid an arm through Lydia's, and together, they walked toward John.

Samuel glanced at his mentor. John's eyes were shiny, his gaze never leaving Dorothy. A wide grin filled his face. When

Dorothy stood before him, he took both her hands in his. "You're beautiful, my love."

Her cheeks flushed a pretty shade of pink.

Lydia slipped to the side, standing beside Alice.

Samuel began the ceremony. "John and Dorothy, we're all honored to be here today to celebrate this special occasion. You've chosen to commit your lives to one another in a second chance at love. That is a gift, one to be cherished."

As he went through the ceremony, he was touched by the genuine emotion behind both older adults' vows. Their love had grown quickly, but it was true. Hopefully, they had many years of wedded bliss ahead.

"I now pronounce you man and wife. John, you may kiss the bride."

John leaned forward, planting a gentle kiss on Dorothy's lips.

Lydia smiled, her hands over her heart. "Congratulations, you two." She hugged Dorothy. "I'm glad you found love again, Mother."

"So am I, dear girl. I'm glad you did too."

Lydia glanced at Samuel, a shy smile on her lips. "I couldn't be happier."

His heart jolted. Would it be inappropriate to kiss his wife in front of a group like this? Before he could decide, Lydia embraced John and wished him happy. Samuel then shook hands with his mentor. "You're a married man again, my friend."

"I'm blessed," John replied, his gaze trained on his new wife.

The other guests rose to offer their congratulations. A swirl of happy exclamations filled the church while the children giggled and caught the excitement of the adults. In the commotion, Samuel slipped an arm around Lydia's waist and pulled her to the side.

She rested a hand on his chest. "You did a beautiful job with the ceremony. I've never seen Dorothy happier."

"Did this bring back memories of our wedding?"

With a chuckle, Lydia nodded. "Ours had a much different tone, but everything turned out well."

"Would you want a vow renewal now that we're in love?"

She shook her head. "We meant those vows, Sam. Things might have changed since our wedding, but that was never in doubt. I don't need a vow renewal—I just need your love from day to day."

He leaned his forehead against hers. "That's all I need too."

Shooting a glance at the others, he smiled when he saw no one looking in their direction. "If you have no objections, I'd like to kiss my beautiful wife."

She smiled and moved closer. "I have no objections."

"Wonderful."

Samuel lowered his lips to hers. For several sweet moments, he lingered, drinking her in. "I love you, Lydi."

She kissed him once more. "I love you too."

They were interrupted by Ruby's little voice. "Ugh. Are you two ever going to stop kissing?"

Samuel pulled back, grinning at Lydia before turning to Ruby. "No, ma'am. I quite enjoy kissing your mama."

"Yuck." Ruby made a face. "I'm never kissing a boy."

Samuel bit back a laugh. "Talk to me in about ten years, sweetie."

Ruby shook her head and skipped away to Alice and Isaiah.

A laugh broke free from Lydia. Her eyes sparkled as she smiled up at Samuel. "I shared her sentiments at that age."

"Thank God you grew out of it." Samuel tugged her close again. "Now, where were we?"

*T*he atmosphere at the café was joyful and relaxed. Cassie had closed it down to give Dorothy and John a dinner reception, complete with a chocolate wedding cake.

Lydia sat with Ella and Cassie, watching Dorothy and John play jacks with the children after they all ate. "I'm not sure if the adults or kids are having more fun with that game."

Cassie adjusted Connor on her lap. "It's a toss up."

"Dorothy's been something of a grandma to all our children," Ella said. "John will probably fill the role of grandpa." She grinned. "It's as though our kids are cousins."

Lydia chuckled. "Well, yours and Cassie's actually are cousins."

"And yours are honorary ones, which is basically the same thing. Some family you're born with. Some family you choose." Cassie took a sip of her tea. "Speaking of family...Ella, you said you had a letter from your sister?"

Ella pulled a folded missive from her pocket. She smoothed it on the table. "I wrote to Tori after Dr. Lewis suggested we advertise for a doctor in our town. She'll finish medical school at the end of spring term."

"Did she say she'd like to come here?" Lydia asked, leaning forward.

"Not exactly." Ella sighed. "She said she'd love to have her own practice in Harmony Springs, but she'll have to pass board exams after graduation and then spend at least a year under a more experienced doctor before she can start a practice of her own. Which I understand. And it's unlikely people here would want a woman fresh out of school as their physician. Still..."

Lydia covered Ella's hand. "You wish you could have your sister here."

"Yes. I miss her terribly. She doesn't want to stay in Boston forever, not with our parents there, but that is where her future is, at least for a time." She brightened. "But she did promise to visit when she could."

"Tori would have been a great addition to town," Lydia said. "I enjoyed getting to know her a bit when she last visited. She's quite vivacious."

Ella laughed. "Yes, that word describes her well." A mischievous smile pulled at her lips. "Maybe we could all pray that God will lead her here sooner than later."

"Hear, hear." Cassie raised her glass. "Perhaps we can find her someone to love as well. There are several eligible men in town."

Hesitation flitted over Ella's face. She shook her head, eyes troubled. "Tori thinks love is a burden, not a blessing."

Lydia cupped her mug with a frown. "I thought she started believing true love was possible after seeing you and Cody together."

"So did I. But the first letter I received from her after she went back to Boston proved her mind hadn't changed." Ella glanced down, fiddling with her sleeve. "If you knew our father, that would come as no surprise."

Cassie put a hand over Ella's. "He can't hurt you anymore."

"No, but he can make Tori's life miserable. I shudder to think of what she might be suffering under his thumb." She sighed, then huffed a small chuckle. "Though she can take care of herself. She never let him rule over her like I did."

Lydia took Ella's other hand. "The past is in the past. Don't let it rob you of your joy now."

Ella chuckled, giving her a knowing look. "Words of wisdom you lived yourself."

"Exactly, so take my word for it."

All three of them laughed.

Two strong hands landed on Lydia's shoulders. Samuel leaned in, his cheek beside hers. "I hate to interrupt, but it might be time to take our girls home. They're starting to yawn."

Sure enough, both girls hid yawns behind their hands. Lydia smiled at her friends. "It's been a pleasure, ladies. See you soon."

They exchanged hugs, and Samuel and Lydia said their goodbyes to Dorothy and John before gathering their children and heading home.

"Did you girls have fun?" Lydia asked.

Alice slipped a hand into hers. "Yes. I liked playing with the other children best."

"Me too. Grandma looked really pretty." Ruby turned to Lydia. "Does this mean Mr. Rivers is our grandpa now?"

"I guess it does. Are you happy about that?"

Ruby clapped her hands. "Yeah. I never had a grandpa before. Now I have two!" She giggled. "Two grandpas and grandmas, a mama and a papa, and a sister. More family than I ever dreamed." After a moment, her face clouded. "But..."

Lydia paused. She lowered herself to one knee. "But what, Ruby?"

Ruby bit her lip and tugged at a black curl. "Is it okay that I still miss Granny?"

"You'll always miss your granny, honey," Samuel said, kneeling beside them. "She's going to have a place in your heart forever."

"So being happy with my new family wouldn't make her sad?"

Lydia shook her head. "Not at all. She'd be happy for you. I think that's why she wanted me and your papa to get together." She smiled at Samuel. "She knew we'd all make each other happy." Lydia pulled Alice closer to her side. "And she'd be thrilled that you girls are sisters."

Alice bumped into Ruby. "I like having a sister."

Ruby hugged her, laughing. "So do I."

Samuel leaned into Lydia, helping her to her feet as the

girls skipped ahead. "I'm thankful we've been given such a beautiful family. We've been blessed."

Lydia slid her arm through his. "Our start wasn't promising, but God brought good out of it."

"A fact I praise Him for every day."

They resumed their walk in companionable silence. Lydia rested her head on his shoulder, gazing up at the sky as stars began twinkling above. "I can't believe we had to come across the country to find each other again."

"It makes our reunion that much more miraculous." Samuel kissed her cheek. "What do you say to trying a new recipe once the girls are in bed?"

Lydia raised a brow in question.

Her husband chuckled. "I might have convinced Cassie to share a recipe with me." He pulled a small notecard from his pocket. "What do you think?"

Lydia squinted, trying to make out the words in the dim twilight. When she finally deciphered the title, she put a hand to her mouth. "Cinnamon jumbles?"

"Yep."

Laughing, Lydia threw her arms around him. "You keep finding ways to surprise me. This is amazing."

"So that's a yes?"

"That's a resounding yes."

He drew her into an embrace, leaving a lingering kiss on her forehead. "Good."

Lydia rested her head against his chest. The warmth from his body fought off the chill in the air. She snuggled close, content to be held in his arms. After everything they'd been through, they were once more where they belonged.

Together.

EPILOGUE

THREE MONTHS LATER

A cool morning breeze rustled Lydia's hair as she stood by the open window in her hotel room. She took in the vast ocean before her, listening to the waves crash against the shore. She inhaled deeply, relishing the salty sea air.

It was more beautiful than she'd ever imagined. Endless blue water stretched into an even bluer sky. Seagulls called to each other, their voices carrying on the wind. White sand covered the beach, beckoning her to sink her toes into the soft depths.

Samuel had surprised her with a summer wedding trip. Dorothy and John agreed to watch the girls, and John was taking over pastoring duties while Lydia and Samuel vacationed in California. They were staying at the new Hotel del Coronado in San Diego, and their room had a stunning view of the ocean. Lydia hadn't been able to see it in all its glory when they arrived last night, but now she drank it in. She'd been awake for thirty minutes and hadn't left her spot at the window.

It warmed her heart that Samuel had made one of her life-long dreams come true.

The door opened to reveal her husband. He smiled, holding something behind his back. "Are you ready for your surprise?"

She chuckled. "Sam, you've already given me the best surprise. What more could there be?"

"Close your eyes."

He sounded so excited, Lydia laughed as she complied. She had a surprise of her own, but she'd wait until he revealed his.

His footsteps approached before he placed a package in her hands. Her eyes flew open, and she eagerly tore off the paper.

A strange outfit lay beneath the wrapping. She held it up, tilting her head back and forth. It was a navy-blue dress, of sorts, with long sleeves and a high neck, but with a skirt that would only reach her knees at most. Her gaze fell to the other wad of fabric—were those bloomers or trousers? Perhaps a combination of both.

She looked up at Samuel. "What is it?"

"A bathing dress. You wear it in the water."

Eyes widening, she clutched the clothes to her chest. "We can go in the water?"

He grinned. "We sure can. I've got a bathing suit as well. Why don't we try these on and then head outside?"

Gratitude swelled in her heart. Dropping the bathing dress and trousers on the bed, Lydia slid her arms around Samuel's neck. "In a moment." She pushed up on tiptoes and pressed her lips to his.

He grunted in surprise, but within seconds, he wrapped her in his arms and delivered a passionate kiss that had her melting against him. When they broke apart, he raised his brows. "Maybe the beach can wait."

She laughed, swatting his chest. "I've been waiting all night to feel the sand under my feet."

"So what's another hour?" He winked and dodged her

second swat. "All right, let's change and get down there. I hear the water calling my name."

As he turned to change into his bathing clothes, Lydia bit her lip. Should she reveal her surprise now? She glanced out the window. No, the outdoor setting would be a better spot. Anticipation welled within as she put on her own bathing outfit. It struck her as strange to don such unfamiliar clothing, but it would feel good to go into the water.

Five minutes later, they stepped out on the sand. Lydia wiggled her toes, burying them as deep as she could. Giggling, she let them stay a few moments before scampering toward the waves. "Race you to the water!" she called to Samuel.

He beat her easily. With a chuckle, he held out a hand and nodded at the beautiful ocean. "Shall we?"

She took his hand, letting him lead her in until their feet were submerged by several inches. Lydia sighed with pleasure. The waves lapped against her legs, soaking the trousers up to her knees. "This feels wonderful."

Samuel adjusted the large hat on her head. "We don't want to stay out too long. I don't want you to burn."

"Okay." She turned hopeful eyes on him. "Maybe tomorrow we can actually swim."

He chuckled. "You don't want to swim now?"

"Not quite. I want to enjoy these first moments getting to know the ocean." She flushed, bringing her hands to her cheeks with a laugh. "That sounds silly."

Samuel took her hands, tugging them down. "No, it doesn't. It sounds like a woman enjoying the sight and feel of a long-time dream." He pulled her close for a sweet kiss. When he pulled back, he searched her eyes. "Do you like your surprise?"

"Very much. I couldn't imagine a better wedding trip."

His blue-green eyes lit with another smile. "I'm glad."

Lydia stepped closer, holding tight to his hand. "I have a surprise for you as well."

"Yeah?"

She cupped his cheek with her free hand. "When I became pregnant with Charlotte, I was terrified. You weren't there to share the news with, and I wasn't sure how my pregnancy would affect us. Then everything happened..."

Pain flickered in his eyes.

Lydia shook her head. "It happened, and there's nothing we can do to change it. Charlotte will always be a part of us, even if we can't be with her in this life. She ended up bringing so much joy to me, but I always wondered, if things were different, what it would have been like to share that joy with you." She brought his hand to her stomach. "Now, we can find out."

He blinked. His gaze flitted from her stomach to her face. Tentative joy flashed in his eyes. "Lydi, are you...?"

She laughed, tears blurring her vision. "We're having a baby."

Samuel whooped. He enveloped her in an exuberant embrace, his laughter mingling with hers.

Lydia held him tight. She'd never felt more thankful. God had brought them back together, mending the pain of the past and bringing them into a present brighter than either of them imagined—a second chance at love, complete with a beautiful family, a wonderful home, and now a baby on the way.

She couldn't wait to see what their future held.

∿

*T*urn the page for a sneak peek of The Doctor's Convenient Marriage, the next book in the Second Chances in Harmony Springs series!

SNEAK PEEK:

Don't miss the next book in the Second Chances in Harmony Springs *series!*

ACKNOWLEDGMENTS

I am so thankful for the opportunity to bring these stories to life, and that is because of wonderful readers like you.

Thank you to my family, immediate and extended, who encourage me and listen to me go on and on about my stories and plotlines and make suggestions for what should come next. I appreciate the support!

Thank you to Denise, who edited this book and let me know what worked, what didn't, and how to make the writing better. You are amazing, and I'm so thankful for your help.

Thank you to Cappy and Candie, who read through this manuscript and gave honest thoughts on the story, thoughts that made it better. Another thank you to Cappy for always being willing to bounce ideas and help me get through writer's block with great suggestions and thoughts on where to take the story and characters.

And finally, thank you to the Lord for the ability to write and tell stories. As the Author of Life, He is the one who wrote the story of all creation, and I am thankful to have a tiny role in mimicking that creative endeavor.

Did you enjoy this book? We hope so!
Would you take a quick minute to leave a review where you purchased the book?
It doesn't have to be long. Just a sentence or two telling what you liked about the story!

Receive a FREE ebook and get updates when new Wild Heart books release: https://wildheartbooks.org/newsletter

ABOUT THE AUTHOR

Lauralyn Keller loves to combine history and romance in stories that touch the heart. She lives in beautiful Colorado and is a member of American Christian Fiction Writers. When she's not writing, she enjoys cooking, hiking, and reading.

If you love historical romance, check out the other Wild Heart books!

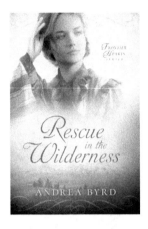

Rescue in the Wilderness by Andrea Byrd

William Cole cannot forget the cruel burden he carries, not with the pock marks that serve as an outward reminder. Riddled with guilt, he assumed the solitary life of a long hunter, traveling into the wilds of Kentucky each year. But his quiet existence is changed in an instant when, sitting in a tavern, he overhears a man offering his daughter—and her virtue—to the winner of the next round of cards. William's integrity and desire for redemption will not allow him to sit idly by while such an injustice occurs.

Lucinda Gillespie has suffered from an inexplicable illness her entire life. Her father, embarrassed by her condition, has subjected her to a lonely existence of abuse and confinement. But faced with the ultimate betrayal on the eve of her eighteenth birthday, Lucinda quickly realizes her trust is better placed in the hands of the mysterious man who appears at her door. Especially when he offers her the one thing she never thought would be within her grasp—freedom.

In the blink of an eye, both lives change as they begin the difficult, danger-fraught journey westward on the Wilderness Trail. But can they overcome their own perceptions of themselves to find love and the life God created them for?

~

A Heart's Gift by Lena Nelson Dooley

Is a marriage of convenience the answer?
Franklin Vine has worked hard to build the ranch he inherited into one of the most successful in the majestic Colorado mountains. If only he had an heir to one day inherit the legacy he's building. But he was burned once in the worst way, and he doesn't plan to open his heart to another woman. Even if that means he'll eventually have to divide up his spread among the most loyal of his hired hands.

When Lorinda Sullivan is finally out from under the control of men who made all the decisions in her life, she promises herself she'll never allow a man to make choices for her again. But without a home in the midst of a hard Rocky Mountain winter, she has to do something to provide for her infant son.

A marriage of convenience seems like the perfect arrangement, yet the stakes quickly become much higher than either of them ever planned. When hearts become entangled, the increasing danger may change their lives forever.

Lone Star Ranger by Renae Brumbaugh Green

Elizabeth Covington will get her man.

And she has just a week to prove her brother isn't the murderer Texas Ranger Rett Smith accuses him of being. She'll show the good-looking lawman he's wrong, even if it means setting out on a risky race across Texas to catch the real killer.

Rett doesn't want to convict an innocent man. But he can't let the Boston beauty sway his senses to set a guilty man free. When Elizabeth follows him on a dangerous trek, the Ranger vows to keep her safe. But who will protect him from the woman whose conviction and courage leave him doubting everything—even his heart?